Robert Williams Buchanan

Selected Poems

With a Frontispiece by Thomas Dalziel

Robert Williams Buchanan

Selected Poems
With a Frontispiece by Thomas Dalziel

ISBN/EAN: 9783337149093

Printed in Europe, USA, Canada, Australia, Japan

Cover: Foto ©Andreas Hilbeck / pixelio.de

More available books at **www.hansebooks.com**

SELECTED POEMS

OF

ROBERT BUCHANAN

WITH A FRONTISPIECE BY THOMAS DALZIEL

London
CHATTO AND WINDUS, PICCADILLY
1882

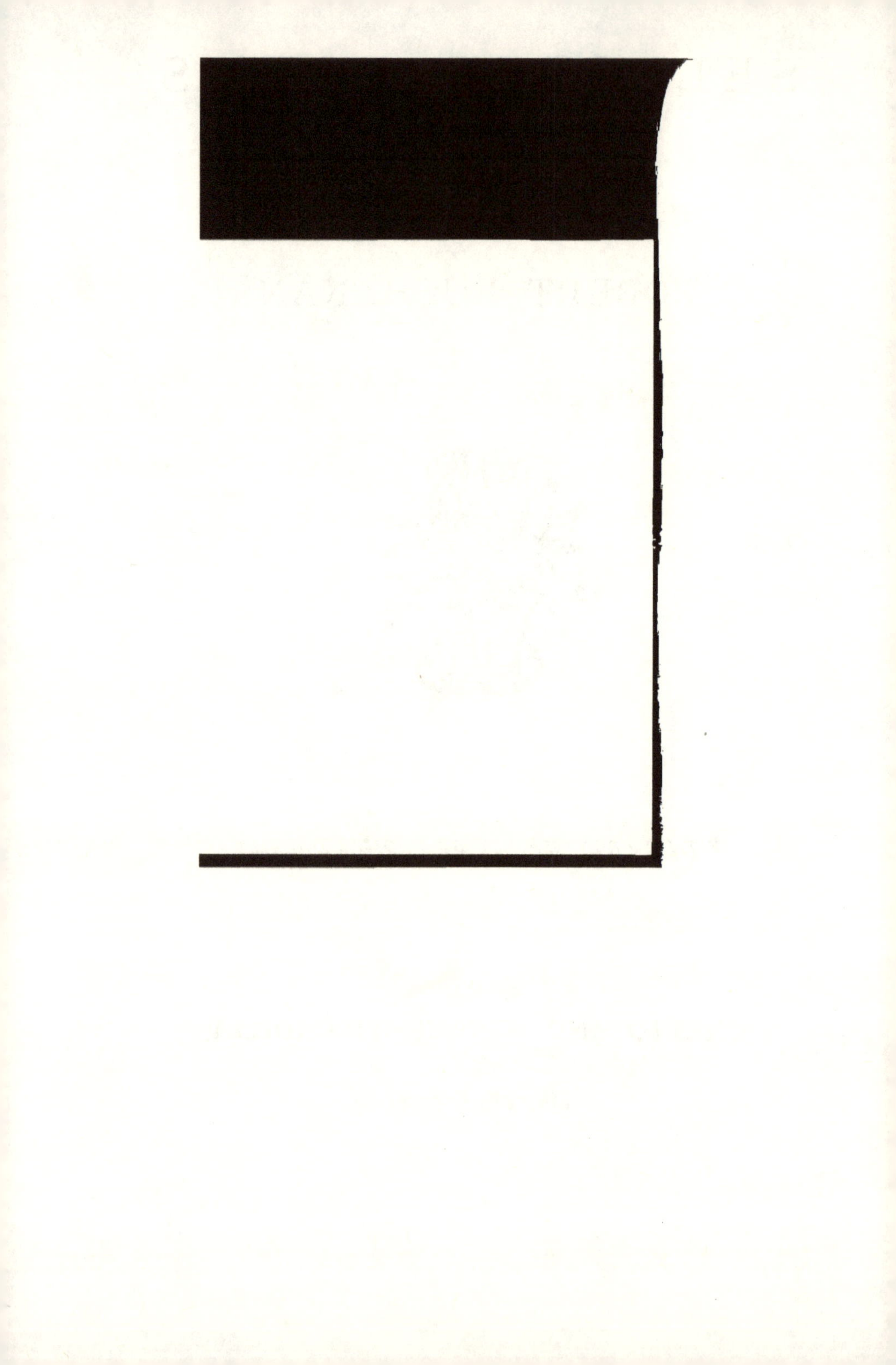

TO MARY.

Weeping and sorrowing, yet in sure and certain hope of a heavenly resurrection, I place these poor flowers of verse on the grave of my beloved Wife, who, with eyes of truest love and tenderness, watched them growing for more than twenty years.

ROBERT BUCHANAN.

Southend, February, 1882.

CONTENTS.

CONTENTS.

BALLADS AND DRAMATIC LYRICS.

TWO SONS.

I.

I HAVE two Sons, Wife—
　　Two, and yet the same ;
One his wild way runs, Wife,
　　Bringing us to shame.
The one is bearded, sunburnt, grim, and fights across
　　the sea,
The other is a little son who sits upon your knee.

II.

One is fierce and cold, Wife,
　　As the wayward Deep ;
Him no arms could hold, Wife,
　　Him no breast could keep.
He has tried our hearts for many a year, not broken
　　them ; for he
Is still the sinless little one that sits upon your knee.

III.

One may fall in fight, Wife—
　　Is he not our son ?
Pray with all your might, Wife,
　　For the wayward one ;
Pray for the dark, rough soldier, who fights across the
　　sea,
Because you love the little son who smiles upon your
　　knee.

IV.

One across the foam, Wife,
　　As I speak may fall ;
But this one at home, Wife,
　　Cannot die at all.
They both are only one ; and how thankful should we
　　be,
We cannot lose the darling Son who sits upon your knee !

CHARMIAN.

Cleo. Charmian.
Char. Madam?
Cleo. Give me to drink mandragora !

Antony and Cleopatra.

IN the time when water-lilies shake

Their green and gold on river and lake,

When the cuckoo calls in the heart o' the heat,

When the Dog-star foams and the shade is sweet,

Where cool and fresh the River ran,

I sat by the side of Charmian,

And heard no sound from the world of man.

All was so sweet and still that day !

The rustling shade, the rippling stream,

All life, all breath, dissolved away

Into a golden dream ;

Warm and sweet the scented shade

Drowsily caught the breeze and stirr'd,

Faint and low through the green glade

Came hum of bee and song of bird.

Our hearts were full of drowsy bliss,
And yet we did not clasp or kiss,
Nor did we break the happy spell
With tender tone or syllable.
But to ease our hearts and set thought free,
We pluckt the flowers of a red rose-tree,
And leaf by leaf, we threw them, Sweet,
Into the River at our feet,
And in an indolent delight
Watch'd them glide onward, slowly, out of sight.

Sweet, had I spoken boldly then,
Then might my love have garner'd thee !
But I had left the paths of men,
And sitting yonder dreamily,
Was happiness enough for me !
Seeking no gift of word or kiss,
But looking in thy face, was bliss !
Plucking the rose-leaves in a dream,
Watching them glimmer down the stream,
Knowing that eastern heart of thine
Shared the dim ecstasy of mine !

But, while we linger'd, cold and gray
Came Twilight, chilling soul and sense ;

And you arose to go away,
Full of a sweet indifference !
I miss'd the spell—I watch'd it break,—
And such come never twice to man :
In a less golden hour I spake,
And did *not* win thee, Charmian !

For wearily we turn'd away
Into the world of everyday,
And from thy heart the fancy fled
Like the rose-leaves on the River shed . . .
But to me that hour is sweeter far
Than the world and all its treasures are :
Still to sit on, so close to thee,
Were happiness enough for me !
Still to sit on, in a green nook,
Nor break the spell by word or look !
To reach out happy hands for ever,
To pluck the rose-leaves, Charmian !
To watch them fade on the gleaming River,
And hear no sound from the world of man !

THE DEATH OF ROLAND.

I.

THEN it grew chiller far, the grass was moist with dew,
The landscape glimmer'd pale, the mournful breezes
   blew,
The many stars above melted like snow-flakes white,
And far behind the hills the east was laced with light,
The dismal vale loom'd clear against a crimson glow,
Clouds spread above like wool, pale steam arose below,
And on the faces dead the frosty morning came,
On mighty men, and foes, and squires unknown to
   fame . . .
And golden mail gleam'd bright, and broken steel
   gleam'd gray,
And cold dew fill'd the wounds of those who sleeping
   lay;
And Roland, rising, drank the dawn with lips apart,
But scents were in the air that sicken'd his proud
   heart!
Yea, all was deathly still; and now, though it was day,
The moon grew small and pale, but did not pass away,

The white mist wreath'd and curl'd over the quick and
    dead,
A cock crew, far among the hills, and echoes answerëd.

II.

Then peering to the east, across the dewy steam,
He spied a naked wood, and there a running stream ;
Thirsting full sore, he rose, and thither did he hie,
Faintly, and panting hard, because his end was nigh ;
But first he stooping loosed from Turpin's fingers cold
The Cross inlaid with gems and wrought about with
    gold,
And bare the holy Cross aloft in one weak hand,
And with the other trail'd great Adalmàr his brand.
Thus wearily he came unto the woody place,
And stooping to the stream did dip therein his face,
And in the pleasant cold let swim his great black curls,
Then swung his forehead up, glittering as with pearls ;
And while the black blood spouted in a burning jet,
He loosed the bandage of his wound and made it wet,
Wringing the silken bands, making them free from
    gore,
Then placed them cool upon the wound, and tighten'd
    them once more.

III.

Eastward rose cloudy mist, drifting like smoke in wind,
Ghastly and round the sun loom'd dismally behind,
High overhead the moon faded with sickle chill,
The frosty wind dropp'd down, and all was deathlier
    still.
Then Roland, drawing deep the breath of vapours
    cold,
Beheld three marble steps, as of a ruin old,
And at the great tree-bolls lay many a carven stone,
Thereto a dial quaint, where slimy grass had grown ;
And frosted were the boughs that gatherëd around,
And cold the runlet crept, with soft and soothing
    sound,
And Roland smilëd sweet, and thought, " Since death
    is nigh,
In sooth, I know no gentler place where gentle man
    could die !"

IV.

Whereon the warrior heard a sound of breaking
    boughs,
And, from the thicket wild, leapt one with painted
    brows ;

Half-naked, glistening dark with oily limbs, he came,

His long-nail'd fingers curl'd, his little eyes aflame,

Shrieking in his own tongue, as on the chief he flew,

"Yield thee thy sword of fame, and thine own flesh
thereto!"

Then Roland gazed and frown'd, though nigh unto his
death,

Sat still, and drew up all his strength in a great
breath,

Pray'd quickly to the saints he served in former days,

With right hand clutch'd the sword he was too weak
to raise,

And in the left swung up the Cross! and, shrieking
hoarse,

Between the eyebrows smote the foe with all his force!

Yea, smote him to the brain, crashing through skin
and bone,

And prone the heathen fell, as heavy as a stone,

And gold and gems of price were loosen'd by the
blow,

And, as he fell, rain'd round the wild hair of the foe;

But Roland kiss'd the cross, and, laughing, backward
fell,

And on the hollow air the laugh rang heavy, like a
knell.

V.

And Roland thought : " I surely die ; but, ere I end,
Let me be sure that thou art ended too, my friend !
For should a heathen hand grasp thee when I am clay,
My ghost would grieve full sore until the judgment
     day !"
Then to the marble steps, under the tall bare trees,
Trailing the mighty sword, he crawl'd on hands and
     knees,
And on the slimy stone he struck the blade with
     might—
The bright hilt, sounding, shook, the blade flash'd
     sparks of light ;
Wildly again he struck, and his sick head went round,
Again there sparkled fire, again rang hollow sound ;
Ten times he struck, and threw strange echoes down
     the glade,
Yet still unbroken, sparkling fire, glitter'd the peerless
     blade.

VI.

Then Roland wept, and set his face against the
     stone—
" Ah, woe, I shall not rest, though cold be flesh and
     bone !"

And pain was on his soul to die so cheerless death;
When on his naked neck he felt a touch like breath!
He did not stir, but thought, "O God, that madest
    me,
And shall my sword of fame brandish'd by heathens
    be?
And shall I die accursed, beneath a heathen's heel,
Too weak to slay the slave whose hated breath I
    feel!"
Then, clenching teeth, he turn'd to look upon the foe,
His great eyes growing dim with coming death; and lo!
His life shot up in fire, his heart arose again,
For no unhallow'd face loom'd dark upon his ken,
No heathen-breath he felt,—though he beheld, indeed,
The white arch'd head and round brown eyes of Veillin-
    tif, his steed!

VII.

And pressing his moist cheek on his who gazed beneath,
Curling the upper lip to show the large white teeth,
The white horse, quivering, look'd with melancholy eye,
Then waved his streaming mane, and utter'd up a cry:
And Roland's bitterness was spent—he laugh'd, he
    smiled,

He clasp'd his darling's neck, wept like a little child ;
He kiss'd the foamy lips, and hugg'd his friend, and
    cried :
" Ah, nevermore, and nevermore, shall we to battle ride!
Ah, nevermore, and nevermore, shall we sweet comrades
    be.
And Veillintif, had I the heart to die forgetting thee ?
To leave thy mighty heart to break, in slavery to the foe ?
I had not rested in the grave, if it had ended so.
Ah, never shall we conquering ride, with banners bright
    unfurl'd,
A shining light 'mong lesser lights, a wonder to the
    world !"

VIII.

And Veillintif neigh'd low, breathing on him who died,
Wild rock'd his great strong heart beneath his silken side,
Tears roll'd from his brown eyes upon his master's cheek,
And Roland, gathering strength, though wholly worn and
    weak,
Held up the point of Adalmàr the peerless brand,
And at his comrade's heart push'd with his dying hand ;
And the black blood sprang forth, while heavily as lead,
With quivering, silken side, the mighty steed fell dead !

And Roland, since his eyes with frosty film were dim,
Groped for the steed, crept close, and smiled, embracing
    him,
And, pillow'd on his neck, kissing the pure white hair,
Clasp'd Adalmàr the brand, and tried to say a prayer,
And that he conquering died, wishing all men to know,
Set firm his lips, and turn'd his face towards the foe,
And closëd eyes, and slept, and never woke again.

Roland is dead, the gentle knight! dead is the crown
    of men!

THE DEAD MOTHER.

I.

As I lay asleep, as I lay asleep,
Under the grass as I lay so deep,
As I lay asleep in my white death-serk
Under the shade of Our Lady's Kirk,
I waken'd up in the dead of night,
I waken'd up in my shroud o' white,
And I heard a cry from far away,
And I knew the voice of my daughter May:
" Mother, mother, come hither to me !
Mother, mother, come hither and see !
Mother, mother, mother dear,
Another mother is sitting here :
My body is bruised, in pain I cry,
All night long on the straw I lie,
I thirst and hunger for drink and meat,
And mother, mother, to sleep were sweet !"
I heard the cry, though my grave was deep,
And awoke from sleep, and awoke from sleep.

II.

I awoke from sleep, I awoke from sleep,
Up I rose from my grave so deep!
The earth was black, but overhead
The stars were yellow, the moon was red;
And I walk'd along all white and thin,
And lifted the latch and enter'd in.
I reach'd the chamber as dark as night,
And though it was dark my face was white:
"Mother, mother, I look on thee!
Mother, mother, you frighten me!
For your cheeks are thin and your hair is gray!"
But I smiled, and kiss'd her fears away;
I smooth'd her hair and I sang a song,
And on my knee I rock'd her long.
"O mother, mother, sing low to me—
I am sleepy now, and I cannot see!"
I kiss'd her, but I could not weep,
And she went to sleep, she went to sleep.

III.

As we lay asleep, as we lay asleep,
My May and I, in our grave so deep,
As we lay asleep in the midnight mirk,
Under the shade of Our Lady's Kirk,

I waken'd up in the dead of night,
Though May my daughter lay warm and white,
And I heard the cry of a little one,
And I knew 'twas the voice of Hugh my son :
"Mother, mother, come hither to me !
Mother, mother, come hither and see !
Mother, mother, mother dear,
Another mother is sitting here :
My body is bruised and my heart is sad,
But I speak my mind and call them bad ;
I thirst and hunger night and day,
And were I strong I would fly away !"
I heard the cry, though my grave was deep,
And awoke from sleep, and awoke from sleep !

IV.

I awoke from sleep, I awoke from sleep,
Up I rose from my grave so deep,
The earth was black, but overhead
The stars were yellow, the moon was red ;
And I walk'd along all white and thin,
And lifted the latch and enter'd in.
" Mother, mother, and art thou here ?
I know your face, and I feel no fear ;

Raise me, mother, and kiss my cheek,
For oh, I am weary and sore and weak."
I smooth'd his hair with a mother's joy,
And he laugh'd aloud, my own brave boy;
I raised and held him on my breast,
Sang him a song, and bade him rest.
" Mother, mother, sing low to me—
I am sleepy now and I cannot see!"
I kiss'd him, and I could not weep,
As he went to sleep, as he went to sleep.

V.

As I lay asleep, as I lay asleep,
With my girl and boy in my grave so deep,
As I lay asleep, I awoke in fear,
Awoke, but awoke not my children dear,
And heard a cry so low and weak
From a tiny voice that could not speak :
I.heard the cry of a little one,
My bairn that could neither talk nor run,
My little, little one, uncaress'd,
Starving for lack of the milk of the breast;
And I rose from sleep and enter'd in,
And found my little one pinch'd and thin,

And croon'd a song and hush'd its moan,
And put its lips to my white breast-bone ;
And the red, red moon that lit the place
Went white to look at the little face,
And I kiss'd, and kiss'd, and I could not weep.
As it went to sleep, as it went to sleep.

VI.

As it lay asleep, as it lay asleep,
I set it down in the darkness deep,
Smooth'd its limbs and laid it out,
And drew the curtains round about ;
Then into the dark, dark room I hied,
Where awake *he* lay, at the woman's side ;
And though the chamber was black as night,
He saw my face, for it was so white !
I gazed in his eyes, and he shriek'd in pain,
And I knew he would never sleep again,
And back to my grave crept silently,
And soon my baby was brought to me ;
My son and daughter beside me rest,
My little baby is on my breast ;
Our bed is warm and our grave is deep,
But he cannot sleep, he cannot sleep !

Lo, we are side by side !—one white arm furls
   Around me like a serpent, warm and bare ;
The other, lifted 'mid a gleam of pearls,
   Holds a full golden goblet in the air :
Her face is shining through her cloudy curls
   With light that makes me drunken unaware,
And with my chin upon my breast I smile
Upon her, darkening inwardly the while.

And thro' the chamber curtains, backward roll'd
   By spicy winds that fan my fever'd head,
I see a sandy flat slope yellow as gold
   To the brown banks of Nilus wrinkling red
In the slow sunset; and mine eyes behold
   The West, low down beyond the river's bed,
Grow sullen, ribb'd with many a brazen bar,
Under the swart smile of the Cyprian star.

A bitter Roman vision floateth black
    Before me, in my busy brain's despite ;
The Roman armour brindles on my back,
    My swelling nostrils drink the fumes of fight :
But then, she smiles upon me !—and I lack
    The warrior will that frowns on lewd delight,
And, passionately proud and desolate,
I smile an answer to the joy I hate.

Joy coming uninvoked, asleep, awake,
    Makes sunshine on the grave of buried powers;
Ofttimes I wholly loathe her for the sake
    Of manhood slipt away in easeful hours :
But from her lips wild words and kisses break,
    Till I am like a ruin mock'd with flowers ;
I think of Honour's face—then turn to hers—
Dark, like the splendid shame that she confers.

Lo, how her white arm holds me !—I am bound
    By the soft touch of fingers light as leaves :
I drag my face aside, but at the sound
    Of her low voice I turn—and she perceives
The cloud of Rome upon my face, and round
    My neck she twines her odorous arms and grieves,

Shedding upon a heart as soft as they
Tears 'tis a hero's task to kiss away !

And then she loosens from me, trembling still
    Like a bright throbbing snake, and bids me " go ! "—
When pearly tears her drooping eyelids fill,
    And her bold beauty saddens into snow ;
And lost to use of life and hope and will,
    I gaze upon her with a warrior's woe,
And turn, and watch her sidelong in annoy—
Then snatch her to me, flush'd with shame and joy !

Once more, O Rome ! I would be son of thine—
    This constant prayer my chain'd soul ever saith—
I thirst for honourable end—I pine
    Not thus to kiss away my mortal breath.
But comfort such as this may not be mine—
    I cannot even die a Roman death :
I seek a Roman's grave, a Roman's rest—
But, dying, I would die upon her breast !

THE LAST SONG OF APOLLO.

O Lyre!   O Lyre!
Strung with celestial fire!
A living soul of sound that answereth
   These fingers that have troubled it so long
With passion, and with beauty, and with breath
   Of melancholy song,—
      Answer, answer, answer me,
      With thy mournful melody!
      For the earth is old, and strange
      Mysteries are working change,
      And the Dead who slumber'd deep
      Startle sobbing in their sleep,
      And the ancient gods divine,
      Wan and weary o'er their wine,
Wail in their ghastly banquet-halls, with large eyes fix'd
      on mine!

      Ah me! ah me!
      The earth and air and sea

Are shaken ; and the great pale gods sit still,
   The roseate mists around them roll away :—
Lo ! Hebe falters in the act to fill,
   And groweth wan and gray ;
     On the banquet-table spread,
     Fruits and flowers grow black and dead,
     Nectar cold in every cup
     Gleams to blood and withers up ;
     Aphrodité breathes a charm,
     Gripping Pallas' bronzëd arm ;
     Zeus the Father clenches teeth,
     While his cloud-throne shakes beneath ;
The passion-flower in Heré's hair melts in a snowy
       wreath !

     Ah, woe ! ah, woe !
     One climbeth from below,—
A mortal shape with pallid smile doth rise,
   Bearing a heavy Cross and crown'd with thorn,—
His brow is moist with blood, his strange sweet eyes
   Look piteous and forlorn :
     Hark ! Oh hark ! his cold foot-fall
     Breaks upon the banquet-hall !
     God and goddess start to hear,
     Earth, air, ocean, moan in fear ;

Shadows of the Cross and Him
Make the banquet-table dim,
Silent sit the gods divine,
Old and haggard over wine,
And slowly to my song they fade, with large eyes fix'd
on mine !

O Lyre !   O Lyre !
Thy strings of golden fire
Fade to their fading, and the hand is chill
That touches thee ; the once glad brow grows
gray—
I faint, I wither, while that conclave still
Dies wearily away !
Ah, the prophecy of old
Sung by Pan to scoffers cold !—
God and goddess droop and die,
Chilly cold against the sky,
There is change and all is done,
Strange look moon and stars and sun !
God and goddess fade, and see !
All their large eyes look on me !
While woe ! ah, woe ! in dying song, I fade, I fade, with
thee !

THE BALLAD OF JUDAS ISCARIOT.

'Twas the body of Judas Iscariot
　　Lay in the Field of Blood;
'Twas the soul of Judas Iscariot
　　Beside the body stood.

Black was the earth by night,
　　And black was the sky;
Black, black were the broken clouds,
　　Tho' the red Moon went by.

'Twas the body of Judas Iscariot
　　Strangled and dead lay there;
'Twas the soul of Judas Iscariot
　　Look'd on it in despair.

The breath of the World came and went
　　Like a sick man's in rest;
Drop by drop on the World's eyes
　　The dews fell cool and blest.

Then the soul of Judas Iscariot
  Did make a gentle moan—
"I will bury underneath the ground
  My flesh and blood and bone.

"I will bury deep beneath the soil,
  Lest mortals look thereon,
And when the wolf and raven come
  The body will be gone !

"The stones of the field are sharp as steel,
  And hard and cold, God wot ;
And I must bear my body hence
  Until I find a spot !"

'Twas the soul of Judas Iscariot,
  So grim, and gaunt, and gray,
Raised the body of Judas Iscariot,
  And carried it away.

And as he bare it from the field
  Its touch was cold as ice,
And the ivory teeth within the jaw
  Rattled aloud, like dice.

As the soul of Judas Iscariot
  Carried its load with pain,
The Eye of Heaven, like a lanthorn's eye,
  Open'd and shut again.

Half he walk'd, and half he seem'd
  Lifted on the cold wind;
He did not turn, for chilly hands
  Were pushing from behind.

The first place that he came unto
  It was the open wold,
And underneath were prickly whins,
  And a wind that blew so cold.

The next place that he came unto
  It was a stagnant pool,
And when he threw the body in
  It floated light as wool.

He drew the body on his back,
  And it was dripping chill,
And the next place he came unto
  Was a Cross upon a hill.

A Cross upon the windy hill,
  And a Cross on either side,
Three skeletons that swing thereon,
  Who had been crucified.

And on the middle cross-bar sat
  A white Dove slumbering;
Dim it sat in the dim light,
  With its head beneath its wing.

And underneath the middle Cross
  A grave yawn'd wide and vast,
But the soul of Judas Iscariot
  Shiver'd, and glided past.

The fourth place that he came unto
  It was the Brig of Dread,
And the great torrents rushing down
  Were deep, and swift, and red.

He dared not fling the body in
  For fear of faces dim,
And arms were waved in the wild water
  To thrust it back to him.

'Twas the soul of Judas Iscariot
    Turn'd from the Brig of Dread,
And the dreadful foam of the wild water
    Had splash'd the body red.

For days and nights he wander'd on
    Upon an open plain,
And the days went by like blinding mist,
    And the nights like rushing rain.

For days and nights he wander'd on,
    All thro' the Wood of Woe;
And the nights went by like moaning wind,
    And the days like drifting snow.

'Twas the soul of Judas Iscariot
    Came with a weary face—
Alone, alone, and all alone,
    Alone in a lonely place!

He wander'd east, he wander'd west,
    And heard no human sound;
For months and years, in grief and tears,
    He wander'd round and round.

For months and years, in grief and tears,
 He walk'd the silent night;
Then the soul of Judas Iscariot
 Perceived a far-off light.

A far-off light across the waste,
 As dim as dim might be,
That came and went like the lighthouse gleam
 On a black night at sea.

'Twas the soul of Judas Iscariot
 Crawl'd to the distant gleam;
And the rain came down, and the rain was blown
 Against him with a scream.

For days and nights he wander'd on,
 Push'd on by hands behind;
And the days went by like black, black rain,
 And the nights like rushing wind.

'Twas the soul of Judas Iscariot,
 Strange, and sad, and tall,
Stood all alone at dead of night
 Before a lighted hall.

And the wold was white with snow,
   And his foot-marks black and damp,
And the ghost of the silver Moon arose,
   Holding her yellow lamp.

And the icicles were on the eaves,
   And the walls were deep with white,
And the shadows of the guests within
   Pass'd on the window light.

The shadows of the wedding guests
   Did strangely come and go,
And the body of Judas Iscariot
   Lay stretch'd along the snow.

The body of Judas Iscariot
   Lay stretch'd along the snow;
'Twas the soul of Judas Iscariot
   Ran swiftly to and fro.

To and fro, and up and down,
   He ran so swiftly there,
As round and round the frozen Pole
   Glideth the lean white bear.

'Twas the Bridegroom sat at the table-head,
   And the lights burnt bright and clear—
" Oh, who is that," the Bridegroom said,
   " Whose weary feet I hear ?"

'Twas one look'd from the lighted hall,
   And answer'd soft and slow,
" It is a wolf runs up and down
   With a black track in the snow."

The Bridegroom in His robe of white
   Sat at the table-head—
" Oh, who is that who moans without ?"
   The blessëd Bridegroom said.

'Twas one look'd from the lighted hall,
   And answer'd fierce and low,
" 'Tis the soul of Judas Iscariot
   Gliding to and fro."

'Twas the soul of Judas Iscariot
   Did hush itself and stand,
And saw the Bridegroom at the door
   With a light in His hand.

The Bridegroom stood in the open door,
  And He was clad in white,
And far within the Lord's Supper
  Was spread so broad and bright.

The Bridegroom shaded His eyes and look'd,
  And His face was bright to see—
" What dost thou here at the Lord's Supper
  With thy body's sins?" said He.

'Twas the soul of Judas Iscariot
  Stood black, and sad, and bare—
" I have wander'd many nights and days;
  There is no light elsewhere."

'Twas the wedding guests cried out within
  And their eyes were fierce and bright—
" Scourge the soul of Judas Iscariot
  Away into the night!"

The Bridegroom stood in the open door,
  And He waved hands still and slow,
And the third time that He waved His hands
  The air was thick with snow.

And of every flake of falling snow,
  Before it touch'd the ground,
There came a dove, and a thousand doves
  Made sweet sound.

'Twas the body of Judas Iscariot
  Floated away full fleet,
And the wings of the doves that bare it off
  Were like its winding-sheet.

'Twas the Bridegroom stood at the open door,
  And beckon'd, smiling sweet;
'Twas the soul of Judas Iscariot
  Stole in, and fell at His feet.

" The Holy Supper is spread within,
  And the many candles shine,
And I have waited long for thee
  Before I pour'd the wine !"

The supper wine is pour'd at last,
  The lights burn bright and fair,
Iscariot washes the Bridegroom's feet,
  And dries them with his hair.

NATURE POEMS.

DAYBREAK.

(*Fragment.*)

But now the first faint flickering ray
Fell from the cold east far away,
The birds awoke and twitter'd, hover'd,
  The dim leaves sparkled in the dew—
Earth slowly her dark head uncover'd
  And held her blind face up the blue,
Till the fresh consecration came
In yellow beams of orient flame,
Touching her, and she breathed full blest
With lilies heaving on her breast.
Seas sparkled, dark capes glimmer'd green,
As Dawn crept on from scene to scene,
Lifting each curtain of the night
With fingers flashing starry-white.

AMONG THE MOUNTAINS.

THE sunlight fades on mossy rocks,
And on the mountain-sides the flocks
  Are spilt like streams ;—the highway dips
Down, narrowing to the path where lambs
Lay to the udders of their dams
  Their soft and pulpy lips.
The hills grow closer ; to the right
The path sweeps round a shadowy bay,
Upon whose sandy fringes, white
And crested wavelets play.
All else is still.   But list, oh list !
Hidden by boulders and by mist,
A shepherd whistles in his fist ;
From height to height the far sheep bleat
In answering iteration sweet ;
Sound, seeking Silence, bends above her,
Within some haunted mountain grot ;
Kisses her, like a trembling lover—
So that she stirs in sleep, but wakens not !

. . . Along this rock I'll lie,
With face turn'd upward to the sky.
A dreamy numbness glows within my brain—
It is not joy and is not pain—
'Tis like the solemn, sweet imaginings
That cast a shade on Music's golden wings.
With face turn'd upward to the sun,
I lie as indolent as one
Who, in a vision sweet, perceives
Spirits thro' mists of lotus leaves;
  And as I lie soft shadows move
Across me, cast by clouds so small
Mine eyes perceive them scarce at all
  In the unsullied blue above.
I hear the streams that thrill and fall,
The straggling shepherd's frequent call,
  The cattle lowing as they pass,
The dark lake stirring with the breeze,
The melancholy hum of bees,
  The very murmur of the waving grass.

THE LOWLAND VILLAGE.

SEVEN pleasant miles by wood, and stream, and moor,
Seven miles along the country road that wound
Uphill and downhill in a dusty line,
Then from the forehead of a hill, behold—
Lying below me, sparkling ruby-like—
The village !—quaint old gables, roofs of thatch,
A glimmering spire that peep'd above the firs,
The sunset lingering orange-red on all,
And nearer, tumbling thro' a mossy bridge,
The river that I knew !   No wondrous peep
Into the faëry land of Oberon,
Its bowers, its glowworm-lighted colonnades
Where pigmy lovers wander two by two,
Could weigh upon the city wanderer's heart
With peace so pure as this !   Why, yonder stood,
A fledgling's downward flight beyond the spire,
The grey old manse, endear'd by memories
Of Jean the daughter of the minister ;
And in the cottage with the painted sign,
Hard by the bridge, how many a winter night

Had I with politicians sapient-eyed
Discuss'd the county paper's latest news
And read of toppling thrones!—And nought seem'd
  changed!
The very gig before the smithy door,
The barefoot maiden with the milking pail
Pausing and looking backward from the bridge,
The last rook wavering homeward to the wood,
All seem'd a sunset-picture, every tint
Unchanged, since I had bidden it farewell.
My heart grew garrulous of olden times,
And my face sadden'd, as I saunter'd down.
Then came a rural music on my ears,—
The waggons in the lanes, the waterfall
With cool sound plunging in its wood-nest wild,
The rooks amid the windy rookery,
The shouts of children, and more far away
The crowing of a cock.   Then o'er the bridge
I bent, above the river gushing down
Thro' mossy boulders, making underneath
Green-shaded pools where now and then a trout
Sank in the ripple of its own quick leap;
And like some olden and familiar tune,
Half humm'd aloud, half tinkling in the brain,
Troublously, faintly, came the buzz of looms.

And here I linger'd, nested in the shade
Of Peace that makes a music as she grows ;
And when the vale had put its glory on
The bitter aspiration was subdued,
And Pleasure, tho' she wore a woodland crown,
Look'd at me with Ambition's serious eyes.
Amid the deep green woods of pine, whose boughs
Made a sea-music overhead, and caught
White flakes of sunlight on their highest leaves,
I foster'd solemn meditations ;
Stretch'd on the sloping river banks, fresh strewn
With speedwell, primrose, and anemone,
I watch'd the bright king-fisher dart about,
His quick small shadow with an azure gleam
Startling the minnows in the pool beneath ;
Or later on the moors, where far away
Across the waste the sportsman with his gun
Stood a dark speck across the blue sky, while
The heath-hen tower'd with beating wings and fell,
I caught the solemn wind that wander'd down
With thunder-echoes heaved among the hills.
Nor lack'd I, in the balmy summer nights,
Or on the days of rain, such counterpoise
As books can give. The honey-languaged Greek
Who gently piped the sweet bucolic lay,

The wit who raved of Lesbia's loosen'd zone
And loved divinely what was less than earth,
Were with me; others, of a later date:
The eagle-eyed comedian divine;
The English Homer, not the humpback'd one
Who sung Belinda's curl at Twickenham,
But Chapman, master of the long strong line;
Moreover, those few singers who have lit
The beacon-lights of these our latter days—
Chief, young Hyperion, who setting soon
Sent his pale look along the future time,
And the tall figure on the hills, that stoopt
To see the daisy's shadow on the grass.

A SUMMER POOL.

THERE is a singing in the summer air,
The blue and brown moths flutter o'er the grass,
The stubble bird is creaking in the wheat,
And perch'd upon the honeysuckle-hedge
Pipes the green linnet.   Oh, the golden world!
The stir of life on every blade of grass,
The motion and the joy on every bough,
The glad feast everywhere, for things that love
The sunshine, and for things that love the shade!

Aimlessly wandering with weary feet,
Watching the wool-white clouds that wander by,
I come upon a lonely place of shade,—
A still green Pool, where with soft sound and stir
The shadows of o'erhanging branches sleep,
Save where they leave one dreamy space of blue
O'er whose soft stillness ever and anon
The mirror'd cirrus blows.   Here unaware
I pause, and leaning on my staff I add

A shadow to the shadows ; and behold !
Dim dreams steal down upon me, with a hum
Of little wings, a murmuring of boughs,—
The dusky stir and motion dwelling here,
Within this small green world.   O'ershadowëd
By dusky greenery, tho' all around
The sunshine throbs on fields of wheat and bean,
Downward I gaze into the dreamy blue,
And pass into a waking sleep, wherein
The green boughs rustle, feathery wreaths of cloud
Pass softly, piloted by golden airs :
The air is still,—no birds sing any more,—
And, helpless as a tiny flying thing,
I am alone in all the world with God.

The wind dies—not a leaf stirs—on the Pool
The fly scarce moves ; earth seems to hold her breath
Until her heart stops, listening silently
For the far footsteps of the coming Rain !

While thus I pause, it seems that I have gained
New eyes to see ; my brain grows sensitive
To trivial things that, at another hour,
Would pass unheeded.   Suddenly the air
Shivers, the shadows in whose midst I stand

Tremble and blacken—the blue eye o' the Pool
Is closed and clouded ; with a sudden gleam,
Oiling its wings, a swallow darteth past,
And weedling flowers beneath my feet thrust up
Their leaves to feel the fragrant shower.   Oh, hark !
The thirsty leaves are troubled into sighs,
And up above me, on the glistening boughs,
Patters the summer Rain !

                 Into a nook,
Screen'd by thick foliage of oak and beech,
I creep for shelter ; and the happy shower
Murmurs around me.   Oh, the drowsy sounds !
The pattering dew, the numerous sigh of leaves,
The deep, warm breathing of the scented air,
Sink sweet into my soul—until at last
Comes the soft ceasing of the gentle fall,
And lo ! the eye of blue within the Pool
Opens again ! while with a silvern gleam
Dew-diamonds twinkle moistly on the leaves,
Or, shaken downward by the summer wind,
Fall melting on the Pool in rings of light !

THE INDIAN STREAM.

(*From* "*St. Abe.*")

FROM pool to pool the wild beck sped
Beside us, dwindled to a thread.
With mellow verdure fringed around
It sang along with summer sound :
Here gliding into a green glade ;
Here darting from a nest of shade
With sudden sparkle and quick cry,
As glad again to meet the sky ;
Here whirling off with eager will
And quickening tread to turn a mill ;
Then stealing from the busy place
With duskier depths and wearier pace.
In the blue void above the beck
Sailed with us, dwindled to a speck,
The hen-hawk ; and from pools below
The blue-wing'd heron oft rose slow,
And upward pass'd with measured beat

Of wing to seek some new retreat.
Blue was the heaven and darkly bright,
Suffused with throbbing golden light,
And in the burning Indian ray
A million insects humm'd at play.

THE COMING OF BALDER.*

(From " Balder the Beautiful.")

O WHO cometh sweetly
  With singing of showers?—
The wild wind runs fleetly
  Before his soft tread,
The sward stirs asunder
  To radiance of flowers,
While o'er him and under
  A glory is spread—
A white cloud above him
  Moves on thro' the blue,
And all things that love him
  Are dim with its dew:
The lark is upspringing,
  The merle whistles clear,
There is sunlight and singing
  For Balder is here!

---

* Balder is—conceived in a certain sense, and for the purpose of the present
poem read apart from its context—simply the Sun-god, or Spirit of Summer.

He walks on the mountains,
　He treads on the snows;
He loosens the fountains
　And quickens the wells;
He is filling the chalice
　Of lily and rose,
He is down in the valleys
　And deep in the dells—
He smiles, and buds spring to him,
　The bright and the dark;
He speaks, and birds sing to him,
　The finch and the lark,—-
He is down by the river,
　He is up by the mere,
Woods gladden, leaves quiver,
　For Balder is here.

There is some divine trouble
　On earth and in air—
Trees tremble, brooks bubble,
　Ants loosen the sod;
Warm footfalls awaken
　Whatever is fair;
Sweet rain-dews are shaken
　To quicken each clod.

The wild rainbows o'er him
  Are melted and fade,
The grass runs before him
  Thro' meadow and glade ;
Green branches close round him,
  The leaves whisper near—
" He is ours—we have found him —
  Bright Balder is here !"

The forest glows golden
  Where'er he is seen,
New flowers are unfolden,
  New voices arise ;
Flames flash at his passing
  From boughs that grow green,
Dark runlets gleam, glassing
  The stars of his eyes.
The Earth wears her brightest
  Wherever he goes,
The hawthorn its whitest,
  Its reddest the rose ;
The days now are sunny,
  The white storks appear,
And the bee gathers honey,
  For Balder is here.

He is here on the heather,
　And here by the brook,
And here where together
　　The lilac boughs cling;
He is coming and going
　With love in his look,
His white hand is sowing
　　Warm seeds, and they spring!
He has touch'd with new silver
　The lips of the stream,
And the eyes of the culver
　Are bright from his beam,
He has lit the great lilies
　Like lamps on the mere;
All happy and still is,
　For Balder is here.

Still southward with sunlight
　He wanders away—
The true light, the one light,
　The new light, is he!
With music and singing
　The mountains are gay,
And the peace he is bringing
　Spreads over the sea.

All night, while stars twinkling
  Gleam down on the glade,
His white hands are sprinkling
  With harebells the shade ;
And when day hath broken,
  All things that dwell near
Will know, by that token,
  That Balder is here.

In the dark deep dominions
  Of pine and of fir,
Where the dove with soft pinions
  Sits still on her nest,
He sees her, and by her
  The young doves astir,
And smiling sits nigh her,
  His hand on her breast
The father-dove lingers
  With love in its eyes,
Alights on his fingers,
  And utters soft cries,
And the sweet colours seven
  Of the rainbow appear
On its neck, as in heaven,
  Now Balder is here.

He sits by a fountain
  Far up near the snow,
And high on the mountain
  The wild reindeer stand;
On crimson moss near to him
  They feed walking slow,
Or come with no fear to him,
  And eat from his hand.
He sees the ice turning
  To columns of gold,
He sees the clouds burning
  On crags that were cold;
The great snows are drifting
  To cataracts clear,
All shining and shifting,
  For Balder is here.

O who sitteth singing,
  Where sunset is red,
And wild ducks are winging
  Against the dark gleam?
It is he, it is Balder,
  He hangeth his head
Where willow and alder
  Droop over the stream;

And the purple moths find him
  And hover around,
And from marshes behind him
  He hears a low sound :
The frogs croak their greeting
  From swamp and from mere,
And their faint hearts are beating,
  For Balder is here.

The round moon is peeping
  Above the low hill ;
Her white light, upcreeping
  Against the sun's glow,
On the black shallow river
  Falls silvern and chill,
Where bulrushes quiver
  And wan lilies grow.
The black bats are flitting,
  Owls pass on soft wings,
Yet silently sitting
  He lingers and sings—
He sings of the Maytime,
  Its sunlight and cheer,
And the night like the daytime
  Knows Balder is here.

He is here with the moonlight,
  With night as with day,
The true light, the one light,
  The new light, is he;
The moon-bows above him
  Are melted away,
And the things of night love him,
  And hearken and see.
He sits and he ponders,
  He walks and he broods,
Or singing he wanders
  'Neath star-frosted woods;
And the spheres from afar, light
  His face shining clear:
Yea, the moonlight and starlight
  Feel Balder is here.

He is here, he is moving
  On mountain and dale,
And all things grow loving,
  And all things grow bright:
Buds bloom in the meadows,
  Milk foams in the pail,
There is scent in the shadows,
  And sound in the light:

O listen ! he passes
  Thro' valleys of flowers,
With springing of grasses
  And singing of showers.
Earth wakes—he has call'd her,
  Whose voice she holds dear;
She was waiting for Balder,
  And Balder is here !

THE FINDING OF BALDER.

(From " Balder the Beautiful.")

BEFORE her lay a vast and tranquil lake,
And wading in its shallows silently
Great storks of golden white and light green cranes
Stood sentinel, while, far as eye could see,
Swam the wild water-lily's oilëd leaves.
Still was that place as sleep, yet evermore
A stir amid its stillness ; for behold,
At every breath of the warm summer wind
Blown on the beating bosom of the lake,
The white swarms of the new-born lily-flowers,
A pinch of gold-dust in the heart of each,
Rose from the bubbling depths, and open'd up,
And floated luminous with cups of snow.
Across that water came so sweet an air,
It fell upon the immortal mother's brow
Like coolest morning dew, and tho' she stood
Beneath the open arch of heaven, the light

Stole thro' the gauze of a soft summer mist
Most gentle and subdued.　Then while she paused
Close to the rippling shallows sown with reeds,
Those cranes and storks arose above her head
In one vast cloud of flying green and gold ;
And from the under-heaven innumerable
The lilies upward to the surface snow'd,
Till all the waters glitter'd gold and white ;
And lo ! the sun swept shining up the east,
And thro' the cloud of birds, and on the lake,
Shot sudden rays of light miraculous,—
Until the goddess veil'd her dazzled eyes,
And with the heaving whiteness at her feet
Her bosom heaved, till of that tremulous life
She seem'd a throbbing part !

　　　　　　　Tall by the marge
The goddess tower'd, and her immortal face
Was shining as anointed ; then she cried,
" Balder ! " and like the faint cry of a bird
That passeth overhead, the sound was borne
Between the burning ether and the earth.
Then once again she call'd, outstretching arms,
" Balder ! "　Upon her face the summer light
Trembled in benediction, while the voice

Was lifted up and echoed till it died
Far off amid the forest silences.

A space she paused, smiling and listening,
Gazing upon the lilies as they rose
Large, luminously fair, and new-baptized ;
And once again she would have call'd aloud,
When far across the waters suddenly
There shone a light as of the morning star ;
Which coming nearer seem'd as some bright bird
Floating amid the lilies and their leaves,
And presently, approaching closer still,
Assumed the likeness of a shining shape,
Who, with white shoulders from the waters reaching,
And sunlight burning on his golden hair,
Swam like a swan.   Upon his naked arms
The amber light was melted, while they clove
The crystal depths and softly swept aside
The glittering lilies and their clustering leaves ;
And on the forehead of him burnt serene
A light as of a pearl more wonderful
Than ever from the crimson seas of Ind
Was snatch'd by human hand ; for pearl it seem'd
Tho' blood-red, and as lustrous as a star.
Him Frea breathless watch'd, for all the air

Was golden with his glory as he came ;
And o'er his head hover'd the cloud of birds
With clangour deep ; and thro' the lake he swam
With arm-sweeps swift, till in the shallows bright,
Still dripping from the kisses of the waves,
He rose erect in loveliness divine.
The lustre from his ivory arms and limbs
Stream'd as he stood, and from his yellow hair
A splendour rain'd upon his neck and breast,
While burning unextinguish'd on his brow
Shone that strange star.

       Then as he shining rose,
And on her form the new effulgence fell,
The goddess, with her face beatified,
Yet gentle as a mortal mother's, cried
" Balder ! my Balder !"—and while from all the
    woods,
And from the waters wide, and from the air
Still rainbow'd with the flashing flight of birds,
Innumerable echoes answer'd, " Balder !"—
Clad in his gentle godhead Balder stood,
Bright, beautiful, and palpably divine.

SUNSET IN NEW ENGLAND.

(From " St. Abe.")

ALL was hush'd ; while far away
(As a novelist would say)
Sank the mighty orb of day,
Staring with a hazy glow
On the purple plain below,
Where (like burning embers shed
From the sunset's glowing bed,
Dying out or burning bright,
Every leaf a blaze of light)
Ran the maple swamps ablaze ;
Everywhere amid the haze,
Floating strangely in the air,
Farms and homesteads gather'd fair ;
And the River rippled slow
Thro' the marshes green and low,

Spreading oft as smooth as glass
As it fringed the meadow grass,
Making 'mong the misty fields
Pools like gleaming golden shields.

Thus I walk'd my steed along,
Humming a low scrap of song,
Watching with an idle eye
White clouds on the dreamy sky
Sailing with me in slow pomp.
In the bright flush of the swamp,
While his dogs bark'd in the wood,
Gun in hand the sportsman stood;
And beside me, wading deep,
Stood the angler half asleep,
Figure black against the gleam
Of the bright pools of the stream;
Now and then a wherry brown
With the current drifted down
Sunset-ward, and as it went
Made an oar-splash indolent;
While with solitary sound,
Deepening the silence round,
In a voice of mystery
Faintly cried the chickadee.

Suddenly the River's arm
Rounded, and a lonely Farm
Stood before me blazing red
To the bright blaze overhead;
In the homesteads at its side,
Cattle low'd and voices cried,
And from out the shadows dark
Came a mastiff's measured bark.
Fair and fat stood the abode
On the path by which I rode,
While a mighty orchard, strown
Still with apple-leaves wind-blown,
Raised its branches gnarl'd and bare
Black against the sunset air,
With its greensward deep and dim
Sloping to the River's brim.

DROWSIETOWN.

(From " White Rose and Red.")

O so drowsy !   In a daze
Sweating 'mid the golden haze,
With its smithy like an eye
Glaring bloodshot at the sky,
And its one white row of street
Carpeted so green and sweet,
And the loungers smoking still
Over gate and window-sill ;
Nothing coming, nothing going,
Locusts grating, one cock crowing,
Few things moving up or down,
All things drowsy—Drowsietown !

Thro' the fields with sleepy gleam,
Drowsy, drowsy steals the stream,
Touching with its azure arms
Upland fields and peaceful farms,
Gliding with a twilight tide
Where the dark elms shade its side ;

Twining, pausing sweet and bright,
Where the lilies sail so white ;
Winding in its sedgy hair
Meadow-sweet and iris fair ;
Humming as it hies along
Monotones of sleepy song ;
Deep and dimpled, bright nut-brown,
Flowing into Drowsietown.

Far as eye can see, around,
Upland fields and farms are found,
Floating prosperous and fair
In the mellow misty air :
Apple-orchards,—blossoms blowing
Up above, and clover growing
Red and scented round the knees
Of the old moss-silver'd trees.
Hark ! with drowsy deep refrain,
In the distance rolls a wain ;
As its dull sound strikes the ear,
Other kindred sounds grow clear—
Drowsy all—the soft breeze blowing,
Locusts grating, one cock crowing,
Cries like voices in a dream
Far away amid the gleam,

Then the waggons rumbling down
Thro' the lanes to Drowsietown.

Drowsy? Yea!—but idle? Nay!
Slowly, surely, night and day,
Humming low, well greased with oil,
Turns the wheel of human toil.
Here no grating gruesome cry
Of spasmodic industry;
No rude clamour, mad and mean,
Of a horrible machine !
Strong yet peaceful, surely roll'd,
Winds the wheel that whirls the gold.
Year by year the rich rare land ,
Yields its stores to human hand—
Year by year the stream makes fat
Every field and meadow-flat—
Year by year the orchards fair
Gather glory from the air,
Brighten, ripen, freshly fed,
Their rough balls of golden red.
Thus, most prosperous and strong,
Flows the stream of life along
Six slow days ! wains come and go,
Wheat-fields ripen, squashes grow,

Cattle browse on hill and dale,
Milk foams sweetly in the pail,
Six days : on the seventh day,
Toil's low murmur dies away—
All is husht save drowsy din
Of the waggons rolling in,
Drawn amid the plenteous meads
By small fat and sleepy steeds.
Folk with faces fresh as fruit
Sit therein or trudge afoot,
Brightly drest for all to see,
In their seventh-day finery :
Farmers in their breeches tight,
Snowy cuffs, and buckles bright ;
Ancient dames and matrons staid
In their silk and flower'd brocade,
Prim and tall, with soft brows knitted,
Silken aprons, and hands mitted ;
Haggard women, dark of face,
Of the old lost Indian race ;
Maidens happy-eyed and fair,
With bright ribbons in their hair,
Trip along, with eyes cast down,
Thro' the streets of Drowsietown.

Drowsy thro' the summer day
In the meeting-house sit they;
'Mid the high-back'd pews they doze,
Like bright garden-flowers in rows;
And old Parson Pendon, big
In his gown and silver'd wig,
Drones above in periods fine
Sermons like old home-made wine—
Crusted well with keeping long
In the darkness, and not strong.
Oh! so drowsily he drones
In his rich and sleepy tones,
While the great door, swinging wide,
Shows the still green street outside,
And the shadows as they pass
On the golden sunlit grass.
Then the mellow organ blows,
And the sleepy music flows,
And the folks their voices raise
In old unctuous hymns of praise,
Fit to reach some ancient god
Half asleep with drowsy nod.
Deep and lazy, clear and low,
Doth the oily organ grow!
Then with sudden golden cease

Comes a silence and a peace;
Then a murmur, all alive,
As of bees within a hive;
And they swarm with quiet feet
Out into the sunny street;
There, at hitching-post and gate
Do the steeds and waggons wait.
Drawn in groups, the gossips talk,
Shaking hands before they walk;
Maids and lovers steal away,
Smiling hand in hand, to stray
By the river, and to say
Drowsy love in the old way—
Till the sleepy sun shines down
On the roofs of Drowsietown!

SPRINGTIDE.

(*From " White Rose and Red."*)

DEACON JONES.

WELL, winter's over altogether;
  The loon's come back to Purley Pond;
It's all green grass and pleasant weather
  Up on the marsh and the woods beyond.
It's God Almighty's meaning clear
To give us farmers a prosperous year;
Tho' many a sinner that I could mention
  Is driving his ploughshare now-a-days
Clean in the teeth of the Lord's intention,
  And spiling the land he ought to raise.

BIRD CHORUS.

Chickadee! chickadee!
Green leaves on every tree!
Over field, over foam,
All the birds are coming home.

Honk! honk! sailing low,
Cried the grey goose long ago.
Weet! weet! in the light
Flutes the phœbe-bird so bright.
Chewink, veery, thrush o' the wood,
    Silver treble raise together;
All around their dainty food
    Ripens with the ripening weather.
Hear, oh, hear!
In the great elm by the mere
Whip-poor-will is crying clear.

THE RIVER SINGS.

O willow loose lightly
    Your soft long hair!
I'll brush it brightly
    With tender care;
And past you flowing
    I'll softly uphold
Great lilies blowing
    With hearts of gold.
For spring is beaming,
    The wind's in the south,
And the musk-rat's swimming,
    A twig in its mouth,

To build its nest
Where it loves it best,
In the great dark nook
By the bed o' my brook.
It's spring, bright spring,
And blue-birds sing !
And the fern is pearly
　　All day long,
And the lark rises early
　　To sing a song.
The grass shoots up like fingers of fire,
And the flowers awake to a dim desire.
So willow, willow, shake down, shake down
　Your locks so silvern and long and slight ;
For lovers are coming from Drowsietown,
　And thou and I must be merry and bright !

PHŒBE ANNA.

This is the first fine day this year :
The grass is dry and the sky is clear ;
The sun's out shining ; up to the farm
It looks like summer ; so bright and warm !

There's apple blooms on the boughs already,
Long as your finger the corn-blades shoot,
And father thinks, if the sun keeps steady,
'Twill be a wonderful fall for fruit.

BIRD CHORUS.

Chickadee! chickadee!
Green leaves on every tree;
Winter goes, spring is here;
Little mate, we loved last year.
Cheewink, veery, robin red,
   Shall we take another bride?
We have plighted, we are wed.
   Here we gather happy-eyed.
Little bride, little mate,
Shall I leave you desolate?
Men change; shall we change too?
Men change; but we are true.
If I cease to love thee best,
May a black boy take my nest.

THE CAT-OWL.

Boohoo! boohoo!
White man is not true;

I have seen such wicked ways
That I hide me all the days,
And come from my hole so deep
When the white man lies asleep.
A misanthrope am I,
    And, tho' the skies are blue,
I utter my warning cry—
    Boohoo !
Boohoo ! boohoo ! boohoo !

THE LOON.

(*Chuckling to himself on the pond.*)

Ha ! ha ! ha ! back again,
Thro' the frost, and fog, and rain ;
Winter's over now, that's plain.
Ha ! ha ! ha ! back again !
And I laugh and scream,
    For I love so well
The bright, bright bream,
    And the pickerel !
And soft is my breast,
    And my bill is keen,
And I'll build my nest
    'Mid the sedge unseen.

I've travell'd—I've fish'd in the sunny south,
In the mighty mere, at the harbour mouth ;
I've seen fair countries, all golden and gay ;
   I've seen bright pictures that beat all wishing ;
I've found fine colours afar away—
   But give me Purley Pond, for fishing ;
Of all the ponds, north, south, east, west,
This is the pond I love the best ;
For all is quiet, and few folk peep,
   Save some of the innocent angling people ;
And I like on Sundays, half asleep,
All alone on the pool so deep,
   To rock and hear the bells from the steeple.
And I laugh so clear that all may hear
The loon is back, and summer is near.
Ha ! ha ! ha ! so merry and plain
I laugh with joy to be home again.

   (*A shower passes over; all things sing.*)

The swift is wheeling and gleaming,
   The brook is brown in its bed,
Rain from the cloud is streaming,
   And the Bow bends overhead.
The charm of the winter is broken ! the last of the
      spell is said !

The eel in the pond is quick'ning,
    The grayling leaps in the stream—
What if the clouds are thick'ning?
    See how the meadows gleam!
The sleep of the snowtime is shaken; the world
    awakes from a dream!

The fir puts out green fingers,
    The pear-tree softly blows,
The rose in her dark bower lingers,
    But her curtains will soon unclose,
The lilac will shake her ringlets over the blush of the
    rose.

The swift is wheeling and gleaming,
    The woods are beginning to ring,
Rain from the cloud is streaming;—
    There, where the Bow doth cling,
Summer is smiling afar off, over the shoulder of
    Spring!

THE GREAT SNOW.

(From " White Rose and Red.")

'Twas the year of the Great Snow.

First, the East began to blow
Chill and shrill for many days,
On the wild wet woodland ways.
Then the North, with crimson cheeks,
Blew upon the pond for weeks,
Chill'd the water thro' and thro',
Till the first thin ice-crust grew
Blue and filmy ; then at last
All the pond was frosted fast,
Prison'd, smother'd, fetter'd tight,
Let it struggle as it might.
Then the first Snow drifted down
On the roofs of Drowsietown.

First, the vanguard of the Snow ;
Falling flakes, whirling slow,
Drifting darkness, troubled dream ;
Then a motion and a gleam ;

Covering with a carpet white
   Orchards, swamps, and woodland ways,
Thus the first Snow took its flight,
   And there was a hush for days.

Mid that hush the Spectre dim,
Faint of breath and thin of limb,
HOAR-FROST, like a maiden's ghost,
Nightly o'er the marshes crost
In the moonlight: where she flew,
   At the touch of her chill dress
Cobwebs of the glimmering dew
   Froze to silvern loveliness.

All the night, in the dim light,
Quietly she took her flight;
Thro' the streets she crept, and stay'd
In each silent window shade,
With her finger moist as rain
Drawing flowers upon the pane;—
On the phantom flowers so drawn
   With her freezing breath breathed she;
And each window-pane at dawn
   Turn'd to crystal tracerv!

Then the Phantom Fog came forth,
Following slowly from the North ;
Wheezing, coughing, blown, and damp,
Sullen sat he in the swamp,
Scowling with a blood-shot eye
As the canvas-backs went by ;
Till the North Wind with a shout,
Thrust his pole and poked him out ;
And the Phantom with a scowl,
   Black'ning night and dark'ning day,
Hooted after by the owl,
    Lamely halted on his way.

Now in flocks that ever increase
Honk the armies of the geese,
Silhouetted overhead
On a sky of crimson red.
After them in a dark mass,
Sleet and hail hiss as they pass,
Rattling on the frozen lea
With their chill artillery.
Then a silence : then comes on
Frost, the steel-bright Skeleton !
Silent in the night he steals,

With wolves howling at his heels,
Seeing to the locks and keys
On the lakes and on the leas;
Touching with his tingling wand
Trees and shrubs on every hand,
Till they change, transform'd to sight,
Into dwarfs and druids white,—
Each with icy beard and dress
Frozen into ghastliness;
And on many of their shoulders,
Chill, indifferent to beholders,
Sits the barr'd owl in a heap,
Ruffled, dumb, and fast asleep.
There the legions of the trees
Gather ghost-like round his knees;
While in cloudy cloak and hood,
Cold he creeps to the great wood :—
Lying there in a half doze,
While on finger-tips and toes
Squirrels turn their wheels, and jays
Flutter in a wild amaze,
And the foxes, lean and foul,
Look out of their holes and growl.
There he waited, breathing cold
On the white and silent wold.

In a silence sat the Thing,
Looking north, and listening !
And the farmers drave their teams
Past the woods and by the streams,
Crying as they met together,
With red noses, " *Frosty weather !* "
And along the iron ways
Tinkle, tinkle, went the sleighs.
And the wood-chopper did hie,
Leather stockings to the thigh,
Crunching on the snow that strew'd
Every corner of the wood.
Still Frost waited, very still ;
Then he whistled, loud and shrill ;
Then he pointed north, and lo !
The main Army of the Snow.

Blackly swarm'd the host afar,
Blotting sun, and moon, and star,
Whirling, in confusion driven,
Screaming, straggling, rent and riven,
In an awful wind of War,
Dragging drifts of dead beneath,
 With a melancholy groan,

While the fierce Frost set his teeth,
  Rose erect, and waved them on !

All day long the legions pass'd
On an ever-gathering blast ;
In an ever-gathering night,
Fast they eddied on their flight.
With a rush and with a roar,
Like the waves on a wild shore ;
With a motion and a gleam,
Whirling, driven in a dream ;
On they drave in drifts of white,
Burying Drowsietown from sight,
Covering ponds, and woods, and roads,
Shrouding trees and men's abodes ;
While the great Pond loaded deep,
Turning over in its sleep,
Groan'd !—But when night came, forsooth,
  Grew the tramp unto a thunder ;
Wind met wind with wail uncouth,
Frost and Storm fought nail and tooth,
  Shrieking, and the roofs rock'd under.
Scared out of its sleep that night,
Drowsietown awoke in fright ;

Chimney-pots above it flying,
   Windows crashing to the ground,
Snow-flakes blinding, multiplying,
   Snow-drift whirling round and round;
While, whene'er the strife seemed dying,
The great North Wind, shrilly crying,
   Clash'd his shield in battle-sound!

Multitudinous and vast,
Legions after legions passed.
Still the air behind was drear
With new legions coming near;
Still they waver'd, wander'd on,
Glimmer'd, darken'd, and were gone.
While the drift grew deeper, deeper,
   On the roofs and at the doors,
While the wind awoke each sleeper
   With its melancholy roars.
Once the Moon look'd out, and lo!
Flat against her face the Snow
Like a blinding grave-cloth lay,
Till she shuddering crept away.
Then thro' darkness like the grave,
On and on the legions drave.

When the dawn came, Drowsietown
  Smother'd in the snow-drift lay.
Still the swarms were drifting down
  In a dark and dreadful day.
On the blinds the whole day long,
  Thro' the red light, shadows flitted.
At the inn in a great throng
  Gossips gather'd drowsy-witted.
All around on the white lea
Farm-lamps twinkled drearily;
Not a road was now revealed,
  Drift, deep drift, at every door;
Field was mingled up with field,
  Stream and pond were smother'd o'er,
Trees and fences fled from sight
In the deep wan waste of white.

Many a night, many a day,
Pass'd the wonderful array,
Sometimes in confusion driven,
By the dreadful winds of heaven;
Sometimes gently wavering by
With a gleam and smothered sigh,
While the lean Frost still did stand
Pointing with his skinny hand

Northward, with the shrubs and trees
Buried deep below his knees.
Still the Snow passed ; deeper down
In the snow sank Drowsietown.
Not a bird stay'd, big or small,
Not a team could stir at all.
Round the cottage window-frame
Barking foxes nightly came,
Scowling in a spectral ring
At the ghostly glimmering.
Sly Abe Sinker at the Inn
Heap'd his fire up with a grin,
For the great room, warm and bright,
Never emptied morn or night.
Old folks shiver'd, with their bones
Full of pains and cold as stones.
Nought was doing, nought was done,
From the rise to set of sun.
Yawning in the ale-house heat,
Shivering in the snowy street,
Like dream-shadows, up and down,
  With their footprints black below,
Moved the folk of Drowsietown,
  In the Year of the Great Snow !

THE AURORA.

(From "Balder the Beautiful.")

FAR away across the gloom,
Rose-red like a rose in bloom,
Flashing, changing, ray by ray,
Glorious as the ghost of day,
Gleam'd in one vast aureole
Shifting splendours of the pole.
All across the vault of blue
Shooting lights and colours flew,
And the milky way shone there
Like a bosom white and bare,
Kindling, trembling, softly moved
By some heart that lived and loved.
Night was broken, and grew bright.
All the countless lamps of light
Swinging, flashing, near and far,
  Cast their glittering rays below,—
While the lustrous polar star
  Throbb'd close down upon the snow! . . .

CORUISKEN SONNETS.

I.

CORUISK.

I THINK this is the very stillest place
On all God's earth, and yet no rest is here.
The vapours mirror'd in the black loch's face
Drift on like frantic shapes and disappear;
A never-ceasing murmur in mine ear
Tells me of waters wild that ebb and flow;
There is no rest at all afar or near,
Only a sense of things that moan and go.
And lo! the still small life these limbs contain
Is flowing on as those, restless and proud;
Before that breathing nought within my brain
Pauses, but all drifts on like mist and cloud;
Only the bald peaks and the stones remain,
Frozen and silent, desolate and bow'd.

---

* Written at or near Loch Coruisk, Island of Skye. For a full description of the locality, see the author's "Land of Lorne."

I.

But Whither?

AND whither, O ye Vapours ! do ye wend ?
  Stirr'd by that weary breathing, whither away ?
  And whither, O ye Dreams ! that night and day
Drift o'er the troublous life, tremble, and blend
To broken lineaments of that far Friend,
  Whose strange breath's flux and reflux ye obey ?
  O sleepless Soul ! in the world's waste astray,
Whither ? and will thy wanderings ever end ?
All things that be are full of a quick pain ;
  Onward we fleet, swift as the running rill,—
The vapours drift, the mists within the brain
  Float on obscuringly and have no will.
Only the bare peaks and the stones remain ;
  These only,—and a God sublimely still.

III.

THE HILLS ON THEIR THRONES.

GHOSTLY and livid, robed with shadow, see !
　　Each mighty mountain silent on its throne,
　　From foot to scalp one stretch of livid stone,
Without one gleam of grass or greenery.
Silent they take the immutable decree—
　　Darkness or sunlight come,—they do not stir ;
Each bare brow lifted desolately free,
　　Keepeth the silence of a death-chamber.
Silent they watch each other until doom ;
　　They see each other's phantoms come and go,
Yet stir not.   Now the stormy hour brings gloom,
　　Now all things grow confused and black below,
Specific through the cloudy drift they loom,
　　And each accepts his individual woe.

IV.

KING BLAABHEIN.

MONARCH of these is Blaabhein.   On his height
  The lightning and the snow sleep side by side,
Like snake and lamb; he waiteth in a white
  And wintry consecration.   All his pride
Is husht this dimly-gleaming autumn day—
  He broodeth o'er the things he hath beheld—
Beneath his feet the rains crawl still and grey,
  Like phantoms of the mighty men of eld.
A quiet awe the dreadful heights doth fill,
  The high clouds pause and brood above their King;
The torrent murmurs gently as a rill;
  Softly and low the winds are murmuring;
A small black speck above the snow, how still
  Hovers the eagle, with no stir of wing!

v.

The Fiery Birth of the Hills.

O HOARY Hills, though ye look aged, ye
  Are but the children of a latter time !—
  Methinks I see ye in that hour sublime
When from the hissing cauldron of the Sea
Ye were upheaven, while so terribly
  The clouds boil'd, and the lightning scorch'd you
    bare.
Wild, new-born, blind, Titans in agony,
  Ye glared at heaven through folds of fiery hair ! . . .
Then, in an instant, while ye trembled thus
A Hand from heaven, white and luminous,
  Pass'd o'er your brows, and husht your fiery breath.
Lo ! one by one the still stars gather'd round,
The great Deep glass'd itself, and with no sound
  A cold snow fell, till all was still as death.

VI.

The Changeless Hills.

ALL power, all virtue, is repression—ye
  Are stationary, and God keeps you great ;
Around your heads the fretful winds play free ;
  You change not—you are calm and desolate.
  What seems to us a trouble and a fate
Is but the loose dust streaming from your feet
  And drifting onward—early ye sit and late,
While unseen winds waft past the things that fleet.
So sit for ever, still and passionless
As He that made you !—thought and soul's distress
  Ye know not, though ye contemplate the strife ;
Better to share the Spirit's bitterest aches—
Better to be the weakest wave that breaks
  On a wild Ocean of tempestuous Life.

VI.

O MOUNTAIN PEAK OF A GOD.

FATHER, if imperturbable thou art,
   Passive as these, lords of a lonely land—
If, having labour'd, thou must sit apart—
   If having once open'd the Void, and plann'd
   This tragedy, thou must impassive stand
Spectator of the scenic flow of things,
   Then I—a drop of dew, a grain of sand—
Pity thy lot, poor palsied King of kings.
Better to fail and fail, to shriek and shriek,
   Better to break, break like a wave, and go,—
Impotent godhead, let thy slave be weak!—
   Yea, do not freeze my soul, but let it flow—
Oh, wherefore call to thee, a mountain Peak
   Impassive, beautiful, serene with snow?

VII.

CRY OF THE LITTLE BROOK.

CHRIST help me! whither would my dark thoughts flow?
  I look around me, trembling fearfully;
The dreadful silence of the peaks of snow
    Freezes my lips, and all is sad to see.
    Hark! hark! what small voice murmurs " God made
      me!"
It is the Brooklet, singing all alone,
Sparkling with pleasure that is all its own,
    And running, self-contented, sweet, and free.
O Brooklet, born where never grass is green,
    Finding the stony hill and flowing fleet,
Thou comest as a messenger serene,
    With shining wings and silver-sandall'd feet;
Faint falls thy music on a soul unclean,
    And, in a moment, all the world looks sweet!

VIII.

THE HAPPY HEARTS OF EARTH.

WHENCE thou hast come, thou knowest not, little Brook,
   Nor whither thou art bound.   Yet wild and gay,
Pleased in thyself, and pleasing all that look,
   Thou wendest, all the seasons, on thy way;
   The lonely glen grows gladsome with thy play,
Thou glidest lamb-like through the ghostly shade;
To think of solemn things thou wast not made,
   But to sing on, for pleasure, night and day.
Such happy hearts are wandering, crystal clear,
   In the great world where men and women dwell;
Earth's mighty shows they neither love nor fear,
   They are content to be, while I rebel,
Out of their own delight dispensing cheer,
   And ever softly whispering, " All is well!"

NARRATIVE POEMS.

MEG BLANE.

I.

STORM.

"Lord, hearken to me!
Save all poor souls at sea!
Thy breath is on their cheeks,—
   Their cheeks are wan wi' fear;
Nae man speaks,
   For wha could hear?
The wild white water screams,
   The wind cries loud;
The fireflaught gleams
   On tatter'd sail and shroud!
Under the red mast-light
   The hissing surges slip;
Thick reeks the storm o' night
   Round him that steers the ship,—
And his een are blind

And he kens na where they run.
Lord, be kind !
Whistle back Thy wind,
For the sake of Christ Thy Son !"

.   .   .   And as she pray'd she knelt not on her knee,
But, standing on the threshold, looked to Sea,
   Where all was blackness and a watery roar,
Save when the dead light, flickering far away,
   Flash'd on the line of foam upon the shore,
And show'd the ribs of reef and surging bay !
   There was no sign of life across the dark,
   No piteous light from fishing-boat or bark,
Albeit for such she hush'd her heart to pray.
With tatter'd plaid wrapt tight around her form,
   She stood a space, blown on by wind and rain,
Then, sighing deep, and turning from the storm,
   She crept into her lonely hut again.

'Twas but a wooden hut under the height,
   Shielded in the black shadow of the crag :
One blow of such a wind as blew that night
   Could rend so rude a dwelling like a rag.
There, gathering in the crannies overhead,
Down fell the spouting rain, heavy as lead,—

So that the old roof and the rafters thin
Dript desolately, looking on the surf,
While blacker rain-drops down the walls of turf
  Splash'd momently on the mud-floor within.
There, swinging from the beam, an earthen lamp
Waved to the wind and glimmer'd in the damp,
  And shining on the chamber's wretchedness,
Illumed the household things of the poor place,
And flicker'd faintly on the woman's face,
  Sooted with rain, and on her dripping dress.
        A miserable den wherein to dwell,
        And yet she loved it well.

        "O Mither, are ye there?"
A deep voice fill'd the dark; she thrill'd to hear;
  With hard hand she push'd back her dripping hair,
And kiss'd him.   "Whisht, my bairn, for Mither's near."
  Then on the shuttle bed a figure thin
        Sat rubbing sleepy eyes:
A bearded man, with heavy hanging chin,
  And on his face a light not over-wise.
"Water!" he said; and deep his thirst was quell'd
Out of the broken pitcher she upheld,
And yawning sleepily, he gazed around,
And stretch'd his limbs again, and soon slept sound.

Stooping, she smooth'd the pillow 'neath his head,
  Still looking down with eyes liquid and mild,
And while she gazed, softly he slumberëd,
    That bearded man, her child.
  And a child's dreams were his; for as he lay,
  He uttered happy cries as if at play,
  And his strong hand was lifted up on high
  As if to catch the bird or butterfly;
  And often to his bearded lips there came
        That lonely woman's name;
  And though the wrath of Ocean roar'd so near,
        That one sweet word
        Was all the woman heard,
        And all she cared to hear.

Not old in years, though youth had pass'd away,
And the thin hair was tinged with silver grey,
Close to the noontide of the day of life,
She stood, calm featured like a wedded wife;
And yet no wedded wife was she, but one
  Whose foot had left the pathways of the just,
Yet meekly, since her penance had been done,
  Her soft eyes sought men's faces, not the dust.
Her tearful days were over: she had found
Firm footing, work to do upon the ground;

The Elements had welded her at length
        To their own truth and strength.

This woman was no slight and tear-strung thing,
Whose easy sighs fall soft on suffering,
But one in whom no stranger's eyes would seek
        For pity mild and meek.
Man's height was hers—man's strength and will thereto,
    Her shoulders broad, her step man-like and long ;
'Mong fishermen she dwelt, a rude, rough crew,
    And more than one had found her hand was strong.
And yet her face was gentle, though the sun
        Had made it dark and dun ;
        Her silver-threaded hair
Was comb'd behind her ears with cleanly care ;
And she had eyes liquid and sorrow-fraught,
    And round her mouth were delicate lines, that told
She was a woman sweet with her own thought,
    Though built upon a large, heroic mould.

        Who did not know Meg Blane ?
What hearth but heard the deeds that Meg had done ?
        What fisher of the main
But knew her, and her little-witted son ?
For mid the wildest waves of that mad coast
Her black boat hover'd and her net was tost,

And lonely in the watery solitude
The son and mother fish'd for daily food.
When on calm nights the herring hosts went by,
   Her frail boat follow'd the red smacks from shore,
And steering in the stern the man would lie
   While Meg was hoisting sail or plying oar;
Till, a black speck against the morning sky,
   The boat came homeward, with its silver store.
And Meg was cunning in the ways of things,
   Watching what every changing lineament
   Of Wind and Sky and Cloud and Water meant,
Knowing how Nature threatens ere she springs.
She knew the clouds as shepherds know their sheep,
   To eyes unskill'd alike, yet different each;
She knew the wondrous voices of the Deep;
   The tones of sea-birds were to her a speech.
Much faith was hers in GOD, who was her guide;
   Courage was hers such as GOD gives to few,
For she could face His terrors fearless-eyed,
   Yet keep the woman's nature sweet and true.
   Lives had she snatch'd out of the waste by night,
      When wintry winds were blowing;
   To sick-beds sad her face had carried light,
   When (like a thin sail lessening out of sight)
Some rude, rough life to the unknown Gulf was going;

For men who scorn'd a feeble woman's wail
Would heark to one so strong and brave as *she,*
   Whose face had braved the lightning and the gale,
      And ne'er grown pale,
Before the shrill shrieks of the murderous Sea.

Yet often, as she lay a-sleeping there,
   This woman started up and blush'd in shame,
Stretch'd out her arms embracing the thin air,
      Naming an unknown name;
There was a hearkening hunger in her face
   If sudden footsteps sounded on her ear;
And when strange seamen came unto the place
   She read their faces in a wretched fear;
And finding not the object of her quest,
Her hand she held hard on her heaving breast,
And wore a white look, and drew feeble breath,
     Like one that hungereth. . . .

It was a night of summer, yet the wind
   Had wafted from God's wastes the rain-clouds dank,
Blown out Heaven's thousand eyes and left it blind,
Though now and then the Moon gleamed moist behind
   The rack, till, smitten by the drift, she sank.
     But the Deep roar'd!

Suck'd to the black clouds, spumed the foam-fleck'd
    main,
  While Lightning rent the storm-rack like a sword,
And earthward roll'd the grey smoke of the Rain.

'Tis late, and yet the woman doth not rest,
But sitteth with chin drooping on her breast:
Weary she is, yet will not take repose;
Tired are her eyes, and yet they cannot close;
She rocketh to and fro upon her chair,
     And stareth at the air !

Far, far away her thoughts were travelling:
  They could not rest—they wander'd far and fleet,
As the storm-petrels o'er the waters wing,
  And cannot find a place to rest their feet;
And in her ear a thin voice murmurëd,
    " If he be *dead*—be *dead !*"
Then, even then, the woman's face went white
  And awful, and her eyes were fix'd in fear,
For suddenly all the wild screams of night
  Were hush'd : the Wind lay down ; and she could
    hear
Strange voices gather round her in the gloom,
Sounds of invisible feet across the room,

And after that the rustle of a shroud,
    And then a creaking door,
And last the coronach, full shrill and loud,
Of women clapping hands and weeping sore.

Now Meg knew well that ill was close at hand,
    On water or on land,
Because the Glamour touch'd her lids like breath,
    And scorch'd her heart : but in a waking swoon,
Quiet she stay'd,—not stirring,—cold as death,
    And felt those voices croon ;
Then suddenly she heard a human shout,
The hurried falling of a foot without,
Then a hoarse voice—a knocking at the door—
    " *Meg, Meg! A Ship ashore!*"

Now mark the woman ! She hath risen her height,
Her threadbare shawl is wrapt around her tight,
Tight clenchëd in her palm her fingers are,
Her eye is steadfast as a fixëd star.
One look upon her child—he sleepeth on—
One step unto the door, and she is gone :
Barefooted out into the dark she fares,
    And comes where, rubbing eyelids thick with sleep,
The half-clad fishers mingle oaths and prayers,
    And look upon the Deep.

. . . Black was the oozy lift,
Black was the sea and land ;
Hither and thither, thick with foam and drift,
Did the deep Waters shift,
Swinging with iron clash on stone and sand.
Faintlier the heavy Rain was falling,
Faintlier, faintlier, the Wind was calling
With hollower echoes up the drifting dark !
While the swift rockets shooting through the night
Flash'd past the foam-fleck'd reef with phantom light,
And show'd the piteous outline of a bark,
Rising and falling like a living thing,
Shuddering, shivering,
While, howling beastlike, the white breakers there
Blew blindness in the dank eyes of despair.
Then one cried, "She has sunk !"—and on the shore
Men shook, and on the heights the women cried ;
But, lo ! the outline of the bark once more !
While flashing faint the blue light rose and died.
Ah, God, put out Thy hand ! all for the sake
Of little ones, and weary hearts that wake.
Be gentle ! chain the fierce waves with a chain !
Let the gaunt seaman's little boys and girls
Sit on his knee and play with his black curls
Yet once again !

And breathe the frail lad safely through the foam
Back to the lonely mother in her home!
And spare the bad man with the frenzied eye;
Spare *him*, for CHRIST's sake,—bid Thy Death go by—
  He hath no heart to die!

Now faintlier blew the wind, the thin rain ceased,
 The thick cloud clear'd like smoke from off the strand,
For, lo! a golden glimmer in the east,—
  GOD putting out His hand!
And overhead the rack grew thinner too,
  And through the smoky gorge
The wind drave past the stars, and faint they flew
  Like sparks blown from a forge!
And now the thousand foam-flames o' the sea
  Hither and thither flashing visibly;
And grey lights hither and thither came and fled,
Like dim shapes searching for the drownèd dead;
And where these shapes most thickly glimmer'd by,
 Out on the cruel reef the black hulk lay,
And cast, against the kindling eastern sky,
 Its shape gigantic on the shrouding spray.

Silent upon the shore the fishers fed
　Their eyes on horror, waiting for the close,
When in the midst of them a shrill voice rose :
　　"The boat ! the boat !" it said.

Like creatures startled from a trance, they turn'd
　To her who spake ; tall in the midst stood she,
With arms uplifted, and with eyes that yearn'd
　　Out on the murmuring sea.
Some, shrugging shoulders, homeward turn'd their eyes,
　And others answer'd back in brutal speech ;
But some, strong-hearted, uttering shouts and cries,
　Follow'd the fearless woman up the beach.
A rush to seaward—black confusion—then
　A struggle with the surf upon the strand—
'Mid shrieks of women, cries of desperate men,
　The long oars smite, the black boat springs from land !
　　Around the thick spray flies ;
The surges roll and seem to overwhelm.
　With blowing hair and onward-gazing eyes
The woman stands erect, and grips the helm. . . .

Now fearless heart, Meg Blane, or all must die !
Let not the skill'd hand thwart the steadfast eye.

The crested wave comes near,—crag-like it towers
Above you, scattering round its chilly showers:
One flutter of the hand, and all is done!
Now steel thy heart, thou woman-hearted one!
     Softly the good helm guides;
Up to the liquid ledge the boat leaps light,—
Hidden an instant,—on the foamy height,
  Dripping and quivering like a bird, it rides.
Athwart the ragged rift the moon looms pale,
     Driven before the gale,
And making silvern shadows with her breath,
Where on the sighing sea it shimmereth;
And lo! the light illumes the reef!—'tis shed
  Full on the wreck, as the dark boat draws nigh.
A crash!—the wreck upon the reef is fled!
  A scream!—and all is still beneath the sky,
  Save the wild waters as they clash and cry.

II.

Dead Calm.

Dawn; and the Deep was still.   From the bright strand,
Meg, shading eyes against the morning sun,
Gazed seaward.   After trouble, there was peace.

Smooth, many-colour'd as a ring-dove's neck,
Stretch'd the still sea, and on its eastern rim
The dewy light, with liquid yellow beams,
Gleam'd like a sapphire.   Overhead, soft airs
To feathery cirrus fleck'd the lightening blue;
Beneath, the Deep's own breathing made a breeze;
And up the weedy beach the blue waves crept,
Thinning to one long line of cream-white foam.

Seaward the woman gazed, with keen eye fix'd
On a dark Shape that floated on the calm,
Drifting as seaweed; still and black it lay,—
The outline of a lifeless human form:

And yet it was no drownëd mariner,
For she who look'd was smiling, and her face
Look'd merry; still more merry, when a boat,
With pale and timorous fishermen, drew nigh;
And as the fearful boatmen paused and gazed,
A boat's length distant, leaning on their oars,
The shape took life—dash'd up a dripping head,
Screaming—flung up its limbs with flash of foam,
And, with a shrill and spirit-thrilling cry,
Dived headlong, as a monster of the main
Plunges deep down when startled on its couch
Of glassy waters.   'Twas the woman's child,
The witless water-haunter—Angus Blane.

For Angus Blane, not fearful as the wise
Are fearful, loved the Ocean like a thing
Born amid creatures of the slimy ooze.
A child, he sported on its sands, and crept
Splashing with little feet amid the foam;
And when his limbs were stronger, and he reach'd
A young man's stature, the great gulf had grown
Fair and familiar as his mother's face.
Far out he swam, on windless summer days,
Floating like fabled merman far from land,

Plunging away from startled fishermen
With eldrich cry and wild phantasmic glare;
And in the untrodden halls below the sea,
Awaking wondrous echoes that had slept
Since first the briny Spirit stirr'd and breath'd.
On nights of summer in the gleaming bay
He glisten'd like a sea-snake in the moon,
Splashing with trail of glistening phosphor-fire,
And laughing shrill till echo answer'd him,
While the pale helmsman on the passing boat,
Thinking some Demon of the waters cried,
Shiver'd and pray'd. His playmates were the waves,
The sea his playground. On his ears were sounds
Sweeter than human voices. On his sense,
Tho' saddened with his silent life, there stole
A motion and a murmur that at times
Brake through his lips, informing witless words
With strange sea-music. In his infancy
Children had mock'd him: he had shunn'd their sports,
And haunted lonely places, nurturing
The bright, fierce, animal splendour of a soul
That ne'er was clouded by the mental mists
That darken oft the dreams of wiser men.
Only in winter seasons he was sad;
For then the loving Spirit of the Deep

Repulsed him, and its smile was mild no more ;
And on the strand he wander'd ; from deep caves
Gazed at the Tempest; and from day to day
Moan'd to his mother for the happy time
When swifts are sailing on the wind o' the south,
And summer smiles afar off through the rain,
Bringing her golden circlet to the Sea.

And as the deepening of strange melody,
Caught from the unknown shores beyond the seas,
Was the outspreading of his life to her
Who bare him ; yea, at times, the woman's womb
Seemed laden with the load of him unborn,
So close his being clave unto her flesh,
So link'd was his strange spirit with her own.
The faint forebodings of her heart, when first
She saw the mind-mists in his infant eyes,
And knew him witless, turn'd as years wore on
Into more spiritual, less selfish love
Than common mothers feel ; and he had power
To make her nature deeper, more alive
Unto the supernatural feet that walk
Our dark and troubled waters.   Thence was born
Much of her strength upon the Sea, her trust
In the Sea's MASTER ! thence, moreover, grew

Her faith in visions, warnings, fantasies,
Such as came ever thronging on her heart
When most her eyes look'd inward—to the place
Fraught with her secret sorrow.

                         As she gazed,
Smiling, the bearded face of Angus rose
Nearer to shore, and panting in the sun,
Smiled at the fishers.   Then the woman turn'd,
And took, with man-like step and slow, a path
That, creeping through the shadows of the cliffs,
Wound to the clachan.   In the clear, bright dawn
Lay Thornock glittering, while, thin and blue,
Curl'd peat-smoke from the line of fisher-huts
That parted the high shingle from the land.

The tide was low : amid the tangled weeds
The many-colour'd rocks and sparkling pools,
Went stooping men and women, seeking spoil,
Treasure or drift-wood floating from the wreck ;
Beyond, some stood in fish-boats, peering down
Seeking the drownëd dead ; and, near at hand,
So near, a tall man might have waded thither
With a dry beard, the weedy reef loom'd red,
And there the white fowl ever and anon

Rose like a flash of foam whirl'd in the air,
And, screaming, settled.   But not thitherward
Now look'd Meg Blane.   Along the huts she went —
Among the rainy pools where played and cried
Brown and barefooted bairns—among the nets
Stretch'd steaming in the sun—until she reach'd
The cottage she was seeking.   At the door,
Smoking his pipe, a grizzly Fisher sat,
Looking to sea.   With him she spake awhile,
Then, with a troubled look, enter'd the hut,
And sought the inner chamber.

                              Faint and pale
Light glimmer'd through a loop-hole in the wall,
A deep white streak across the sand-strewn floor,
All else in shadow ; and the room was still,
Save for a heavy breathing, as of one
In troubled sleep.   Within the wall's recess,
On the rude bed of straw the sleeper lay,
His head upon his arm, the sickly light
Touching his upturn'd face ; while Meg drew near,
And gazed upon him with a stranger's eyes,
Quiet and pitying.   Though his sleep was sound,
His dreams were troubled.   Throwing up his arms,
He seem'd to beckon, muttering ; then his teeth

Clench'd tight, a dark frown wrinkled on his brow,
And still he lay like one awaiting doom ;
But suddenly, in agony supreme,
He breathed like one who struggles, sinks, and drowns ;
Strangling, with wavering arms and quivering limbs,
And screaming in his throat, he fought for life ;
Till, half-awakening with the agony,
His glazèd eyes he open'd, glaring round,
While Meg drew shivering back into the shade ;
Again, with deeper breath, as if relieved,
He dropp'd his bearded face upon his arm,
And dream'd again.

            Then Meg stole stilly forth,
And in the outer chamber found a lamp,
And lit the same in silence, and return'd
On tiptoe to the sleeper.   As she went,
White as a murder'd woman's grew her face,
Her teeth were clench'd together ; and her eyes
With ring on ring of widening wonder glared
In fever'd fascination upon him
Who slumber'd.   Closer still she crept,
Holding the lamp aloft, until his breath
Was hot upon her cheek,—so gaunt, so white,
It seem'd her time was come.   Yet in her look

Was famine.   As one famish'd looks on food
After long agony, and thinks it dream,
She gazed and gazed, nor stirr'd, nor breathed, nor lived,
Save in her spirit's hunger flashing forth
Out of her face ; till suddenly the man,
Half-opening his eyes, reached out his arms
And gript her, crying, "Silence ! pray to GOD !
She's sinking !" then, with shrill and awful groan,
Awaken'd.

    And the woman would have fled,
Had he not gript her.   In her face he gazed,
Thrusting one hand into his silver'd hair,
Seeking to gather close his scatter'd thoughts,
And his eye brighten'd, and he murmur'd low,
"Where am I?   Dead or living?   Ah, I live !
The ship? the ship?"   Meg answer'd not, but shrank
Into the shadow ; till she saw the mists
Pass from his bearded face and leave it clear,
And heard his voice grow calmer, measured now
By tranquil heart-beats.   Then he ask'd again,
" The ship? How many live of those aboard?"
And when she answer'd he alone was saved,
He groan'd ; but with a sailor's fearless look,
" Thank GOD for that !" he said ; " and yet He might

Have spared a better man.   Where am I, friend?"
"On the north coast," said Meg, " upon the shore
At Thornock."

        Could the seaman, while she spake,
Have mark'd the lurid light on that pale face,
All else,—the Storm, the terrible fight for life,—
Had been forgotten ; but his wearied eye
Saw dimly.   Grasping still her quivering wrist,
He question'd on ; and, summoning strength of heart,
In her rude speech she told him of the storm :
How from the reef the rending Ship had rolled
As aid drew nigh ; how, hovering near its tomb,
The fishers from the whirling waters dragg'd
Two drownèd seamen, and himself, a corpse
In seeming ; how by calm and tender care,
They wound his thin and bloody thread of life
Out of the slowly-loosening hands of Death.

III.

A Troubled Deep.

Then, with strange trouble in her eyes, Meg Blane
Stole swiftly back unto her hut again,
Like one that flyeth from some fearful thing;
Then sat and made a darkness, covering
Her face with apron old, thinking apart;
And yet she scarce could think, for ache of heart,
But saw dead women and dead men go by,
And felt the wind, and heard the waters cry,
And on the waters, as they wash'd to shore,
Saw one face float alone and glimmer hoar
Through the green darkness of the breaking brine.

And Meg was troubled deep, nor could divine
The wherefore of her trouble, since 'twas clear
The face long wearied for at last was near,
Since all her waiting on was at an end.
Ay, Meg was dull, and could not comprehend
How God put out His breath that day, and blew
Her lover to her feet before she knew,

Yet misted the dull future from her sight;
Wherefore she stared stark down on her delight
As on a dead face washing in from sea.
But when she understood full certainly
The thing had come according to her prayer,
Her strength came back upon her unaware,
And she thank'd GOD, albeit the pleasure seem'd
Less absolute a bliss than she had dream'd
When it was a sweet trouble far away;
For she was conscious how her hair was gray,
Her features worn, her flesh's freshness gone,
Through toiling in the sun and waiting on;
And quietly she murmur'd, weeping not,
" Perchance—for men forget—he hath forgot ! "

And two long days she was too dazed and weak
To step across the sands to him, and speak;
But on the third day, pale with her intent,
She took the great hand of her son, and went,
Not heeding while the little-witted one
Mouth'd at the sea and mutter'd in the sun;
And firmly stepping on along the shore,
She saw, afar off at the cottage door,
The figure of her shipwreck'd mariner;

When, deeply troubled by a nameless fear,
She linger'd, and she linger'd, pale and wan.

Then, coming near, she noted how the man
Sat sickly, holding out his arm to please
A fisher child he held between his knees,
Whose eyes look'd on the mighty arm and bare,
Where ships, strange faces, anchors, pictured were,
Prick'd blue into the skin with many a stain ;
And, sharply marking the man's face, Meg Blane
Was cheer'd and holpen, and she trembled less,
Thinking, " His heart is full of kindliness."
And, feeling that the thing if to be done
Must be done straight, she hasten'd with her son,
And though she saw the man's shape growing dim,
Came up with sickly smile and spake to him,
Pausing not, though she scarce could hear or see —
" Has Angus Macintyre forgotten me ? "
And added quickly, " I am Maggie Blane ! "

Whereat the man was smit by sudden pain
And wonder—yea, the words he heard her speak
Were like a jet of fire upon his cheek ;
And, rising up erect, " Meg Blane ! " he cried,
And, white and chilly, thrust the bairn aside,

And peer'd upon the woman all amazed,
While, pressing hard upon her heart, she gazed
Blankly at the dim mist she knew was he.

For a short space both stood confusedly,
In silence ; but the man was first to gain
Calmness to think and power to speak again ;
And, though his lips were bloodless and prest tight,
Into his eyes he forced a feeble light,
Taking her shivering hand, naming her name
In forced kind tones, yet with a secret shame ;—
Nor sought to greet her more with touch or kiss.
But she, who had waited on so long for this,
Feeling her hand between his fingers rest,
Could bear no more, but fell upon his breast,
Sobbing and moaning like a little bairn.

Then, with her wild arms round him, he looked stern,
With an unwelcome burden ill at ease,
While her full heart flow'd out in words like these—
" At last ! at last ! O Angus, let me greet ![1]
God's good ! I ever hoped that we would meet !
Lang, lang hae I been waiting by the Sea,
Waiting and waiting, praying on my knee ;

------

[1] *To greet ;* anglicè, to weep.

And God *said* I should·look again on you,
And, though I scarce believed, God's word comes true,
And He hath put an end to my distress ! "—
E'en as she spoke, her son pluck'd at her dress,
Made fierce grimaces at the man, and tried
To draw her from the breast whereon she cried ;
But looking up, she pointed to her child,
And look'd into her lover's eyes and smiled.
" God help him, Angus ! 'Tis *the Bairn !* " she said ;—
Nor noted how the man grew shamed and red,
With child and mother ill at ease and wroth,
And wishing he were many a mile from both.

For now Meg's heart was wandering far away,
And to her soul it seem'd but yesterday
That, standing inland in a heathery dell,
At dead of night, she bade this man farewell,
And heard him swear full fondly in her ear
Sooner or late to come with gold and gear,
And marry her in church by holy rite ;
And at the memory a quiet light,
Rose-like and maiden, came upon her face,
And soften'd her tall shape to nameless grace,
As warm winds blowing on a birk-tree green
Make it one rippling sheet of radiant sheen.

But soon from that remembrance driven again
By the man's silence and his pallid pain,
She shiver'd for a moment as with cold,
And left his bosom, looking grieved and old,
Yet smiling, forcing a strange smile, and seeking
For tokens in his face more sweet than speaking.

But he was dumb, and with a gloomy frown,
Twitching his fingers quick, was looking down.
" What ails thee, Angus?" cried the woman, reading
His face with one sharp look of interceding ;
Then, looking downward too, she paused apart,
With blood like water slipping through her heart,
Because she thought, " Alas, if it should be
That Angus cares no more for mine and me,
Since I am old and worn with sharp distress,
And men like pretty looks and daintiness ;
And since we parted twenty years have past,
And that, indeed, is long for a man's love to last ! "

But, agonized with looking at her woe,
And bent to end her hope with one sharp blow,
The troubled man, uplifting hands, spake thus,
In rapid accents, sharp and tremulous :

"Too late, Meg Blane! seven years ago I wed
Another woman, deeming you were dead,—
And I have bairns!"   And there he paused, for fear.

As when, with ghostly voices in her ear,
While in her soul, as in a little well
The silver moonlight of the Glamour fell,
She had been wont of nights to hark alone,
So stood she now, not stirring, still as stone,
While in her soul, with desolate refrain,
The words, "*Too late!*" rang o'er and o'er again;
Into his face she gazed with ghastly stare;
Then raising her wild arms into the air,
Pinching her face together in sharp fear,
She quiver'd to the ground without a tear,
And put her face into her hands, and thrust
Her hair between her teeth, and spat it forth like dust.

And though, with pity in his guilty heart,
The man spake on, and sought to heal her smart,
She heard not, but was dumb and deaf in woe;
But when in pain, to see her grieving so,
Her son put down his hand, and named her name,
And whisper'd, "Mither! mither! let us hame!"

K

She seized the hand, and smoothed her features wan,
And rose erect, not looking at the man,
But, gazing down, moved slowly from the spot.

    Over this agony I linger not,
Nor shall I picture how on that sad shore
They met and spoke and parted yet once more,
So calmly that the woman understood
Her hope indeed had gone away for good.
But ere the man departed from the place
It seem'd to Meg, contemplating his face,
Her love for him had ne'er been so intense
As it had seem'd when he was far from thence;
And many a thing in him seem'd little-hearted
And mean and loveless; so that ere they parted
She seem'd unto her sorrow reconciled.
And when he went away, she almost smiled,
But bitterly, then turn'd to toil again,
And felt most hard to all the world of men.

IV.

"And the Spirit of God moved upon the waters."

LORD, with how small a thing
Thou canst prop up the heart against the grave !
A little glimmering
Is all we crave !
The lustre of a love
That hath no being ;
The pale point of a little star above
Flashing and fleeing,
Contents our seeing.
The house that never will be built ; the gold
That never will be told ;
The task we leave undone when we are cold ;
The dear face that returns not, but is lying,
Lick'd by the leopard, in an Indian cave ;
The coming rest that cometh not, till, sighing,
We turn our tremulous gaze upon the grave.
And, Lord, how should we dare
Thither in peace to fall,
But for a feeble glimmering even *there*—
Falsest, some sigh, of all ?

We are as children in Thy hands indeed,
And Thou hast easy comfort for our need,—
The shining of a lamp, the tinkling of a bell,
Content us well.

And even when Thou bringest to our eyes
A thing long-sought, to show its worthlessness,
Anon we see another thing arise,
And we are comforted in our distress ;
And, waiting on, we watch it glittering,
Till in its turn it seems a sorry thing ;
And even as we weep
Another rises, and we smile again !
Till, wearied out with watching on in vain,
We fall to sleep.

And oft one little light that *looks* divine
Is all some strong Soul seeks on mortal ground ;
There are no more to shine
When that one thing is found.
If it be worthless, then what shall suffice ?
The lean hand grips a speck that was a spark,
The heart is turned to ice,
And all the world is dark.

Hard are Thy ways when that one thing is sought,
    Found, touch'd and proven nought.
Far off it is a mighty magic strong
    To lead a life along.
But lo ; it shooteth hitherward, and now
    Droppeth, a rayless stone, upon the sod.—
The world is lost : perchance not even Thou
    Survivest it, Lord God !

    In poverty, in pain
    For weary years and long,
One faith, one fear, had comforted Meg Blane,
    Yea, made her brave and strong ;
A faith so faint, it seem'd not faith at all,
    Rather a trouble, and a dreamy fear,—
A hearkening for a voice, for a footfall,
    She never hoped in sober heart to hear :
    This had been all her cheer !
    Yet with this balm
    Her Soul might have slept calm
For many another year.
In terror and in desolation, she
    Had been sustain'd,
And never felt abandon'd utterly
    While that remain'd.

Lord, in how small and poor a space can hide
The motives of our patience and our pride,—
The clue unto the fortunate man's distress,
The secret of the hero's fearlessness!
What had sustain'd this Woman on the sea
      When strong men turn'd to flee?
        Not courage, not despair,
        Not pride, not household care,
      Not faith in Thee!
Nought but a hungry instinct blind and dim—
      A fond pathetic pain:
A dreamy wish to gaze again on him
  She never wholly hoped to see again!

Not all at once,—not in an hour, a day,
  Did the strong Woman feel her force depart,
Or know how utterly had pass'd away
      The strength of her sad heart.
It was not Love she miss'd, for Love was dead,
  And surely had been dead long ere she knew;
She did not miss the man's face when it fled,
      As passionate women do.
She saw him walk into the world again,
      And had no pain;
She shook him by the hand, and watch'd him go,

And thought it better so.
She turn'd to her hard task-work as of old,
Tending her bearded child with love tenfold,
Hoisted the sails and plied the oar,
Went wandering out from shore,
And for a little space,
Wore an unruffled face,
Though wind and water help'd her heart no more.
But, mark : she knelt less often on her knees,
For, labour as she might,
By day or night,
She could not toil enough to give her ease.
And presently her tongue, with sharper chimes,
Chided at times.
And she who had endured such sore distress
Grew peevish, pain'd at her own peevishness ;
And though she did not weep,
Her features grew disfigur'd, dark, and dead,
And in the night, when bitterest mourners sleep,
She feverishly toss'd upon her bed.

Slowly the trouble grew, and soon she found
Less pleasure in the fierce yet friendly Sea ;
The wind and water had a wearier sound,
The Moon and Stars were sick as corpse-lights be ;

Then more and more strange voices filled her ear,
And ghostly feet came near,
And strange fire blew her eyelids down, and then
Dead women and dead men
Dripping with phosphor, rose, and ere she wist
Went by in a cold mist;
Nor left her strengthen'd in her heart and bold,
As they had done of old;
But ever after they had pass'd away
She had no heart to pray.
Bitter and dull and cold,
Her Soul crawl'd back into the common day.

Out of the East by night
Drew the dark drifting cloud;
The air was hush'd with snow-flakes wavering white;
But the seas below were loud;
And out upon the reef the piteous light
Rose from a shipwreck'd bark
Into the dark.
Pale stood the fishers, while the wind wail'd by,
Till suddenly they started with one cry,
And fearless to their places leapt the crew,
And forth into the foam the black boat flew.

Then one call'd out, "*Meg Blane!*"
  But Meg stood by, and trembled and was dumb,
Till, smit unto the heart by sudden pain,
  Into her hair she thrust her fingers numb,
    And fell upon the sands,
Nor answer'd while the wondering fishers call'd,
  But tore the slippery seaweed with her hands,
    And scream'd, and was appall'd.

For lo! the Woman's spiritual strength
      Snapt like a thread at length,
And tears, ev'n such as suffering women cry,
      Fell from her eyes anon;
And she knew well, although she knew not *why*,
  The charm she had against the Deep was gone!
      And after that dark hour,
        She was the shadow of a strong Soul dead,
      All terrible things of power
      Turn'd into things of dread,
And all the peace of all the world had fled.

Then only in still weather did she dare
  To seek her bread on Ocean, as of old,
And oft in tempest time her shelf was bare,
  Her hearth all black and cold;

Then very bitterly, with heart gone wild,
   She clung about her child,
And hated all the Earth beneath the skies,
Because she saw the hunger in his eyes.
For on his mother's strength the witless wight
   Had leant for guide and light,
And food had ever come into his hand,
 And he had known no thought of suffering;
Yea, all his life and breath on sea and land
   Had been an easy thing.
And now there was a change in his sole friend
   He could not comprehend.
Yet slowly to the shade of her distress
His nature shaped itself in gentleness!
And when he found her weeping, he too wept,
 And, if she laugh'd, laugh'd out in company;
Nay, often to the fisher-huts he crept,
 And begg'd her bread, and brought it tenderly,
Holding it to her mouth, and till she ate
 Touching no piece, although he hunger'd sore.
And these things were a solace to her fate,
 But wrung her heart the more.

 Thus, to the bitter dolour of her days,
In witless mimicry he shaped his ways!

They fared but seldom now upon the Sea,
　　But wander'd mid the marshes hand in hand,
　Hunting for faggots on the inland lea,
　　Or picking dulse for food upon the strand.
Something had made the world more sad and strange,
But easily he changëd with the change.
For in the very trick of woe he clad
His features, and was sad since she was sad,
Yea, leant his chin upon his hands like her,
　Looking at vacancy ; and when the Deep
　Was troublous, and she started up from sleep,
He too awoke, with fearful heart astir ;
And still, the more her bitter tears she shed
　Upon his neck, marking that mimic-woe,
The more in blind, deep love he fashionëd
　His grief to hers, and was contented so.

But as a tree inclineth weak and bare
Under an unseen weight of wintry air,
Beneath her load the weary Woman bent,
And, stooping double, waver'd as she went ;
And the days snow'd their snows upon her head
　　　As they went by,
　　And ere a year had fled
　　She felt that she must die.

Then like a thing whom very witlessness
　　Maketh indifferent, she linger'd on,
Not caring to abide with her distress,
　　Not caring to be gone;
But gazing with a dull and darkening eye,
　　And seeing Dreams pass by.
Not speculating whither she would go,
But feeling there was nought she cared to know,
　　And melting even as Snow.
Save when the man's hand slipp'd into her own,
　　And flutter'd fondly there,
And she would feel her life again, and groan,
" O God ! when I am gone, how will he fare ? "
　　And for a little time, for Angus' sake,
　　　Her hopeless heart would ache,
　　And all life's stir and anguish once again
　　　Would swoon across her brain.

　　　" O bairn, when I am dead,
　　　　How shall ye keep frae harm ?
　　　What hand will gie ye bread ?
　　　　What fire will keep ye warm ?
How shall ye dwell on earth awa' frae me ? "—
　　　　" O Mither, dinna dee ! "

"O bairn, by night or day
  I hear nae sounds ava',
  But voices of winds that blaw,
And the voices of spirits that say
  'Come awa! come awa!'
The Lord that made the Wind, and made the Sea,
  Is sore on my son and me,
  And I melt in His breath like snaw "—
  "O Mither, dinna dee!"

"O bairn, it is but closing up the een,
  And lying down never to rise again.
Many a strong man's sleeping hae I seen.—
  There is nae pain;
I am weary, weary, and I scarce ken why;
  My summer has gone by,
And sweet were sleep but for the sake o' thee."—
  "O Mither, dinna dee!"

When summer scents and sounds were on the Sea,
And all night long the silvern surge plash'd cool,
Outside the hut she sat upon a stool,
And with thin fingers fashion'd carefully,
While Angus leant his head against her knee,
  A long white dress of wool.

"O Mither," cried the man, " what make ye there ? "
    " A blanket for our bed ! "
"O Mither, is it like the shroud folk wear
    When they are drown'd and dead ? "
And Meg said nought, but kiss'd him on the lips,
    And looked with dull eye seaward, where the Moon
Blacken'd the white sails of the passing ships,
    Into the land where she was going soon.

And in the reaping time she lay abed,
And by her side the dress unfinishëd,
And with dull eyes that knew not even her child
She gazed at vacancy and sometimes smiled;
And ever her fingers work'd, for in her thought,
Stitching and stitching, still the dress she wrought ;
And then a beldame old, with blear-eyed face,
For CHRIST and Charity came to the place,
And stilly sew'd the woollen shroud herself,
And set the salt and candle on a shelf.
And like a dumb thing crouching moveless there,
    Gripping the fingers wan,
Marking the face with wild and wondering stare,
    And whining beast-like, watch'd the witless man.

Then like a light upon a headland set,
In winds that come from far-off waters blowing,

The faint light glimmer'd—fainter—fainter yet !

But suddenly it brighten'd, at its going ;

And Meg sat up, and, lo ! her features wore

The stately sweetness they had known of yore ;

And delicate lines were round her mouth ; mild rest

   Was in her eyes, though they were waxing dim ;

And when the man crept close unto her breast,

        She brighten'd kissing him.

        And it was clear

She had heard tidings it was sweet to hear,

And had no longer any care or fear.

" I go my bairn, and thou wilt come to me !"

      "O Mither, dinna dee !"

But as she spake she dropt upon the bed,

And darken'd, while the breath came thick and fleet :

" O Jessie, see they mind my Bairn !" she said,

And quiver'd,—and was sleeping at God's Feet.

When on her breast the plate of salt was laid,

   And the corse-candle burnt with sick blue light,

The man crouch'd, fascinated and afraid,

   Beside her, moaning through the night ;

And answer'd not the women who stole near,

      And would not see nor hear;

And when a day and night had come and gone,

Ate at the crusts they brought him, gazing on ;
And when they took her out upon a bier,
He follow'd quietly without a tear ;
And when on the hard wood fell dust and stone,
    He murmur'd a thin answer to the sound,
And in the end he sat, with a dull moan,
        Upon the new-made mound.

Last, as a dog that mourns a master dead,
    The man did haunt that grave in dull dumb pain ;
Creeping away to beg a little bread,
        Then stealing back again ;
And only knaves and churls refused to give
The gift of bread or meal that he might live—
        Till, pale and piteous-eyed,
He moan'd beneath a load too hard to bear.
        " Mother !" he cried,—
And crawled into the Dark, to seek her *there*.

WILLIE BAIRD.

" An old man's tale, a tale for men grey-hair'd,
   Who wear, thro' second childhood to the Lord."

'TIS two-and-thirty summers since I came
To school the village lads of Inverburn.

My father was a shepherd old and poor,
Who, dwelling 'mong the clouds on norland hills,
His tartan plaidie on, and by his side
His sheep-dog running, redden'd with the winds
That whistle southward from the Polar seas:
I follow'd in his footsteps when a boy,
And knew by heart the mountains round our home;
But when I went to Edinglass, to learn
At college there, I look'd about the place,
And heard the murmur of the busy streets
Around me, in a dream;—and only saw
The clouds that snow around the mountain tops,
The mists that chase the phantom of the moon
In lonely mountain tarns,—and heard the while,

Not footsteps sounding hollow to and fro,
But wild winds, wailing thro' the woods of pine.
Time pass'd; and day by day those sights and sounds
Grew fainter,—till they troubled me no more.

 O Willie, Willie, are you sleeping sound?
And can you feel the stone that I have placed
Yonder above you? Are you dead, my doo?
Or did you see the shining Hand that parts
The clouds above, and becks the bonnie birds,
Until they wing away, and human eyes,
That watch them while they vanish up the blue,
Droop and grow tearful? Ay, I ken, I ken,
I'm talking folly, but I loved the child!
He was the bravest scholar in the school!
He came to teach the very Dominie—
Me, with my lyart locks and sleepy heart!

 Oh, well I mind the day his mother brought
Her tiny trembling tot with yellow hair,
Her tiny poor-clad tot six summers old,
And left him seated lonely on a form
Before my desk. He neither wept nor gloom'd;
But waited silently with shoeless feet
Swinging above the floor; in wonder eyed
The maps upon the walls, the big black board,

The slates and books and copies, and my own
Grey hose and clumpy boots ; last, fixing gaze
Upon a monster spider's web that fill'd
One corner of the whitewash'd ceiling, watch'd
The speckled traitor jump and jink about,
Till he forgot my unfamiliar eyes,
Weary and strange and old.   " Come here, my bairn ! "
And timid as a lamb he seedled up.
" What do they call ye ? "   " Willie," coo'd the wean,
Up-peeping slily, scraping with his feet.
I put my hand upon his yellow hair,
And cheer'd him kindly.   Then I bade him lift
The small black bell that stands behind the door,
And ring the shouting laddies from their play.
" Run, Willie ! "   And he ran, and eyed the bell,
Stoop'd o'er it, seem'd afraid that it would bite,
Then grasp'd it firm, and as it jingled gave
A timid cry—next laugh'd to hear the sound—
And ran full merry to the door and rang,
And rang, and rang, while lights of music lit
His pallid cheek, till, shouting, panting hard,
In ran the big rough laddies from their play.

Then, rapping sharply on the desk, I drove
The scholars to their seats, and beckon'd up

The stranger ; smiling, bade him seat himself
And hearken to the rest.   Two weary hours
Buzz-buzz, boom-boom, went on the noise of school.
While Willie sat and listen'd open-mouth'd ;
Till school was over, and the big and small
Flew home in flocks.   But Willie stay'd behind.
I beckon'd to the mannock with a smile,
Took him upon my knee, and crack'd and talk'd.

    First, he was timid ; next, grew bashful ; next,
He warm'd, and told me stories of his home,
His father, mother, sisters, brothers, all ;
And how, when strong and big, he meant to buy
A gig to drive his father to the kirk ;
And how he long'd to be a dominie !
Such simple prattle as I plainly see
Your wisdom smiles at. . . . Weel ! the laddie still
Was seated on my knee, when at the door
We heard a sound of scraping : Willie prick'd
His ears and listen'd, then he clapt his hands—
" Hey, Donald, Donald, Donald ! "   [See ! the rogue
Looks up and blinks his eyes—he knows his name !]
" Hey, Donald, Donald ! " Willie cried.   At that
I saw beneath me, at the door, a Dog—
The very collie dozing at your feet,

His nose between his paws, his eyes half closed.
At sight of Willie, with a joyful bark
He leapt and gamboll'd, eyeing *me* the while
In queer suspicion ; and the mannock peep'd
Into my face, while patting Donald's back—
" It's Donald !   He has come to take me home ! "

An old man's tale, a tale for men grey-hair'd,
Who wear, thro' second childhood, to the grave !
I'll hasten on.   Thenceforward Willie came
Daily to school, and daily to the door
Came Donald trotting ; and they homeward went
Together—Willie walking slow but sure,
And Donald trotting sagely by his side.
[Ay, Donald, he is dead !   Be still, old man !]

What link existed, human or divine,
Between the tiny tot six summers old,
And yonder life of mine upon the hills
Among the mists and storms ?   'Tis strange, 'tis strange !
But when I look'd on Willie's face, it seem'd
That I had known it in some beauteous life
Which I had left behind me in the North !
This fancy grew and grew, till oft I sat—
The buzzing school around me—and would seem

To be among the mists, the tracks of rain,
Nearing the silence of the sleeping snow.
Slowly and surely I began to feel
That I was all alone in all the world,
And that my mother and my father slept
Far, far away, in some forgotten grave—
Remember'd but in dreams.   Alone at nights,
I read my Bible more and Euclid less.
For, mind you, like my betters, I had been
Half scoffer, half believer; on the whole,
I thought the life beyond a useless dream,
Best left alone, and shut my eyes to themes
That puzzled mathematics.   But at last,
When Willie Baird and I grew friends, and thoughts
Came to me from beyond my father's grave,
I found 'twas *pleasant* late at e'en to read
The Scripture—haply, only just to pick
Some easy chapter for my pet to learn—
Yet night by night my soul was guided on
Like a blind man some angel-hand convoys.

　　I cannot frame in speech the thoughts that fill'd
This grey old brow, the feelings dim and warm
That soothed the throbbings of this weary heart !
But when I placed my hand on Willie's head,

Warm sunshine tingled from the yellow hair
Thro' trembling fingers to my blood within !
And when I look'd in Willie's stainless eyes
I saw the empty ether, floating grey
O'er shadowy mountains murmuring low with winds !
And often when, in his old-fashion'd way,
He question'd me, I seem'd to hear a voice
From far away, that mingled with the cries
Haunting the regions where the round red sun
Is all alone with God among the snow !

Who made the stars ? and if within his hand
He caught and held one, would his fingers burn ?
If I, the grey-hair'd dominie, was dug
From out a cabbage garden such as *he*
Was found in ? if, when bigger, he would wear
Grey homespun hose and clumsy boots like mine,
And have a house to dwell in all alone ?
Thus would he question, seated on my knee,
While Donald [*Wheesht, old man !*] stretch'd lyart limbs
Under my chair, contented.   Open-mouth'd
He hearken'd to the tales I loved to tell
About Sir William Wallace and the Bruce,
And the sweet Lady on the Scottish throne,
Whose crown was colder than a band of ice,

Yet seem'd a sunny crown whene'er she smiled ;
With many tales of genii, giants, dwarfs,
And little folk that play at jing-a-ring
On beds of harebells 'neath the silver moon ;
Stories and rhymes and songs of Wonder-land :
How Tammas Ercildoune in Elfland dwelt,
How Galloway's mermaid comb'd her golden hair,
How Tammas Thumb stuck in the spider's web,
And fought and fought, a needle for his sword,
Dying his weapon in the crimson blood
Of the foul traitor with the poison'd fangs !

And when we read the Holy Book, the lad
Would think and think o'er parts he loved the best :—
The draught of fish, the Child that sat so wise
In the great Temple, Herod's cruel law
To slay the babes, or—oftenest of all—
The crucifixion of the Good Kind Man
Who loved the babes and was a babe himself.
He speir'd of death ; and were the sleepers *cold*
Down in the dark wet earth? and was it *God*
That put the grass and flowers in the kirk-yard?
What kind of dwelling-place was heaven above?
And was it full of *flowers?* and were there *schools*
And *dominies* there? and was it *far awa'?*

Then, with a look that made your eyes grow dim,
Clasping his wee white hands round Donald's neck,
" Do *doggies* gang to heaven ? " he would ask ;
" Would Donald gang ? " and keek'd in Donald's face,
While Donald blink'd with meditative gaze,
As if he knew full brawly what he said,
And ponder'd o'er it, wiser far than we.
But how I answer'd, how explain'd, these themes,
I know not.   Oft, I could not speak at all
Yet every question made me think of things
Forgotten, puzzled so, and when I strove
To reason puzzled me so much the more,
That, flinging logic to the winds, I went
Straight onward to the mark in Willie's way,
Took most for granted, laid down premises
Of Faith, imagined, gave my wits the rein,
And often in the night, to my surprise,
Felt palpably an Angel's glowing face
Glimmering down upon me, while mine eyes
Dimm'd their old orbs with tears that came unbid
To bear the glory of the light they saw !

So summer pass'd.   Yon chestnut at the door
Scatter'd its burnish'd leaves and made a sound
Of wind among its branches.   Every day

Came Willie, seldom going home again
Till near the sunset : wet or dry he came :
Oft in the rainy weather carrying
A big umbrella, under which he walk'd—
A little fairy in a parachute,
Blown hither, thither, at the wind's wild will.
Pleased was my heart to see his pallid cheeks
Were gathering rosy-posies, that his eyes
Were softer and less sad.   Then, with a gust,
Old Winter tumbled shrieking from the hills,
His white hair blowing in the wind.

                    The house
Where Willie's mother lives is scarce a mile
From yonder hallan, if you take a cut
Before you reach the village, crossing o'er
Green meadows till you reach the road again ;
But he who thither goes along the road
Loses a reaper's mile.   The summer long
Wee Willie came and went across the fields.
He loved the smell of flowers and grass, the sight
Of cows and sheep, the changing stalks of wheat,
And he was weak and small.   When winter came,
Still caring not a straw for wind or rain
Came Willie and the Collie ; till by night

Down fell the snow, and fell three nights and days,
Then ceased.   The ground was white and ankle-deep;
The window of the school was threaded o'er
With hueless flowers of ice—Frost's unseen hands
Prick'd you from head to foot with tingling heat.
The shouting urchins, yonder on the green,
Play'd snowballs.   In the school a cheery fire
Was kindled every day, and every day
When Willie came he had the warmest seat,
And every day old Donald, punctual, came
To join us, after labour, in the lowe.

Three days and nights the snow had mistily fall'n.
It lay long miles along the country-side,
White, awful, silent.   In the keen cold air
There was a hush, a sleepless silentness,
And mid it all, upraising eyes, you felt
Frost's breath upon your face.   And in your blood,
Though you were cold to touch, was flaming fire,
Such as within the bowels of the earth
Burnt at the bones of ice, and wreath'd them round
With grass ungrown.

One day in school I saw,
Through threaded window-panes, soft snowy flakes
Swim with unquiet motion, mistily, slowly,

At intervals ; but when the boys were gone,
And in ran Donald with a dripping nose,
 The air was clear and grey as glass.   An hour
Sat Willie, Donald, and myself around
The murmuring fire ; and then with tender hand
I wrapt a comforter round Willie's throat,
Button'd his coat around him close and warm,
And off he ran with Donald, happy-eyed
And merry, leaving fairy prints of feet
Behind him on the snow.   I watch'd them fade
Round the white road, and, turning with a sigh,
Came in to sort the room and smoke a pipe
Before the fire.   Here, dreamingly and alone,
I sat and smoked, and in the fire saw clear
The norland mountains, white and cold with snow,
That crumbled silently, and moved, and changed,—
When suddenly the air grew sick and dark,
And from the distance came a hollow sound,
A murmur like the moan of far-off seas.

I started to my feet, look'd out, and knew
The winter wind was whistling from the east
To lash the snow-clothed plain, and to myself
I prophesied a Storm before the night.
Then with an icy pain, an eldritch gleam,

I thought of Willie ; but I cheer'd my heart,
" He's home, and with his mother, long ere this ! "
While thus I stood the hollow murmur grew
Deeper, the wold grew darker, and the snow
Rush'd downward, whirling in a shadowy mist.
I walk'd to yonder door and open'd it.
Whirr ! the wind swung it from me with a clang,
And in upon me with an iron-like crash
Swoop'd in the drift.   With pinch'd sharp face I gazed
Out on the storm !   Dark, dark was all!   A mist,
A blinding, whirling mist, of chilly snow,
The falling and the driven ; for the wind
Swept round and round in spindrift on the earth,
And birm'd the deathly drift aloft with moans,
Till all was swooning darkness.   Far above
A voice was shrieking, like a human cry.

I closed the door, and turn'd me to the fire,
With something on my heart—a load—a sense
Of an impending pain.   Down the broad lum
Came melting flakes, that hiss'd upon the coal ;
Under my eyelids blew the blinding smoke !
And for a time I sat like one bewitch'd,
Still as a stone.   The lonely room grew dark,
The flickering fire threw phantoms of the fog

Along the floor and on the walls around ;
The melancholy ticking of the clock
Was like the beating of my heart.   But, hush !
Above the moaning of the wind I heard
A sudden scraping at the door .   .   .   my heart
Stood still and listen'd . . . and with that there rose
An anguish'd howl, shrill as a dying screech,
And scrape-scrape-scrape, the sound beyond the door !
I could not think—I could not cry nor breathe—
A fierce foreboding gript me like a hand,
As opening the door I gazed straight out,
Saw nothing, till I felt against my knees
Something that moved, and heard a moaning sound—
Then, panting, moaning, o'er the threshold leapt
Donald, the dog, alone, and white with snow.

  Down, Donald ! down, old man !   Sir, look at him !
I swear he knows the meaning of my words,
And tho' he cannot speak, his heart is full !
See now ! see now ! he puts his cold black nose
Into my palm and whines ! he knows, he knows !
Would speak, and cannot, but he minds that night !

  The terror of my heart seem'd choking me :
Wildly I stared in wonder at the dog,
Who gazed into my face and whined and moan'd,

Leap'd at the door, then touch'd me with his paws,
And lastly, gript my coat between his teeth,
And pull'd and pull'd—with stifled howls and whines—
Till fairly madden'd, stupefied with fear,
I let him drag me through the banging door
Out to the whirling Storm.   Bareheaded, wild,
The wind and snow-drift beating on my face,
Blowing me hither, thither, with the dog,
I dashed along the road . . . What followed, seemed
An eeric, eerie dream !—a world of snow,
A sky of wind, a whirling howling mist
Which swam around with countless flashing eyes ;
And Donald dragging, dragging, beaten, bruised,
Leading me on to something that I fear'd—
An awful something, and I knew not what !
On, on, and farther on, and still the snow
Whirling, the tempest moaning ! Then I mind
Of stooping, groping in the shadowy light,
And Donald by me, burrowing with his nose
And whining.   Next a darkness, blank and deep !   ——
But *then* I mind of tearing thro' the storm,
Stumbling and tripping, blind and deaf and dumb,
But holding to my heart an icy load
I clutch'd with freezing fingers. Far away—
It seem'd long miles and miles away—I saw

A yellow light—unto that light I fled—
And last, remember opening a door
And falling, dazzled by a blinding gleam
Of human faces and a flaming fire,
And with a crash of voices in my ears
Fading away into a world of snow !

.   .   .   When I awaken'd to myself, I lay
In mine own bed at home.   I started up
As from an evil dream, and look'd around,
When to my side came one, a neighbour's wife,
Mother to two young lads I taught in school.
With hollow, hollow voice I question'd her,
And soon knew all : how a long night had pass'd
Since, with a lifeless laddie in my arms,
I stumbled, horror-stricken, swooning, wild,
Into a ploughman's cottage : at my side,
My coat between his teeth, a Dog ; and how
Senseless and cold I fell.   Thence, when the storm
Had pass'd away, they bore me to my home.
I listen'd dumbly, catching at the sense ;
But when the woman mention'd Willie's name,
And I was fear'd to phrase the thought that rose,
She *saw* the question in my tearless eyes
And told me—he was dead.

'Twould weary you
To tell the thoughts, the fancies, and the dreams
That weigh'd upon me, ere I rose in bed,
But little harm'd, and sent the wife away,
Rose, slowly drest, took up my staff and went
To Willie's mother's cottage.   As I walk'd,
Though all the air was calm and cold and still,
The blowing wind and dazzled snow were yet   .
Around about.   I was bewilder'd like !
Ere I had time to think, I found myself
Beside a truckle bed, and at my side
· A weeping woman.   And I clench'd my hands,
And look'd on Willie, who had gone to sleep.

In death-gown white lay Willie fast asleep,
His blue eyes closed, his tiny fingers clench'd,
His lips apart a wee as if he breathed,
His yellow hair comb'd back, and on his face
A smile—yet not a smile—a dim pale light
Such as the Snow keeps in its own soft wings.
Ay, he had gone to sleep, and he was sound !
And by the bed lay Donald watching still,
And when I look'd, he whined, but did not move.

I turn'd in silence, with my nails stuck deep
In my clench'd palms ; but in my heart of hearts

I pray'd to God.   In Willie's mother's face
There was a cold and silent bitterness—
I saw it plain, but saw it in a dream,
And cared not.   So I went my way, as grim
As one who holds his breath to slay himself.
What follow'd that is vague as was the rest :
A winter day, a landscape hush'd in snow,
A weary wind, a horrid whiteness borne
On a man's shoulder, shapes in black, o'er all
The solemn clanging of an iron bell,
And lastly me and Donald standing both
Beside a tiny mound of fresh-heap'd earth,
And while around the snow began to fall
Mistily, softly, thro' the icy air,
Looking at one another, dumb and old.

And Willie 's dead !—that 's all I comprehend—
Ay, bonnie Willie Baird has gone before !
I begg'd old Donald hard—they gave him me—
And we have lived together in this house
Long years, with no companions.   There's no need
Of speech between us.   Here we dumbly bide,
But know each other's sorrow,—and we both
Feel weary.   When the nights are long and cold,
And snow is falling as it falleth now,

And wintry winds are moaning, here I dream
Of Willie and the unfamiliar life
I left behind me on those norland hills !
"Do doggies gang to heaven?" Willie ask'd ;
And ah ! what Solomon of modern days
Can answer *that ?*   Yet here at nights I sit,
Reading the Book, with Donald at my side ;
And stooping, with the Book upon my knee,
I sometimes gaze in Donald's patient eyes—
So sad, so human, though he cannot speak—
And think he knows that Willie is at peace,
Far far away beyond the norland hills,
Beyond the silence of the untrodden snow.

*THE SNOWDROP.**

(From " Poet Andrew".)

AND as he nearer grew to God the Lord,
Nearer and dearer day by day he grew
To Mysie and mysel'—our own to love,
The world's no longer.   For the first last time,
We twa, the lad and I, could sit and crack
With open hearts—free-spoken, at our ease ;
I seem'd to know as muckle then as he,
Because I was sae sad.

          Thus grief, sae deep
It flow'd without a murmur, brought the balm
Which blunts the edge of worldly sense and makes
Old people weans again.   In this sad time,
We never troubled at his childish ways ;
We seem'd to *share* his pleasure when he sat
List'ning to birds upon the eaves ; we felt

* See Appendix, " The Life of David Gray."

Small wonder when we found him weeping o'er
His own torn books of pencill'd thought and verse ;
And if, outbye, I saw a bonnie flower,
I pluck'd it carefully and bore it home
To my sick boy.   To me, it somehow seem'd
His care for lovely earthly things had changed—
Changed from the curious love it once had been,
Grown larger, sadder, holier, peacefuller ;
And though he never lost the luxury
Of loving beauteous things for poetry's sake,
His heart was God the Lord's, and he was calm.
Death came to lengthen out his solemn thoughts
Like shadows from the sunset.   So no more
We wonder'd.   What is folly in a lad
Healthy and heartsome, one with work to do,
Befits the freedom of a dying man.   .   .   .
Mother, who chided loud the idle lad
Of old, now sat her sadly by his side,
And read from out the Bible soft and low,
Or lilted lowly, keeking in his face,
The old Scots songs that made his een so dim.
I went about my daily work as one
Who waits to hear a knocking at the door,
Ere Death creeps in and shadows those that watch ;
And seated here at e'en i' the ingleside,

I watch'd the pictures in the fire and smoked
My pipe in silence ; for my head was fu'
Of many rhymes the lad had made of old
(Rhymes I had read in secret, as I said),
No one of which I minded till they came
Unsummon'd, murmuring about my ears
Like bees among the leaves.

                     The end drew near.
Came Winter moaning, and the Doctor said
That Andrew could not live to see the Spring ;
And day by day, while frost was hard at work,
The lad grew weaker, paler, and the blood
Came redder from the lung.   One Sabbath day—
The last of winter, for the caller air
Was drawing sweetness from the barks of trees—
When down the lane, I saw to my surprise
A snowdrop blooming underneath a birk,
And gladly pluckt the flower to carry home
To Andrew.   Ere I reached the bield, the air
Was thick wi' snow, and ben in yonder room
I found him, mother seated at his side,
Drawn to the window in the old arm-chair,
Gazing wi' lustrous een and sickly cheek
Out on the shower, that waver'd softly down

In glistening siller glamour.   Saying nought,
Into his hand I put the year's first flower,
And turn'd awa' to hide my face ; and he . . .
. . . He smiled . . . and at the smile, I knew not why,
It swam upon us, in a frosty pain,
The end was come at last, at last, and Death
Was creeping ben, his shadow on our hearts.
We gazed on Andrew, call'd him by his name,
And touch'd him softly   .   .   .   and he lay awhile,
His een upon the snow, in a dark dream,
Yet neither heard nor saw ; but suddenly,
He shook awa' the vision with a smile,
Raised lustrous een, still smiling, to the sky,
Next upon us, then dropp'd them to the flower
That trembled in his hand, and murmur'd low,
Like one that gladly murmurs to himsel'—
" Out of the Snow, the Snowdrop—out of Death
Comes Life ;" then closed his eyes and made a moan,
And never spake another word again.

LONDON POEMS.

Now, when the catkins of the hazel swing
Wither'd above the leafy nook wherein
The chaffinch breasts her five blue speckled eggs,
All round the thorn grows fragrant, white with may,
And underneath the fresh wild hyacinth-bed
Shimmers like water in the whispering wind;
Now, on this sweet still gloaming of the spring,
Within my cottage by the sea, I sit,
Thinking of yonder city where I dwelt,
Wherein I sicken'd, and whereof I learn'd
So much that dwells like music on my brain.
A melancholy happiness is mine!
My thoughts, like blossoms of the muschatel,
Smell sweetest in the gloaming: and I feel
Visions and vanishings of other years,—
Faint as the scent of distant clover meadows—
Sweet, sweet, though they awaken serious cares—
Beautiful, beautiful, though they make me weep.

The good days dead, the well-belovëd gone
Before me, lonely I abode amid
The buying and the selling, and the strife
Of little natures ; yet there still remain'd
Something to thank the Lord for.—I could live !
On winter nights, when wind and snow were out,
Afford a pleasant fire to keep me warm ;
And while I sat, with homeward-looking eyes,
And while I heard the humming of the town,
I fancied 'twas the sound I used to hear
In Scotland, when I dwelt beside the sea.
I knew not how it was, or why it was,
I only heard a sea-sound, and was sad.
It haunted me and pain'd me, and it made
That little life of penmanship a dream !
And yet it served my soul for company,
When the dark city gather'd on my brain,
And from the solitude came never a voice
To bring the good days back, and show my heart
It was not quite a solitary thing.

The purifying trouble grew and grew,
Till silentness was more than I could bear.
Brought by the ocean murmur from afar,
Came silent phantoms of the misty hills

Which I had known and loved in other days;
And, ah! from time to time, the hum of life
Around me, the strange faces of the streets,
Mingling with those thin phantoms of the hills,
And with that ocean-murmur, made a cloud
That changed around my life with shades and sounds,
And, melting often in the light of day,
Left on my brow dews of aspiring dream.
And then I sang of Scottish dales and dells,
And human shapes that lived and moved therein,
Made solemn in the shadow of the hills.
Thereto, not seldom, did I seek to make
The busy life of London musical,
And phrase in modern song the troubled lives
Of dwellers in the sunless lanes and streets.
Yet ever I was haunted from afar,
While singing; and the presence of the mountains
Was on me; and the murmur of the sea
Deepen'd my mood; while everywhere I saw,
Flowing beneath the blackness of the streets,
The current of sublimer, sweeter life,
Which is the source of human smiles and tears,
And, melodised, becomes the strength of song.

Darkling, I long'd for utterance, whereby
Poor people might be holpen, gladden'd, cheer'd;

Brightening at times, I sang for singing's sake.
The wild wind of ambition grew subdued,
And left the changeful current of my soul
Crystal and pure and clear, to glass like water
The sad and beautiful of human life;
And, even in the unsung city's streets,
Seem'd quiet wonders meet for serious song,
Truth hard to phrase and render musical.
For oh! the weariness and weight of tears,
The crying out to God, the wish for slumber,
They lay so deep, so deep!   God heard them all;
He set them unto music of His own;
But easier far the task to sing of Kings,
Or weave weird ballads where the moon-dew glistens,
Than body forth this life in beauteous sound.
The crowd had voices, but each living man
Within the crowd seem'd silent-smit and hard:
They only heard the murmur of the town,
They only felt the dimness in their eyes,
And now and then turn'd startled, when they saw
Some weary one fling up his arms and drop,
Clay-cold, among them,—and they scarcely grieved,
But hush'd their hearts a time, and hurried on.

'Twas comfort deep as tears to sit alone,
Haunted byshadows from afar away,

And try to utter forth, in tuneful speech,
What lay so musically on my heart.
But, though it sweeten'd life, it seem'd in vain.
For while I sang, much that was clear before—
The souls of men and women in the streets,
The sounding sea, the presence of the hills,
And all the weariness, and all the fret,
And all the dim, strange pain for what had fled—
Turn'd into mist, mingled before mine eyes,
Roll'd up like wreaths of smoke to heaven, and died:
The pen dropt from my hand, mine eyes grew dim,
And the great roar was in mine ears again,
And I was all alone in London streets.

Hither to pastoral solitude I came,
Happy to breathe again serener air
And feel a purer sunshine ; and the woods
And meadows were to me an ecstasy,
The singing birds a glory, and the trees
A green perpetual feast to fill the eye
And shimmer in upon the soul ; but chief,
There came the murmur of the waters, sounds
Of sunny tides that wash on silver sands,
Or cries of waves that anguish'd and went white
Under the eyes of lightnings.   'Twas a bliss

Beyond the bliss of dreaming, yet in time
It grew familiar as my mother's face;
And when the wonder and the ecstasy
Had mingled with the beatings of my heart,
The terrible City loom'd from far away
And gather'd on me cloudily, dropping dews,
Even as those phantoms of departed days
Had haunted me in London streets and lanes.
Wherefore in brighter mood I sought again
To make the life of London musical,
And sought the mirror of my soul for shapes
That linger'd, faces bright or agonised,
Yet ever taking something beautiful
From glamour of green branches, and of clouds
That glided piloted by golden airs.

And if I list to sing of sad things oft,
It is that sad things in this life of breath
Are truest, sweetest, deepest.   Tears bring forth
The richness of our natures, as the rain
Sweetens the leafy world; and I, thank God,
Have anguish'd here in no ignoble tears—
Tears for the pale friend with the singing lips,
Tears for the father with the gentle eyes
(My dearest up in heaven next to God)

Who loved me like a woman.   I have wrought
No garland of the rose and passion-flower,
Grown in a careful garden in the sun ;
But I have gather'd samphire dizzily,
Close to the hollow roaring of a Sea.

PAN.

"Pan, Pan is dead!"—E. B. BROWNING.

THE broken goblets of the Gods
  Lie scatter'd in the Waters deep,
Where the tall sea-flag blows and nods
  Over the shipwreck'd seaman's sleep;
The gods like phantoms, come and go
  Amid the wave-wash'd ocean-hall,
Above their heads the bleak winds blow;
They sigh, and shiver to and fro—
  'Pan, Pan!' those phantoms call.

O Pan, great Pan, thou art not dead,
  Nor dost thou haunt that weedy place,
Tho' blowing winds hear not thy tread,
  And silver runlets miss thy face;
Where ripe nuts fall thou hast no state,
  Where eagles soar, thou now art dumb,
By lonely meres thou dost not wait;—
But *here*, 'mid living waves of fate,
  We feel thee go and come!

O piteous one !—In wintry days
   Over the City falls the snow,
And, where it whitens stony ways,
   I see a Shade flit to and fro ;
Over the dull street hangs a cloud—
   It parts, an ancient Face flits by,
'Tis thine ! 'tis thou !   Thy gray head bow'd,
Dimly thou flutterest o'er the crowd,
   With a thin human cry.

Ghost-like, O Pan, thou glimmerest still,
   A spectral Face, with sad, dumb stare ;
On rainy nights thy breath blows chill
   In the street-walker's dripping hair ;
Thy ragged woe from street to street
   Goes mist-like, constant day and night ;
But often, where the black waves beat,
Thou hast a smile most strangely sweet
   For honest hearts and light !

Where'er thy shadowy vestments fly
   There comes across the waves of strife,
Across the souls of all close by,
   The gleam of some forgotten life ;

There is a sense of waters clear,
    An odour faint of flowery nooks ;
Strange plumaged birds seem flitting near,
The cold brain blossoms, lives that hear
    Ripple like running brooks.

And as thou pässest, human eyes
    Look in each other and are wet—
Simple or gentle, weak or wise,
    Alike are full of tender fret ;
And mean and noble, brave and base
    Raise common glances to the sky ;—
And lo ! the phantom of thy Face,
While sad and low thro' all the place
    Thrills thy thin human cry !

Christ help thee, Pan ! canst *thou* not go
    Now all the other gods have fled ?
Why dost thou flutter to and fro
    When all the sages deem thee dead ?
Or if thou still must live and dream,
    Why leave the fields of harvest fair—
Why quit the peace of wood and stream—
And haunt the streets with eyes that gleam
    Thro' white and holy hair ?

THE CITY ASLEEP.

Still as the sea serene and deep
    When all the winds are laid,
The City sleeps—so still, its sleep
    Maketh the soul afraid.

Over the living waters, see !
    The seraphs shining go,—
The moon is gliding hushfully
    Through stars like flakes of snow.

In pearl-white silver here and there
    The fallen moon-rays stream ;
Hark ! a dull stir is in the air,
    Like the stir of one in dream.

Through all the thrilling waters creep
    Deep throbs of strange unrest,
Like washings of the windless deep
    When it is peacefullest.

A little while—God's breath will go,
    And hush the flood no more ;
The dawn will break—the wind will blow,
    The ocean rise and roar.

Each day with sounds of strife and death
　　The waters rise and call;
Each midnight, conquer'd by God's breath,
　　To this dead calm they fall.

Out of his heart the fountains flow,
　　The brook, the running river;
He marks them strangely come and go,
　　For ever and for ever.

Till darker, deeper, one by one,
　　After a weary quest,
'They, from the light of moon and sun,
　　Flow back into his breast.

Love, hold my hand! be of good cheer!
　　For His would be the cost,
If, out of all the waters here,
　　One little drop were *lost.*

Heaven's eyes above the waters dumb
　　Innumerably yearn;
Out of His heart each drop hath come,
　　And thither *must* return!

UP IN AN ATTIC.

"Do you *dream* yet, on your old rickety sofa, in the dear old ghastly bankrupt garret at No. 66?"—*Gray to Buchanan* (see "The Life of David Gray").

HALF of a gold ring bright,
  Broken in days of old,
One yellow curl, whose light
  Gladden'd my gaze of old !
A sprig of thyme thereto,
Pluckt on the mountains blue,
When in the gloaming dew
  We roam'd erratic ;
Last, an old Book of Song,—
These have I treasured long,
  Up in an Attic.

Held in one little hand,
  They gleam in vain to me :
Of Love, Fame, Fatherland,
  All that remain to me !
Love, with thy wounded wing,
Up the skies lessening,

Sighing, too sad to sing !
  Fame, dead to pity !
Land,—that denied me bread,
Count me as lost and dead,
  Tomb'd, in the City.

Daily the busy roar,
  Murmur and motion here ;
Surging against its shore,
  Sighs a great Ocean here !
But night by night it flows
Slowly to strange repose,
Calm and more calm it grows
  Under the moonshine :
Then, only then, I peer
On each old souvenir
  Shut from the sunshine.

Half of a ring of gold,
  Tarnish'd and yellow now,
Broken in days of old,
  Where is thy fellow now ?
Upon the heart of *her* ?
Feeling the sweet blood stir,
Still (though the mind demur)

Kept as a token?
Ah! doth her heart forget?
Or, with the pain and fret,
Is *that*, too, broken?

Thin threads of yellow hair,
Clipt from the brow of her,
Lying so faded there,—
Why whisper *now* of her?
Strange lips are press'd unto
The brow o'er which ye grew,
Strange fingers flutter through
The loose long tresses.
Doth she remember still,
Trembling, and turning chill
From his caresses?

Sprig from the mountains blue
Long left behind me now,
Of moonlight, shade, and dew.
Wherefore remind me now?
Cruel and chill and gray,
Looming afar away,
Dark in the light of day,

Shall the Heights daunt me?
My footsteps on the hill
Are overgrown,—yet still
Hill-echoes haunt me !

Book of Byronic Song,
Put with the dead away,
Wherefore wouldst *thou* prolong
Dreams that have fled away ?
Thou art an eyeless skull,
Dead, fleshless, cold, and null,
Complexionless, dark, dull,
And superseded ;
Yet, in thy time of pride,
How loudly hast thou lied
To all who heeded !

Now, Fame, thou hollow Voice,
Shriek from the heights above !
Let all who will rejoice
In those wild lights above !
When all are false save you,
Yet were so beauteous too,
O Fame, canst *thou* be true,

And shall I follow?
Nay! for the song of man
Dies in his throat, since Pan
   Hath slain Apollo!

O Fame, thy hill looks tame,
   No vast wings flee from thence,—
Were *I* to climb, O Fame,
   What could I see from thence?
Only, afar away,
The mountains looming gray,
Crimson'd at close of day,
   Clouds swimming by me;
And in my hand a ring
And ringlet glimmering,—
   And no one nigh me!

Better the busy roar,
   Best the mad motion here!
Surging against its shore,
   Groans a great Ocean here.
O Love,—thou wouldst not wait!
O Land,—thou art desolate!
O Fame,—to others prate
   Of flights ecstatic!

Only, at evenfall,
Touching these tokens small,
I think about you all,
   Up in an Attic!

THE FIRST GLIMPSE OF GREEN FIELDS.

(*From " Liz."*)

I.

AND so the baby's come, and I shall die !
   And though 'tis hard to leave poor baby here,
   Where folk will think him bad, and all's so drear,
The great LORD GOD knows better far than I.
Ah, don't !—'tis kindly, but it pains me so !
You say I'm wicked, and I *want* to go !
" GOD's kingdom," Parson dear ?   Ah nay, ah nay !
   That must be like the country—which I fear :
I *saw* the country once, one summer day,
   And I would rather die in London here !

2.

For I was sick of hunger, cold, and strife,
   And took a sudden fancy in my head
   To try the country, and to earn my bread
Out among fields, where I had heard one's life

Was easier and brighter.   So, that day,
I took my basket up and stole away,
Just after sunrise.   As I went along,
  Trembling and loath to leave the busy place,
I felt that I was doing something wrong,
  And fear'd to look policemen in the face.
And all was dim : the streets were gray and wet
  After a rainy night : and all was still ;
  I held my shawl around me with a chill,
And dropt my eyes from every face I met ;
Until the streets began to fade, the road
  Grew fresh and clean and wide,
Fine houses where the gentlefolk abode,
  And gardens full of flowers, on every side.
That made me walk the quicker—on, on, on—
  As if I were asleep with half-shut eyes,
  And all at once I saw, to my surprise,
The houses of the gentlefolk were gone ;
And I was standing still,
Shading my face, upon a high green hill,
  And the bright sun was blazing,
And all the blue above me seem'd to melt
  To burning, flashing gold, while I was gazing
On the great smoky cloud where I had dwelt !

3.

I'll ne'er forget that day.   All was so bright
  And strange.   Upon the grass around my feet
The rain had hung a million drops of light;
  The air, too, was so clear and warm and sweet,
It seem'd a sin to breathe it.   All around
  Where hills and fields and trees that trembled through
  A burning, blazing fire of gold and blue:
And there was not a sound,
  Save a bird singing, singing, in the skies,
And the soft wind, that ran along the ground,
  And blew so sweetly on my lips and eyes.
Then, with my heavy hand upon my chest,
  Because the bright air pain'd me, trembling, sighing,
I stole into a dewy field to rest;
  And oh, the green, green grass where I was lying
Was fresh and living—and the bird sang loud,
Out of a golden cloud—
  And I was looking up at him, and crying!

4.

How swift the hours slipt on !—and by and by
The sun grew red, big shadows fill'd the sky,
  The air grew damp with dew,
  And the dark night was coming down, I knew.

Well, I was more afraid than ever, then,
    And felt that I should die in such a place,—
    So back to London town I turn'd my face,
And crept into the cheerful streets again ;
And when I breathed the smoke and heard the roar,
    Why, I was better, for in London here
    My heart was busy, and I felt no fear.
I never saw the country any more.
And I have stay'd in London, well or ill—
    I would not stay out yonder if I could,
    For one feels dead, and all looks pure and good—
I could not bear a life so bright and still.
All that I want is sleep,
Under the flags and stones, so deep, so deep !
God won't be hard on one so mean, but He,
    Perhaps, will let a tired girl slumber sound
    There in the deep cold darkness under ground ;
And I shall waken up in time, may be,
Better and stronger, not afraid to see
    The burning Light that folds Him round and round !

5.

See ! there's the sunset creeping through the pane —
How cool and moist it looks amid the rain !

I like to hear the splashing of the drops,

On the house-tops,

And the loud murmur of the folk that go

Along the streets below !

I like the smoke and roar—I love them yet—

    They seem to still one's cares . . .

    There's Joe !   I hear his foot upon the stairs !—

Poor lad, he must be wet !

He will be angry, like enough, to find

    Another little life to clothe and keep.

But show him baby, Parson—speak him kind—

    And tell him Doctor thinks I'm going to sleep.

A hard, hard life is his ! He need be strong

And rough, to earn his bread and get along.

I think he will be sorry when I go,

    And leave the little one and him behind . . .

    I hope he'll see another to his mind,

To keep him straight and tidy . . . Poor old Joe !

THE STARLING.

THE little lame Tailor
    Sat stitching and snarling—
Who in the world
    Was the Tailor's darling?
To none of mankind
Was he well inclined,
    But he doted on Jack the Starling.

For the bird had a tongue,
    And of words good store,
And his cage was hung
    Just over the door;
And he saw the people,
    And heard the roar,—
Folk coming and going
    Evermore,—
And he looked at the Tailor—
    And swore !

From a country lad
    The Tailor bought him,—
His training was bad,
    For tramps had taught him;
On alehouse benches
    His cage had been,
While louts and wenches
    Made jests obscene,—
But he learn'd, no doubt,
    His oaths from fellows
Who travel about
    With kettle and bellows;
And three or four
    [The roundest by far
That ever he swore!]
    Were taught by a Tar.
And the Tailor heard—
    " We'll be friends!" thought he;
" You're a clever bird,
    And our tastes agree.
We both are old,
    And esteem life base,
The whole world cold,
    Things out of place;

And we're lonely too,
　　And full of care—
So what can we do
　　But swear?

The devil take you,
　　How you mutter!
Yet there's much to make you
　　Fluster and flutter.
You want the fresh air
　　And the sunlight, lad,
And your prison there
　　Feels dreary and sad;
And here *I* frown
　　In a prison as dreary,
Hating the town,
　　And feeling weary:
We're too confined, Jack,
　　And we want to fly,
And you blame mankind, Jack,
　　And so do I !"

A haggard and ruffled
　　Old fellow was Jack,
With a grim face muffled
　　In ragged black,

And his coat was rusty
    And never neat,
And his wings were dusty
    With grime of the street,
And he sidelong peer'd,
    With eyes of soot,
And scowl'd and sneer'd,—
    And was lame of a foot !
And he longed to go
    From whence he came ;—
And the Tailor, you know,
    Was just the same.

All kinds of weather
    They felt confined,
And swore together
    At all mankind ;
For their mirth was done,
    And they felt like brothers,
And the railing of one
    Meant no more than the other's.
'Twas just a way
    They had learn'd, you see,—
Each wanted to say
    Only *this*—" Woe's me ;

I'm a poor old fellow,
        And I'm prison'd so,
While the sun shines mellow,
And the corn waves yellow,
        And the fresh winds blow,—
And the folk don't care
        If I live or die,
But I long for air,
        And I wish to fly !"
Yet unable to utter it,
        And too wild to bear,
They could only mutter it,
        And swear.

Many a year
        They dwelt in the City,
In their prisons drear,
        And none felt pity,—
Nay, few were sparing
        Of censure and coldness,
To hear them swearing
        With such plain boldness.
But at last, by the Lord,
        Their noise was stopt,—

For down on his board
    The Tailor dropt,
And they found him, dead,
    And done with snarling,
Yet over his head
    Still grumbled the Starling.
But when an old Jew
    Claim'd the goods of the Tailor,
And with eye askew
    Eyed the feathery railer,
And with a frown
    At the dirt and rust,
Took the old cage down,
    In a shower of dust,—
Jack, with heart aching,
    Felt life past bearing,
And shivering, quaking,
All hope forsaking,
    Died, swearing.

NELL.

I.

You're a kind woman, Nan! ay, kind and true!
God will be good to faithful folk like you!
The neighbours all look black, and snap me short—
Well, I shall soon be gone from Camden Court.
You knew my Ned?
    A better, kinder lad never drew breath—
We loved each other true, though never wed
    In church, like some who took him to his death:
A lad as gentle as a lamb, but lost
    His senses when he took a drop too much—
Drink did it all—drink made him mad when cross'd—
    He was a poor man, and they're hard on such.
So kind! so true! that life should come to this!
    Gentle and good!—the very week before
The fit came on him, and he went amiss,
He brought me home, and gave me, with a kiss,
    That muslin gown as hangs behind the door.

II.

O Nan ! that night ! that night !
  When I was sitting in this very chair,
Watching and waiting in the candle-light,
  And heard his foot come creaking up the stair,
And turn'd, and saw him standing yonder, white
  And wild, with staring eyes and rumpled hair !
And when I caught his arm and call'd, in fright,
  He push'd me, swore, and pass'd
  Back to the door, and lock'd and barr'd it fast !
Then dropp'd down heavy as a lump of lead,
  Holding his brow, shaking, and growing whiter,
  And—Nan !—just then the candle-light grew brighter,
And I could see the hands that held his head,
All red ! all bloody red !
What could I do but scream ?   He groan'd to hear,
  Jump'd to his feet, and gripp'd me by the wrist !
  " Be still, or I shall kill thee, Nell ! " he hiss'd.
And I *was* still for fear.
" They're after me—I've knifed a man ! " he said.
" Be still !—the drink—drink did it—he is *dead !* "
And as he said the word, the wind went by
With a whistle and cry—
The room swam round—the babe unborn seem'd to
    scream out and die !

III.

Then we grew still, so still.   I couldn't weep—
  All I could do was to cling to Ned and hark—
And Ned was cold, cold, cold, as if asleep,
But breathing hard and deep ;
  The candle flicker'd out—the room grew dark—
And—Nan !—although my heart was true and tried,—
  When all grew cold and dim,
I shudder'd—not for fear of them outside,
  But just afraid to be alone with *him :*
And he was hard, he was—the wind it cried—
A foot went hollow down the court and died—
What could I do but clasp his knees and cling ?
  And call his name beneath my breath in pain ?
Until he raised his head a-listening,
  And gave a groan, and hid his face again :
"Ned ! Ned !" I whisper'd—and he moan'd and
        shook—
But did not heed or look !
"Ned ! Ned ! speak, lad ! tell me it is not true !"
  At that he raised his head and look'd so wild ;
Then, with a stare that froze my blood, he threw
  His arms around me, sobbing like a child,
And held me close—and not a word was spoken—
  While I clung tighter to his heart and press'd him—

And did not fear him, though my heart was broken—
  But kiss'd his poor stain'd hands, and cried, and
    bless'd him !

IV.

Then, Nan, the dreadful daylight, coming cold
  With sound o' falling rain,—
When I could see his face, and it look'd old,
  Like the pinch'd face of one as dies in pain ;
Well, though we heard folk stirring in the sun,
We never thought to hide away or run,
Until we heard those voices in the street,
That hurrying of feet.
And Ned leap'd up, and knew that they had come.
" Run, Ned !" I cried, but he was deaf and dumb !
" Hide, Ned !" I scream'd, and held him—" hide thee,
    man !"
He stared with bloodshot eyes, and hearken'd, Nan !
And all the rest is like a dream—the sound
  Of knocking at the door—
A rush of men—a struggle on the ground—
  A mist—a tramp—a roar ;
For when I got my senses back again,
  The room was empty,—and my head went round !
The neighbours talk'd and stirr'd about the lane,
  And Seven Dials made a moaning sound ;

And as I listen'd, lass, it seem'd to me
Just like the murmur of a great dark sea,
   And Ned a-lying somewhere, stiff and drown'd!

V.

God help him?   God *will* help him!   Ay, no fear!
   It was the drink, not Ned—he meant no wrong;
So kind! so good!—and I am useless here,
   Now he is lost as loved me true and long.
Why, just before the last of it, we parted,
And Ned was calm, though I was broken-hearted;
And ah, my heart *was* broke! and ah, I cried
And kiss'd him,—till they took me from his side;
And though he died *that way*, (God bless him!) Ned
   Went through it bravely, calm as any there;
They've wrought their fill of spite upon his head,
   And—there's the hat and clothes he used to wear!

VI.

. . . That night before he died,
I didn't cry—my heart was hard and dried;
But when the clocks went "one," I took my shawl
   To cover up my face, and stole away,
And walk'd along the moonlight streets, where all
   Look'd cold and still and gray,—

Only the lamps of London here and there
   Scatter'd a dismal gleaming ;
And on I went, and stood in Leicester Square,
   Just like a woman dreaming :
But just as "three" was sounded close at hand,
   I started and turn'd east, before I knew,—
Then down Saint Martin's Lane, along the Strand,
   And through the toll-gate, on to Waterloo.
How I remember all I saw, although
   'Twas only like a dream !—
The long still lines o' lights, the chilly gleam
   Of moonshine on the deep black stream below ;
While far, far, far away, along the sky
   Streaks soft as silver ran,
And the pale moon looked paler up on high,
   And little sounds in far-off streets began !
Well, while I stood, and waited, and look'd down,
And thought how sweet 'twould be to drop and drown,
Some men and lads went by,
   And I turn'd round, and gazed, and watch'd 'em go,
Then felt that they were going to see him die,
   And drew my shawl more tight, and follow'd slow.
How clear I feel it still !
   The streets grew light, but rain began to fall ;
I stopp'd and had some coffee at a stall,

Because I felt so chill;
A cock crew somewhere, and it seem'd a call
    To wake the folk who kill !
The man who sold the coffee stared at me !
I must have been a sorry sight to see !
    More people pass'd—a country cart with hay
Stopp'd close beside the stall,—and two or three
    Talk'd about *it !*   I moan'd and crept away !

VII.

Ay, nearer, nearer to the dreadful place,
    All in the falling rain,
I went, and kept my shawl upon my face,
    And felt no grief or pain—
Only the wet that soak'd me through and through
    Seem'd cold and sweet and pleasant to the touch—
It made the streets more drear and silent, too,
    And kept away the light I fear'd so much.
Slow, slow the wet streets fill'd, and all were going,
    Laughing and chatting, the same way,
And grayer, sadder, lighter, it was growing,
    Though still the rain fell fast and darken'd day !
Nan !—every pulse was burning—I could feel
    My heart was made o' steel—

As, crossing Ludgate Hill, where many stirr'd,
  I saw Saint Paul's great clock and heard it chime,
And hadn't power to count the strokes I heard,
  But strain'd my eyes and saw it was not time;
Ah! then I felt I dared not creep more near,
  But went into a lane off Ludgate Hill,
And sitting on a doorstep, I could hear
  The people gathering still!
And still the rain was falling, falling,
  And deadening the hum I heard from *there;*
And wet and stiff, I heard the people calling,
  And watch'd the rain-drops glistening down my hair,
My elbows on my knees, my fingers dead,—
My shawl thrown off, now none could see,—my head
  Dripping and wild and bare.
I heard the murmur of a crowd of men,
  And next, a hammering sound, I knew full well,
For something gripp'd me round the heart!—and then
  There came the solemn tolling of a bell!
O God! O God! how could I sit close by
And neither scream nor cry?
As if I had been stone, all hard and cold,
  But listening, listening, listening, still and dumb,
While the folk murmur'd, and the death-bell toll'd,
  And the day brighten'd, and his time had come. . .

. . . Till Nan !—all else was silent, but the knell
Of the slow bell !
And I could only wait, and wait, and wait,
   And what I waited for I couldn't tell,—
At last there came a groaning deep and great—
Saint Paul's struck " eight "—
   I scream'd and seem'd to turn to fire, and fell !

VIII.

God bless him, live or dead !
   He never meant no wrong, was kind and true—
They've wrought their fill of spite upon his head—
   Why didn't they be kind, and take me too ?
And there's the dear old things he used to wear,
And here's a lock o' hair !
And they're more precious far than gold galore,
   Than all the wealth and gold in London town !
He'll never wear the hat and clothes no more,
   And I shall never wear the muslin gown !
And Ned ! my Ned !
   Is fast asleep, and cannot hear me call ;—
God bless you, Nan, for all you've done and said,
   But don't mind *me !* My heart is broke—that's all '

THE BOOKWORM.

WITH spectacles upon his nose,
   He shuffles up and down ;
Of antique fashion are his clothes,
   His napless hat is brown.
A mighty watch, of silver wrought,
   Keeps time in sun or rain
To the dull ticking of the thought
   Within his dusty brain.

To see him at the bookstall stand
   And bargain for the prize,
With the odd sixpence in his hand
   And greed in his gray eyes !
Then, conquering, grasp the book, half blind,
   And take the homeward track,
For fear the man should change his mind,
   And want the bargain back !

The waves of life about him beat,
　He scarcely lifts his gaze,
He hears within the crowded street
　The wash of ancient days.
If ever his short-sighted eyes
　Look forward, he can see
Vistas of dusty Libraries
　Prolong'd eternally !

But think not as he walks along
　His brain is dead and cold ;
His soul is thinking in the tongue
　Which Plato spake of old ;
And while some grinning cabman sees
　His quaint shape with a jeer,
He smiles,—for Aristophanes
　Is joking in his ear.

Around him stretch Athenian walks,
　And strange shapes under trees ;
He pauses in a dream and talks
　Great speech, with Socrates.
Then, as the fancy fails—still mesh'd
　In thoughts that go and come—
Feels in his pouch, and is refresh'd
　At touch of some old tome.

The mighty world of humankind
  Is as a shadow dim,
He walks thro' life like one half blind,
  And all looks dark to him;
But put his nose to leaves antique,
  And hold before his sight
Some press'd and wither'd flowers of Greek,
  And all is life and light.

A blessing on his hair so gray,
  And coat of dingy brown!
May bargains bless him every day,
  As he goes up and down;
Long may the bookstall-keeper's face,
  In dull times, smile again,
To see him round with shuffling pace
  The corner of the lane!

A good old Ragpicker is he,
  Who, following morn and eve
The quick feet of Humanity,
  Searches the dust they leave.
He pokes the dust, he sifts with care,
  He searches close and deep;
Proud to discover, here and there,
  A treasure in the heap!

BARBARA GRAY.

A mourning woman, robed in black,
Stands in the twilight, looking back ;
Her hand is on her heart, her head
Bends musingly above the Dead,
Her face is plain, and pinch'd, and thin,
But splendour strikes it from within.

I.

" Barbara Gray !

Pause, and remember what the world will say,"

I cried, and turning on the threshold fled,

When he was breathing on his dying bed ;

But when, with heart grown bold,

I cross'd the threshold cold,

Here lay John Hamerton, and he was dead.

II.

And all the house of death was chill and dim,

The dull old housekeeper was looking grim,

The hall-clock ticking slow, the dismal rain

Splashing by fits against the window-pane.

The garden shivering in the twilight dark,

Beyond, the bare trees of the empty park,

And faint gray light upon the great cold bed,
And I alone ; and he I turn'd from—dead.

III.

Ay, "dwarf" they called this man who sleeping lies ;
No lady shone upon him with her eyes,
No tender maiden heard his true-love vow,
And press'd her kisses on the great bold brow.
What cared John Hamerton ? With light, light laugh,
He halted through the streets upon his staff ;
Halt, lame, not beauteous, yet with winning grace
And sweetness in his pale and quiet face ;
Fire, hell's or heaven's, in his eyes of blue ;
Warm words of love upon his tongue thereto ;
Could win a woman's Soul with what he said ;—
And I am here ; and here he lieth dead.

IV.

I would not blush if the bad world saw now
How by his bed I stoop and kiss his brow !
Ah, kiss it, kiss it, o'er and o'er again,
With all the love that fills my heart and brain.

V.

For where was man had stoop'd to me before,
Though I was maiden still, and girl no more ?

Where was the spirit that had deign'd to prize
The poor plain features and the envious eyes?
What lips had whisper'd warmly in mine ears?
When had I known the passion and the tears?
Till he I look on sleeping came unto me,
Found me among the shadows, stoop'd to woo me,
Seized on the heart that flutter'd withering here,
Strung it and wrung it, with new joy and fear,
Yea, brought the rapturous light, and brought the day,
Waken'd the dead heart withering away,
Put thorns and roses on the unhonour'd head,
That felt but roses till the roses fled!
Who, who but he crept to that sunless ground,
Content to prize the faded face he found?
John Hamerton, I pardon all—sleep sound, my love,
    sleep sound!

VI.

What fool that crawls shall prate of shame and sin?
Did he not think me fair enough to win?
Yea, stoop and smile upon my face as none,
Living or dead, save he alone, had done?
Bring the bright blush unto my cheek, when ne'er
The full of life and love had mantled there?
And I am all alone; and here lies he,—
The only man that ever smiled on me.

VII.

Here, in his lonely dwelling-house he lies,
The light all faded from his winsome eyes:
Alone, alone, alone, he slumbers here,
With wife nor little child to shed a tear!
Little, indeed, to him did nature give;
Nor was he good and pure as some that live,
But pinch'd in body, warp'd in limb,
He hated the bad world that loved not him!

VIII.

Barbara Gray!
Pause, and remember how he turn'd away;
Think of your wrongs, and of your sorrows.   Nay!
Woman, think rather of the shame and wrong
Of pining lonely in the dark so long;
Think of the comfort in the grief he brought,
The revelation in the wrong he wrought.
Then, Barbara Gray!
Blush not, nor heed what the cold world will say;
But kiss him, kiss him, o'er and o'er again,
In passion and in pain,
With all the love that fills your heart and brain!
Yea, kiss him, bless him, pray beside his bed,
For you have loved, and here your love lies dead.

THE WAKE OF O'HARA.

(SEVEN DIALS).

To the Wake of O'Hara
Came company ;
All St. Patrick's Alley
Was there to see,
With the friends and kinsmen
Of the family.
On the long deal table lay Tim in white,
And at his pillow the burning light.
Pale as himself, with the tears on her cheek,
The mother received us, too full to speak ;
But she heap'd the fire, and on the board
Set the black bottle with never a word,
While the company gather'd, one and all,
Men and women, big and small—
Not one in the Alley but felt a call
To the Wake of Tim O'Hara.

At the face of O'Hara,
All white with sleep,

Not one of the women
But took a peep,
And the wives new-wedded
Began to weep.
The mothers gather'd round about,
And praised the linen and laying-out,—
For white as snow was his winding-sheet,
And all was peaceful, and clean, and sweet ;
And the old wives, praising the blessëd dead,
Were thronging around the old press-bed,
Where O'Hara's widow, tatter'd and torn,
Held to her bosom the babe new-born,
And stared all around her, with eyes forlorn,
At the Wake of Tim O'Hara.

For the heart of O'Hara
Was good as gold,
And the life of O'Hara
Was bright and bold,
And his smile was precious
To young and old !
Gay as a guinea, wet or dry,
With a smiling mouth, and a twinkling eye !
Had ever an answer for chaff and fun ;
Would fight like a lion, with any one !

Not a neighbour of any trade
But knew some joke that the boy had made;
Not a neighbour, dull or bright,
But minded *something*—frolic or fight,
And whisper'd it round the fire that night,
      At the Wake of Tim O'Hara!

      " To God be glory
            In death and life,
      He's taken O'Hara
            From trouble and strife!"
      Said one-eyed Biddy,
            The apple-wife.
"God bless old Ireland!" said Mistress Hart,
Mother to Mike of the donkey-cart;
"God bless old Ireland till all be done,
She never made wake for a better son!"
And all join'd chorus, and each one said
Something kind of the boy that was dead;
And the bottle went round from lip to lip,
And the weeping widow, for fellowship,
Took the glass of old Biddy and had a sip,
      At the Wake of Tim O'Hara.

      Then we drank to O'Hara,
            With drams to the brim,

While the face of O'Hara
Look'd on so grim,
In the corpse-light shining
Yellow and dim.
The cup of liquor went round again,
And the talk grew louder at every drain;
Louder the tongues of the women grew!—
The lips of the boys were loosening too!
The widow her weary eyelids closed,
And, soothed by the drop o' drink, she dozed;
The mother brighten'd and laugh'd to hear
Of O'Hara's fight with the grenadier,
And the hearts of all took better cheer,
At the Wake of Tim O'Hara.

Tho' the face of O'Hara
Lookt on so wan,
In the chimney-corner
The row began—
Lame Tony was in it,
The oyster-man;
For a dirty low thief from the North came near,
And whistled " Boyne Water " in his ear,
And Tony, with never a word of grace,
Flung out his fist in the blackguard's face;

And the girls and women scream'd out for fright,
And the men that were drunkest began to fight,—
Over the tables and chairs they threw,—
The corpse light tumbled,—the trouble grew,—
The new-born join'd in the hullabaloo,—
  At the Wake of Tim O'Hara.

  " Be still ! be silent !
   Ye do a sin !
  Shame be his portion
   Who dares begin !"
  'Twas Father O'Connor
   Just enter'd in !—
All look'd down, and the row was done—
And shamed and sorry was every one ;
But the Priest just smiled quite easy and free—
" Would ye wake the poor boy from his sleep ? " said he :
And he said a prayer, with a shining face,
Till a kind of brightness fill'd the place ;
The women lit up the dim corpse-light,
The men were quieter at the sight,
And the peace of the Lord fell on all that night
  At the Wake of Tim O'Hara !

SPRING SONG IN THE CITY.

WHO remains in London,
  In the streets with me,
Now that Spring is blowing
  Warm winds from the sea ;
Now that trees grow green and tall,
  Now the Sun shines mellow,
And with moist primroses all
  English lanes are yellow?

Little barefoot maiden,
  Selling violets blue,
Hast thou ever pictured
  Where the sweetlings *grew ?*—
Oh, the warm wild woodland ways,
  Deep in dewy grasses,
Where the wild-blown shadow strays,
  Scented as it passes !

Pedlar breathing deeply,
  Toiling into town,
With the dusty highway
  You are dusky brown,—

Have you seen by daisied leas,
  And by rivers flowing,
Lilac-ringlets which the breeze
  Loosens lightly blowing?

Out of yonder wagon
  Pleasant hay-scents float,
He who drives it carries
  A daisy in his coat :
Oh, the English meadows, fair
  Far beyond all praises !
Freckled orchids everywhere
  Mid the snow of daisies !

Now in busy silence
  Broods the nightingale,
Choosing his love's dwelling
  In a dimpled dale ;
Round the leafy bower they raise
  Rose-trees wild are springing ;
Underneath, thro' the green haze,
  Bounds the brooklet singing.

And his love is silent
  As a bird can be,
For the red buds only
  Fill the red rose-tree,—

Just as buds and blossoms blow
  He'll begin his tune,
When all is green and roses glow
  Underneath the Moon.

Nowhere in the valleys
  Will the wind be still,
Everything is waving,
  Wagging at his will
Blows the milkmaid's kirtle clean,
  With her hand prest on it !
Lightly o'er the hedge so green
  Blows the ploughboy's bonnet !

Oh, to be a-roaming
  In an English dell !
Every nook is wealthy,
  All the world looks well,
Tinted soft the Heavens glow,
  Over Earth and Ocean,
Brooks flow, breezes blow,
  All is light and motion !

TO DAVID IN HEAVEN.

"Quem Di diligunt, adolescens moritur."

SEE ! the slow Moon roaming
Thro' gray mists of gloaming,
Furrowing with pearl-bright edge the jewel-powder'd sky !
See, the Bridge moss-laden,
Arch'd like foot of maiden,
And on the Bridge, in silence, looking upwards, you
and I !
'Tis the pleasant season
Of reaping and of mowing—
The mournful Moon above—beneath, the River duskily
flowing !

Blown from scented meadows,
Violet-colour'd shadows
Pass o'er us to the pine-wood dark from yonder dim
corn-ridge ;
The River gleams and gushes
Thro' shady sedge and rushes,

And gray gnats gather o'er the pools, beneath the mossy
      Bridge ;—
      And you and I stand darkly,
      O'er the keystone leaning,
And watch the pale mesmeric Moon, in the time of
      reaping and gleaning.

      Do I *dream*, I wonder?
      As, sitting sadly under
A lonely roof in London, thro' the grim square pane I
      gaze ?
      Here of thee I ponder,
      In a dream, and yonder
The sad streets seem to stir and breathe beneath the
      white Moon's rays.
      By the vision cherish'd,
      By the battle bravëd,
Do I but dream a hopeless dream, in the City that
      slew you, David?

      Is it fancy also,
      That the light which falls so
Faintly upon the stony street below me, as I write,
      Near tall mountain passes,
      Thro' churchyard weeds and grasses,

Barely a mower's mile away from that small Bridge, this
night?
And, where you are lying,—
Grass and flowers above you—
Is mingled with your sleeping face, as calm as the hearts
that love you?

Poet gentle-hearted,
Are you then departed,
Have you ceased to dream the dream we loved of old so
well?
Has the deeply cherish'd
Aspiration perish'd,
And are you happy, David, in that heaven where you
dwell?
Have you won the wisdom
We so wildly fought for,
Is your young Soul enswathed, at last, in the singing
robes you sought for?

In some Heaven star-lighted,
Are you now united
Unto the poet spirits that you loved, of English race?
Is Chatterton still dreaming?
To give it stately seeming,

Hath the music of his last strong song flash'd into
  Keats's face?
  Is Wordsworth there? and Spenser?
  Beyond the grave's black portals,
Can the grand eye of Milton *see* the glory he sang to
  mortals?

  You at least could teach me,
  Could your low voice reach me,
Where I sit and copy out for men my Soul's strange
  speech,
  Whether it be bootless,
  Profitless and fruitless,—
The weary aching upward strife to heights we cannot
  reach,
  The fame we seek in sorrow,
  The agony we forego not,
The haunting singing sense that makes us climb—whither
  we know not!

  Must it last for ever,
  The passionate endeavour,
Ay, have you, there in heaven, hearts to throb and still
  aspire?
  In the life you know now,
  Render'd white as snow now,

Doth a fresh mountain-range arise, and beckon higher—
    higher?
      Are you dreaming, dreaming,
      Is your Soul still roaming,
Still gazing upward as we gazed, of old, in the autumn
    gloaming!

      Upward my face I turn to you,
      I long for you, I yearn to you,
The spectral vision trances me to utt'rance wild and
    weak;
      It is not that I mourn you,
      To mourn you were to scorn you,
For you are one step nearer to the secret Singers seek.
      But I want, and cannot see you,
      I seek, and cannot find you,
And, see! I touch the Book of Songs you tenderly left
    behind you!

      Ay me! I bend above it
      With tearful eyes, and love it,
With tender hand I touch the leaves, but cannot find
    you *there!*
      My sad eyes ever and only
      Behold that gloaming lonely,

The shadows on the mossy Bridge, the glamour in the
    air !
    I touch the leaves, and only
    See rays which *they* retain not—
The Moon that is a lamp to Hope, who glorifies—what
    we gain not !

    The aching and the yearning,
    The hollow, undiscerning,
Uplooking want I still retain, darken the leaves I touch—
    Pale promise, with much sweetness
    Solemnizing incompleteness,
But ah ! you knew so little then—and now, you know so
    much !
    By the vision cherish'd,
    By the battle bravëd,
Have you, in Heaven, shamed the song, by a mightier
    music, David ?

    I, who loved and knew you,
    In the City that slew you,
Still hunger on, and thirst, and climb, proud-hearted and
    alone :
    Serpent-fears enfold me,
    Syren-visions hold me,

And, like a wave, I gather strength, and gathering
      strength, I moan ;
      Yea, the pale Moon beckons,
      Still I follow, aching,
And gather strength, only to make a louder moan, in
      breaking.

      Tho' the world could turn from you,
      This, at least, I learn from you :
Beauty and Truth, tho' never found, are worthy to be
      sought ;
      The Singer, upward-springing,
      Is grander than his singing,
And tranquil self-sufficing joy illumes the Poet's thought.
      This, at least, you teach me,
      In a revelation :
The Gods *still* snatch, as worthy death, the Soul in its
      aspiration.

      And I think, as you thought,
      Poesy and Truth ought
Never to lie silent in the Singer's heart on earth ;
      Tho' they be discarded,
      Slighted, unrewarded,—

'Tho', unto vulgar seeming, they appear of little worth,—
 Yet tender brother-singers,
 Young or yet unborn to us,
May seek there, for the Singer's sake, that love which
 sweetcneth scorn to us !

 While I sit in silence,
 Ccmes from mile on mile hence,
From English Keats's Roman grave, a voice that lightens
 toil ;
 Think you, no fond creatures
 Draw comfort from the features
Of Chatterton, that Phaëthon pale, struck down to sunless
 soil :
 Scorch'd with sunlight lying,
 Eyes of sunlight hollow,
But see ! upon the lips a gleam of the chrism of Apollo !

 Noble thought produces
 Noble ends and uses,
Noble hopes are part of Hope wherever she may be,
 Noble thought enhances
 Life and all its chances,
And noble self is noble song,—all this I learn from
 thee !

And I learn, moreover,

'Mid the City's strife too,

That such faint song as sweetens Death can sweeten the

Singer's life too !

Lo ! thy Book !—I hold it

In weary hands, and fold it

Unto my heart, if only as a token *I* aspire

And, by Song's assistance,

Unto your dim distance,

My Soul upwafted is on wings, and beckon'd higher,

nigher.

By the sweeter wisdom

You retain unspeaking,

Though endless, hopeless, be the search, we exalt our

Souls in seeking.

Higher, yet, and higher,

Ever nigher, ever nigher,

To glory we conceive not yet, let us still strive and

strain !—

The agonizëd yearning.

The imploring and the burning,

Grown awfuller, intenser, at each vista we attain ;

And clearer, brighter, growing,

By heavenly waters wander,

Higher, higher yet, and higher, to the Mystery we ponder ;
    Up ! higher yet, and higher,
    Ever nigher, ever nigher,
Thro' voids that Milton and the rest beat still with seraph-
        wings ;
    Out thro' the dark Gate creeping
    Where God hath put his sleeping—
A quiet cloud detaining not the Soul that soars and sings,
    Up ! higher yet, and higher,
    Fainting nor retreating,
Beyond the sun, beyond the stars, to the far bright realm
        of meeting !

    O Mystery ! O Passion !
    To sit on earth, and fashion
What floods of music and of light may fill that fancied
        place !
    To think, the least that singeth,
    Aspireth and upspringeth,
May weep glad tears on Keats's breast and look in Shak-
        speare's face !
    When human power and failure
    Are equalised for ever,
And the one great Light that haloes all is the passionate
        bright endeavour !

   . . . But ah ! that pale Moon roaming
     Thro' the gray mists of gloaming,
Furrowing with pearl-bright edge the jewel-powder'd sky !
     And ah ! the days departed
     With friendships gentle-hearted,
And ah ! the dream we dreamt that night, together, you
       and I !
     Is it fashion'd wisely,
     To help us or to blind us,
At every height we gain, we turn, and behold our Heaven
      —*behind* us ?

SPIRITUAL POEMS.

THE STRANGE COUNTRY.

I HAVE come from a mystical Land of Light
    To a Strange Country ;
The Land I have left is forgotten quite
    In the Land I see.

The round earth rolls beneath my feet,
    And the still stars glow,
The murmuring waters rise and retreat,
    The winds come and go.

Sure as a heart-beat all things seem
    In this Strange Country ;
So sure, so still, in a dazzle of dream,
    All things flow free.

'Tis life, all life, be it pleasure or pain,
    In the field and the flood,
In the beating heart, in the burning brain,
    In the flesh and the blood.

Deep as Death is the daily strife
    Of this Strange Country :
All things thrill up till they blossom in Life,
    And flutter and flee.

Nothing is stranger than the rest,
    From the pole to the pole,
The weed by the way, the eggs in the nest,
    The flesh and the soul.

Look in mine eyes, O Man I meet
    In this Strange Country !
Lie in mine arms, O Maiden sweet,
    With thy mouth kiss me !

Go by, O King, with thy crownèd brow
    And thy sceptred hand—
Thou art a straggler too, I vow,
    From the same strange Land.

O wondrous faces that upstart
    In this Strange Country !
O souls, O shades, that become a part
    Of my soul and me !

What are ye working so fast and fleet,
  O Humankind?
" We are building cities for those whose feet
  Are coming behind ;

" Our stay is short, we must fly again
  From this Strange Country ;
But others are growing, women and men,
  Eternally ! "

Child, what art *thou ?* and what am *I ?*
  But a breaking wave !
Rising and rolling on, we hie
  To the shore of the grave.

I have come from a mystical Land of Light
  To this Strange Country ;
This dawn I came, I shall go to-night,
  Ay me ! ay me !

I hold my hand to my head and stand
  'Neath the air's blue arc,
I try to remember the mystical Land,
  But all is dark ;

And all around me swim shapes like mine
    In this Strange Country ;—
They break in the glamour of gleams divine,
    And they moan, " Ay me ! "

Like waves in the cold Moon's silvern breath
    They gather and roll,
Each crest of white is a birth or a death,
    Each sound is a soul.

Oh, whose is the Eye that gleams so bright
    O'er this Strange Country ?
It draws us along with à chain of light,
    As the Moon the Sea !

A SONG OF A DREAM.

OH, what is this cry in our burning ears,
   And what is this light on our eyes, dear love?
The cry is the cry of the rolling years,
   As they break on the Sun-rock far above;
And the light is the light of that rock of gold
   As it burneth bright in a starry sea;
And the cry is clearer a hundredfold,
   And the light more bright, when I gaze on *thee.*
My weak eyes dazzle beneath that gleam,
   My sad ears deafen to hear that cry:
I was born in a dream, and I dwell in a dream,
   And I go in a dream to die!

Oh, whose is this hand on my forehead bare,
   And whose are these eyes that look in mine?
The hand is the Earth's soft hand of air,
   The eyes are the Earth's—thro' tears they shine;
And the touch of the hand is so soft, so light,
   As the ray of the blind orbs blesseth me;

R

But the touch is softest, the eyes most bright,
    When I sit and smile by the side of *thee.*
For the mortal Mother's blind eyes beam
    With the long-lost love of a life gone by,
On her breast I woke in a beauteous dream,
    And I go in a dream to die !

Oh, what are these voices around my way,
    And what are these shadows that haunt me so ?
The voices of waifs in a world astray,
    The shadows of souls that come and go.
And I hear and see, and I wonder more,
    For their features are fair and strange as mine,
But most I wonder when most I pore
    On the passionate peace of this face of thine.
We walk in silence by wood and stream,
    Our gaze upturn'd to the same blue sky :
We move in a dream, and we love in a dream,
    And we go in our dream to die !

Oh, what is this music of merry bells,
    And what is this laughter across the wold?
'Tis the mirth of a market that buys and sells,
    'Tis the laughter of men that are counting gold.

I walk thro' Cities of silent stone,
    And the public places alive I see ;
The wicked flourish, the weary groan,
    And I think it real, till I turn to *thee !*
And I smile to answer thine eyes' bright beam,
    For I know all's vision that blackens by :
That they buy in a dream, and they sell in a dream,
    And they go in a dream to die.

Oh, what are these shapes on their thrones of gold,
    And what are those clouds around their feet ?
The shapes are kings with their hearts clay-cold,
    The clouds are armies that ever meet ;
I see the flames of the crimson fire,
    I hear the murder'd who moan, "Ah me ! "—
My bosom aches with its bitter ire,
    And I think it real, till I turn to *thee !*
And I hear thee whisper, " These shapes but seem—
    They are but visions that flash and fly,
While we move in a dream, and love in a dream,
    And go in our dream to die !"

Oh, what are these Spirits that o'er us creep,
    And touch our eyelids and drink our breath ?

The first, with a flower in his hand, is Sleep;
   The next, with a star on his brow, is Death.
We fade before them whene'er they come,
   (And never single those spirits be !)
A little season my lips are dumb,
   But I waken ever,—and look for *thee.*
Yea ever each night when the pale stars gleam
   And the mystical Brethren pass me by,
This cloud of a trance comes across my dream,
   As I seem in my dream to die !

Oh, what is this grass beneath our feet,
   And what are these beautiful under-blooms ?
The grass is the grass of the churchyard, sweet,
   The flowers are flowers on the quiet tombs.
I pluck them softly, and bless the dead,
   Silently o'er them I bend the knee,
But my tenderest blessing is surely said,
   Tho' my tears fall fast, when I turn to *thee.*
For our lips are tuned to the same sad theme,
   We think of the loveless dead, and sigh ;
Dark is the shadow across our dream,
   For we go in that dream to die !

Oh, what is this moaning so faint and low,
  And what is this crying from night to morn?
The moaning is that of the souls that go,
  The crying is that of the souls new-born.
The life-sea gathers with stormy calls,
  The wind blows shrilly, the foam flies free,
The great wave rises, the great wave falls,
  I swim to its height by the side of *thee!*
With arms outstretching and throats that scream,
  With faces that flash into foam and fly,
Our beings break in the light of a dream,
  As the great waves gather and die!

Oh, what is this Spirit with silvern feet,
  His bright head wrapt in a saffron veil?
Around his raiment our wild arms beat,
  We cling unto it, but faint and fail.
'Tis the Spirit that sits on the twilight star,
  And soft to the sound of the surge sings he:
He leads the chaunt from his crystal car,
  And I join in the mystical chaunt with *thee;*
And our beings burn with the heavenly theme,
  For he sings of wonders beyond the sky,
Of a god-like dream, and of gods in a dream,
  Of a dream that cannot die!

Oh, closer creep to this breast of mine ;
  We rise, we mingle, we break, dear love !
A space on the crest of the wave we shine,
  With light and music and mirth we move ;
Before and behind us (fear not, sweet !)
  Blackens the trough of the surging sea—
A little moment our mouths may meet,
  A little moment I cling to thee ;
Onward the wonderful waters stream,
  'Tis vain to struggle, 'tis vain to cry—
We wake in a dream, and we ache in a dream,
  And we break in a dream and die !

But who is this other with hair of flame,
  The naked feet and the robe of white ?
A Spirit too, with a sweeter name,
  A softer smile, a serener light.
He wraps us both in a golden cloud,
  He thrills our frames with a fire divine,
Our souls are mingled, our hearts beat loud,
  My breath and being are blent with thine ;
And the Sun-rock flames with a flash supreme,
  And the starry waves have a stranger cry—
We climb to the crest of our golden dream,
  For we dream that we cannot die !

Aye ! the cry rings loud in our burning ears,
  And the light flames bright on our eyes, dear love,
And we know the cry of the rolling years,
  As they break on the Sun-rock far above ;
And we know the light of the rock of gold
  As it burneth bright in a starry sea ;
And the glory deepens a thousandfold
  As I name the immortal gods and thee !
We shrink together beneath that gleam,
  We cling together before that cry ;
We were made in a dream, and we fade in a dream,
  And if death be a dream, we die !

FLOWER OF THE WORLD.

WHEREVER men sinn'd and wept,
I wander'd in my quest;
At last in a Garden of God
I saw the Flower of the World.

This Flower had human eyes,
Its breath was the breath of the mouth;
Sunlight and starlight came,
And the Flower drank bliss from both.

Whatever was base and unclean,
Whatever was sad and strange,
Was piled around its roots,
It drew its strength from the same.

Whatever was formless and base
Pass'd into fineness and form;
Whatever was lifeless and mean
Grew into beautiful bloom.

Then I thought, "O Flower of the World,
Miraculous Blossom of things,
Light as a faint wreath of snow
Thou tremblest to fall in the wind.

" O beautiful Flower of the World,
Fall not nor wither away ;
He is coming—He cannot be far—
The Lord of the Flowers and the Stars.

And I cried, " O Spirit divine !
That walkest the Garden unseen,
Come hither, and bless, ere it dies,
The beautiful Flower of the World."

THE FIRST SONG OF THE VEIL.

(*From " The Book of Orm."*)

I.

THE VEIL WOVEN.

In the beginning,
　Ere Man grew,
The Veil was woven
　Bright and blue ;
Soft mist and vapours
Gather'd and mingled
Over the black world
　Stretch'd below,
While winds of heaven
Blew from all places,
Shining luminous,
　A starry snow.
Blindly, dumbly,
Darken'd under
Ocean and river,

Mountain and dale,
While over his features,
Wondrous, terrible,
The beautiful Master
Drew the Veil :
Then starry, luminous,
Roll'd the Veil of azure
O'er the first dwellings
Of mortal race ;
—And since the beginning
No mortal vision,
Pure or sinning,
Hath seen the Face !

II.

EARTH THE MOTHER.

Beautiful, beautiful, she lay below,
The mighty Mother of humanity,
Turning her sightless eyeballs to the glow
Of light she could not see,
Feeling the happy warmth, and breathing slow
As if her thoughts were shining tranquilly.
Beautiful, beautiful the Mother lay,
Crownëd with silver spray,

The greenness gathering hushfully around
　　The peace of her great heart, while on her breast
The wayward Waters, with a weeping sound,
　　Were sobbing into rest.
For all day long her face shone merrily,
And at its smile the waves leapt mad and free;
But at the darkening of the Veil, she drew
　　The wild things to herself, and husht their cries—
Then, stiller, dumber, search'd the deepening Blue
　　With passionate blind eyes;
And went the old life over in her thought,
Dreamily praying as her memory wrought
　　The dimly guess'd at, never utter'd tale,
　　　While, over her dreaming,
　　　Deepen'd the luminous,
　　　Star-inwrought, beautiful,
　　Folds of the wondrous Veil.

For more than any of her children of clay
　　The beautiful Mother knows—
　　　She is so old !
Ye would go wild to hearken, if this day
　　Her dumb lips should unclose,
　　　And the tale be told :

Such unfathomable things,
Such mystic vanishings,
  She knoweth about God—she is so old.
For oft, in the beginning, long ago,
Without a Veil look'd down the Face ye know,
And Earth, an infant happy-eyed and bright,
Look'd smiling up, and gladden'd in its sight.
But later, when the Man-Flower from her womb
Burst into brightening bloom,
In her glad eyes a golden dust was blown
Out of the Void, and she was blind as stone.

And since that day
She hath not seen, nor spoken,—lest her say
  Should be a sorrow and fear to mortal race,
And doth not know the Lord hath hid away,
  But turneth up blind orbs—to feel the Face.

III.

CHILDREN OF EARTH.

So dumbly, blindly,
So cheerly, sweetly,
The beautiful Mother
  Of mortals smiled ;

Her children marvell'd
And look'd upon her—
Her patient features
  Were bright and mild ;
And on her eyeballs
  Night and day,
A sweet light glimmer'd
  From far away.
Her children gather'd
  With sobs and cries,
To see the sweetness
  Of sightless eyes ;
But though she held them
  So dear, so dear,
She could not answer,
  She could not hear.
She felt them flutter
  Around her knee,
She felt their weeping,
Yet knew not wherefore—
  She could not see.
" O Mother ! Mother
  Of mortal race !
Is there a Father ?
  Is there a Face ? "

She felt their sorrow
  Against her cheek,—
She could not hearken,
  She could not speak ;
With thin lips fluttering,
With blind eyes tearful,
  With features pale,
She clasp'd her children,
And look'd in silence
  Upon the Veil.

Her hair grew silvern,
  The swift days fled,
Her lap was heavy
  With children dead ;
To her heart she held them,
But could not warm them—
The life within them
  Was gone like dew.
Whiter, stiller,
  The Mother grew.

The World grew hoary,
The World was weary,

The children cried at
The empty air :
" Father of mortals ! "
The children murmur'd,
" Father ! father !
Art Thou there ? "

Then the Master answer'd·
From the thunder-cloud :
" I am God the Maker !
I am God the Master ;
I am God the Father ! "
He cried aloud.
Further, the Master
Made sign on sign—
Footprints of his spirits,
Voices divine ;
His breath was a water,
His cry was a wind.

But the people heard not,
The people saw not,—
Earth and her children
Were deaf and blind.

IV.

THE WISE MEN.

" Call the great philosophers !
Call them all hither,—
   The good, the wise !"
Their robes were snowy,
Their hearts were holy,
   They had cold still eyes.
To the mountain-summits
Wearily they wander'd,
Reaching the desolate
   Regions of snow,
Looming there lonely,
They search'd the Veil wonderful
With tubes fire-fashion'd
   In caverns below . . .
God withdrew backward,
And darker, dimmer,
   Deepen'd the day :
O'er the philosophers
Looming there lonely
   Night gather'd gray.
Then the wise men gazing
Saw the lights above them

Thicken and thicken,
　　And all went pale—
Ah! the lamps numberless,
The mystical jewels of God,
The luminous, wonderful,
　　Beautiful lights of the Veil!

Alas for the Wise Men!
The snows of the mountain
　　Drifted about them,
And the wind cried round them,
As the lights of wonder
　　Multiplied!
The breath of the mountain
Froze them into stillness,—
　　They sighed and died.
Still in the desolate
　　Heights overhead,
Stand their shapes frozen,
　　Frozen and dead.
But a weary few,
　　Weary and dull and cold,
Crept faintly down again,
　　Looking very old;
And when the people

Gather'd around them,
The heart went sickly
  At their dull blank stare—
"O Wise Men answer!
Is there a Father?
Is there a beautiful
  Face up there?"
The Wise Men answer'd and said:
"Bury us deep when dead—
  We have travell'd a weary road,
We have seen no more than ye.
'Twere better not to be—
  There is no God!"
And the people, hearkening,
Saw the Veil above them,
And the darkness deepen'd,
  And the Lights gleam'd pale.
Ah! the lamps numberless,
The mystical jewels of God,
The luminous, wonderful,
  Beautiful Lights of the Veil!

THE SOUL AND THE DWELLING.

(From " The Book of Orm.")

Come to me! clasp me!
Spirit to spirit!
Bosom to bosom !
Tenderly, clingingly,
   Mingle to one ! . . .

Now, from my kisses
Withdrawing, and blushing,
Why dost thou gaze on me?
Why dost thou weep?
Why dost thou cling to me,
Imploring, adoring?
What are those meanings
   That flash from thine eyes?

   Pitiful! pitiful!
Now I conceive thee !—
Yea, it were easier
Striking two swords,

To weld them together,
Than spirit with spirit
To mingle, though rapture
  Be perfect as this.
Shut in a tremulous
 Prison, each spirit
Hungers and yearns—
Never, ah never,
Belovëd, belovëd,
 Have these eyes look'd on
  The face of thy Soul.

Ours are two dwellings,
Wondrously beautiful,
Made in the darkness
  Of soft-tinted flesh:
In the one dwelling,
Prison'd I dwell,
And lo ! from the other
  Thou beckonest me !
I am a Soul !
 Thou art a Soul !
These are our dwellings !
  O to be free !

Beauteous, belovëd,
Is thy dear dwelling;
All o'er it blowing
The roses of dawn—
Bright is the portal,
The dwelling is scented
　　Within and without;
Strange are the windows,
So clouded with azure,
The faces are hidden
　　That look from within.

Now I approach thee,
Sweetness and odour
Tremble upon me—
Wild is the rapture!
Thick is the perfume!
Sweet bursts of music
Thrill from within!
Closer, yet closer!
Bosom to bosom!
Tenderly, clingingly,
　　Mingle to one.　.　.　.
Ah! but what faces
　　Are those that look forth!　.

Faces! What faces? As I speak they die,
And all my gaze is empty as of old.
O love! the world was fair, and everywhere
Rose wondrous human dwellings like mine own,
And many of these were foul and dark with dust,
Haunted by things obscene, not beautiful,
But most were very royal, meet to serve
Angels for habitation. All alone
Brooded my soul by a mysterious fire
Dim-burning, never-dying, from the first
Lit in the place by God; the winds and rains
Struck on the abode and spared it; day and night
Above it came and went; and in the night
My Soul gazed from the threshold silently,
And saw the congregated lamps that swung
Above it in the dark and dreamy blue;
And in the day my soul gazed on the earth,
And sought the dwellings there for signs, and lo!
None answer'd; for the Soul's inhabitant
Drew coldly back and darken'd; and I said,
" In all the habitations I behold,
Some old, some young, some fair, and some not fair,
There dwells no soul I know." But as I spake
I saw beside me in a dreamy light
Thy habitation, so serene and fair,

So stately in a rosy dawn of day,
That all my soul look'd forth and cried, " Behold
The sweetest dwelling in the whole wide world !"
And thought not of the inmate, but gazed on,
Lingeringly, hushfully, for as I gazed
Something came glistening up into thine eyes,
And beckon'd, and a murmur from the portal,
A murmur and a perfume, floated hither,
Thrill'd thro' my dwelling, making every chamber
                Tremble with mystical,
                Dazzling desire !

            .   .   Come to me ! close to me !
            Bosom to bosom !
            Tenderly, clingingly,
                Mingle to one !
            Wildly within me
            Some eager inmate
            Rushes and trembles,
            Peers from the eyes
            And calls in the ears,
            Yearns to thee, cries to thee !
            Claiming old kinship
            In lives far removed !   .   .   .
            Vainly, ah vainly !

Pent in its prison
Must each miraculous
   Spirit remain,—
Yet inarticulate,
Striving to language
Music and memory,
   Rapture and dream !

Rapture and dream !   Belovëd one, in vain
My spirit seeks for utterance.   Alas,
Not yet shall there be speech.   Not yet, not yet,
One dweller in a mortal tenement
Can know what secret faces hide away
Within the neighbouring dwelling.   Ah belovëd,
The mystery, the mystery !   We cry
For God's face, who have never look'd upon
The poorest Soul's face in the wonderful
Soul-haunted world.   A spirit once there dwelt
Beside me, close as thou—two wedded souls,
We mingled—flesh was mix'd with flesh—we knew
All joys, all unreserves of mingled life—
Yea, not a sunbeam fill'd the house of one
But touch'd the other's threshold.   Hear me swear
I never knew that Soul !   All touch, all sound,
All light was insufficient.   The Soul, pent

In its strange chambers, cried to mine in vain—
We saw each other not : but oftentimes
When I was glad, the windows of my neighbour
Were dark and drawn, as for a funeral ;
And sometimes, when, most weary of the world,
My soul was looking forth at dead of night,
I saw the neighbouring dwelling brightly lit,
The happy windows flooded full of light,
As if a feast were being held within.
Yet were there passing flashes, random gleams,
Low sounds, from the inhabitant divine
I knew not ; and I shrunk from some of these
In a mysterious pain.   At last, belovëd,
The frail fair mansion where that spirit dwelt
Totter'd and trembled, through the wondrous flesh
A dim sick glimmer from the fire within
Grew fainter, fainter.   " I am going away,"
The spirit seem'd to cry ; and as it cried,
Stood still and dim and very beautiful
Up in the windows of the eyes—there linger'd,
First seen, last seen, a moment, silently—
So different, more beautiful tenfold
Than all that I had dream'd—I sobb'd aloud
" Stay ! stay ! " but at the one despairing word
The spirit faded, from the hearth within

The dim fire died with one last quivering gleam—
The house became a ruin ; and I moan'd
" God help me ! 'twas herself that look'd at me !
First seen !   I never knew her face before !
Too late ! too late ! too late ! "

> . . . Yea, from my forehead
> Kiss the dark fantasy !
> Tenderly, clingingly,
>   Mingle to one !
> Is not this language ?
> Music and memory,
>   Rapture and dream ?—
> Oh, in the dewy-bright
>   Day-dawn of love,
> Is it not wondrous,
> Blush-red with roses,
> The beautiful, mystical
>   House of the Soul !
> Lo, in my innermost
> Chambers is floating
> Soft perfume and music
>   That tremble from *thee.* . . .
> Ah, but what faces
>   Are these that look forth ?

.　.　.　Sit, still, belovëd, while I search thy looks
For memories.　O thou art beautiful !
Crownëd with silken gold,—soft amber tints
Coming and going on thy peach-hued flesh,—
Thy breath a perfume—thy blue eyes twin stars—
Thy lips like dewy rosebuds to the eye,
Though living to the touch.　O royal abode,
Flooded with music, light, and precious scent,
Curtainëd soft with subtle mystery !
Nay, stir not, but gaze on, still and serene,
Possessing me with thy superb still sweep
Of eyes ineffable—sit still, my queen,
And let me, clinging on thee, count the ways
Wherein I know thee.　Nay, even now, belovëd,
When all the world like some vast tidal wave
Withdraws and leaves us on a golden shore
Alone together—when thou most art mine—
When the winds blow for us, and the soft stars
Are shining for us, where we dream apart,—
Now our two dwellings in a dizzy hour
Have mingled their foundations—clinging thus
And hungering round me in mine ecstasy,—
Belovëd, do I know thee ?　Hath my Soul
Spoken to thine the imperial speech of Souls,
Perfect in meaning and in melody ?

Tell me, belovëd, while thou sittest so,
Mine own, my queen, my palace of delights,
What lights are these that pass and come again
Within thee?   Is the Spirit looking forth,
Or is it but the glittering gleams of time
Playing on vacant windows?   Can I swear
Thou thinkest of me now at all?   Behold
Now all thy beauty is suffused with brightness—
Thou blushest and thou smilest.   Tell me true,
Thou then wast far within, and with that cry
I woke thee out of dream.   O speak to me —
Soul's speech, belovëd!   Do not smile that way—
A flood of brightness issues from thy door,
But mine is scarcely bright.   Lovest thou me,
Belovëd, my belovëd?   Soul belovëd,
Do I possess thee?   Sight and scent and touch
Are insufficient.   Open! let me in
To the strange chambers I have never seen!
Heart of the rose, blow open! or I die!

THE CITY OF MAN.

COMFORT, O free and true !
Soon shall there rise for you
A City fairer far than all ye plan ;
    Built on a rock of strength,
    It shall arise at length,
Stately and fair and vast, the City meet for Man !

    Towering to yonder skies
    Shall the fair City rise,
Dim in the dawning of a day more pure :
    House, mart, and street, and square
    Yea, and a Fane for prayer—
Fair, and yet built by hands, strong, for it shall endure.

    In the fair City then
    Shall walk white-robëd men,
Wash'd in the river of peace that watereth it ;
    Woman with man shall meet
    Freely in mart and street —
At the great council-board woman with man shall sit.

Hunger and Thirst and Sin
Shall never pass therein ;
Fed with pure dews of love, children shall grow.
Fearless and fair and free,
Honour'd by all that see,
Virgins in golden zones shall walk as white as snow.

There, on the fields around,
All men shall till the ground,
Corn shall wave yellow, and bright waters stream '
Daily, at set of sun,
All, when their work is done,
Shall watch the heavens yearn down and the strange
starlight gleam.

In the fair City of men
All shall be silent then,
While, on a reverent lute, gentle and low,
Some holy Bard shall play
Music divine, and say
Whence those that hear have come, whither in time
they go.

No man of blood shall dare
Wear the white mantle there ;
No man of lust shall walk in street or mart ;—

Yet shall the Magdalen
Walk with the citizen ;
Yet shall the sinner stand gracious and pure of heart.

Now, while days come and go,
Doth the fair City grow,
Surely its stones are laid in sun and moon.
Wise men and pure prepare
Ever this City fair.
Comfort, O ye that weep ; it shall arise full soon.

When, stately, fair, and vast,
It doth uprise at last,
Who shall be King thereof, say, O ye wise ?—
When the last blood is spilt,
When the fair City is built,
Unto the throne thereof the Monarch shall arise.

Flower of blessedness,
Wrought out of heart's distress,
Light of all dreams of saintly men who died,
He shall arise some morn
One Soul of many born,
Lord of the realms of peace, Heir of the Crucified !

Oh, but he lingereth,
Drawing mysterious breath
In the dark depths where he was cast as seed.
Strange was the seed to sow,
Dark is the growth and slow ;
Still hath he lain for long—now he grows quick indeed.

Quicken, O Soul of Man !
Perfect the mystic plan—
Come from the flesh where thou art darkly wrought ;
Wise men and pure prepare
Ever thy City fair —
Come when the City is built, sit on the Throne of
Thought.

Earth and all things that be,
Wait, watch, and yearn for thee,
To thee all loving things stretch hands bereaven ;—
Perfect and sweet and bright,
Lord of the City of Light,
Last of the flowers of Earth, first of the fruits of
Heaven !

T

THE VISION OF THE MAN ACCURST.

(From the " Book of Orm.")

Judgment was over ; all the world redeem'd
Save one Man,—who had sinn'd all sins, whose soul
Was blackness and foul odour.   Last of all,
When all was lamb-white, thro' the summer Sea
Of ministering Spirits he was drifted
On to the white sands ; there he lay and writhed,
Worm-like, black, venomous, with eyes accurst
Looking defiance, dazzled by the light
That gleam'd upon his clench'd and blood-stain'd hands ;
While, with a voice low as a funeral bell,
The Seraph, sickening, read the sable scroll,
And as he read, the Spirits ministrant
Darken'd and murmur'd, " Cast him forth, O Lord ! "
And, from the shrine where unbeheld He broods,
The Lord said, " 'Tis the basest mortal born—
Cast him beyond the Gate ! "

                      The wild thing laugh'd
Defiant, as from wave to wave of light

He drifted, till he swept beyond the Gate,
Past the pale Seraph with the silvern eyes;
And there the wild Wind, that for ever beats
About the edge of brightness, caught him up,
And, like a straw, whirl'd round and wafted him,
And on a dark shore in the Underworld
Cast him, alone and shivering; for the Clime
Was sunless, and the ice was like a sheet
Of glistening tin, and the faint glimmering peaks
Were twisted to fantastic forms of frost,
And everywhere the frozen moonlight steam'd
Foggy and blue, save where the abysses loom'd
Sepulchral shadow.   But the Man arose,
With teeth gnash'd beast-like, waved wild feeble hands
At the white Gate (that glimmer'd far away,
Like to the round ball of the Sun beheld
Through interspaces in a wood of pine),
Cast a shrill curse at the pale Judge within
Then groaning, beast-like crouch'd.

Like golden waves

That break on a green island of the south,
Amid the flash of many plumaged wings,
Pass'd the fair days in Heaven.   By the side
Of quiet waters perfect Spirits walk'd,

Low singing, in the star-dew, full of joy
In their own thoughts and pictures of those thoughts
Flash'd into eyes that loved them ; while beside them,
After exceeding storm, the Waters of Life
With soft sea-sound subsided.   Then God said,
"'Tis finish'd—all is well!"   But as He spake
A voice, from out the lonely Deep beneath,
Mock'd !

   Then to the pale Seraph at the Gate,
Who looketh on the Deep with steadfast eyes
For ever, God cried, " What is he that mocks ? "
The Seraph answer'd, "'Tis the Man accurst ! "
And, with a voice of most exceeding peace,
God ask'd, " What doth the Man ? "

      The Seraph said :
" Upon a desolate peak, with hoar-frost hung,
Amid the steaming vapours of the Moon,
He sitteth on a throne, and hideously
Playeth at judgment ; at his feet, with eyes
Slimy and luminous, squats a monstrous Toad ;
Above his head pale phantoms of the Stars
Fulfil cold ministrations of the Void,
And in their dim and melancholy lustre
His shadow, and the shadow of the Toad

Beneath him, linger.   Sceptred, throned, and crown'd,
The foul judgeth the foul, and sitting grim,
Laughs ! "

        With a voice of most exceeding peace
The Lord said, " Look no more ! "

                    The Waters of Life
Broke with a gentle sea-sound gladdening—
God turn'd and blest them ; as He blest the same,
A voice, from out the lonely Void beneath,
Shriek'd !

        Then to the Seraph at the Gate,
Who looketh on the Deep with steadfast eyes
For ever, God cried, " What is he that shrieks ? "
The Seraph answer'd, " 'Tis the Man accurst ! "
And, with a voice of most exceeding peace,
God ask'd, " What doth the Man ? "

                  The Seraph said :
" Around him the wild phantasms of the fog
Moan in the rheumy hoar-frost and cold steam.
Long time, crown'd, sceptred, on his throne he sits
Playing at judgment ; then with shrill voice cries—
' 'Tis finish'd, thou art judged ! ' and, fiercely laughing,
He thrusteth down an iron heel to crush

The foul Toad, that with dim and luminous eyes
So stareth at his soul.   Thrice doth he lift
His foot up fiercely—lo! he shrinks and cowers—
Then, with a wild glare at the far-off gate,
Rushes away, and rushing thro' the dark,
Shrieks!"

      With a voice of most exceeding peace
The Lord said, " Look no more !"
                  The Waters of Life,
The living, spiritual Waters, broke,
Fountain-like, up against the Master's Breast,
Giving and taking blessing.   Overhead
Gather'd the shining legions of the Stars,
Led by the ethereal Moon, with dewy eyes
Of lustre : these have been baptised in fire,
Their raiment is of molten diamond,
And 'tis their office, as they circling move
In their blue orbits, evermore to turn
Their faces heavenward, drinking peace and strength
From that great Flame which, in the core of Heaven,
Like to the white heart of a violet burns,
Diffusing rays and odour.   Blessing all,
God sought their beauteous orbits, and behold !
The Eyes innumerably glistening

Were turn'd away from Heaven, and with sick stare,
Like the blue gleam of salt dissolved in fire,
They search'd the Void, as human faces look
On horror.

       To the Seraph at the Gate,
Who looketh on the Deep with steadfast eyes,
God cried, "What is this thing whereon they gaze?"
The Seraph answer'd, "'Tis the Man accurst."
And, with a voice of most exceeding peace,
God ask'd, "What doth the Man?"

                      The Seraph said:
"O Master! send Thou forth a tongue of fire
To wither up this worm!   Serene and cold,
Flooded with moon-dew, lies the World, and there
The Man roams; and the image of the Man
In the wan waters of the frosty sphere
Falleth gigantic.   Up and down he drifts,
Worm-like, black, venomous, with eyes of hate,
Waving his bloody hands in fierce appeal,
So that the gracious faces of Thy Stars
Are troubled, and the stainless tides of light
Shadow pollution.   With wild, ape-like eyes,
The wild thing whining peers thro' horrent hair,
And rusheth up and down, seeking to find

A face to look upon, a hand to touch,
A heart that beats ; but all the World is void
And awful.   All alone in the Cold Clime,
Alone within the lonely universe,
Crawleth the Man accurst !"

      Then said the Lord,
" Doth he repent ?"   And the fair Seraph said,
" Nay he blasphemeth !   Send Thou forth Thy fire !"
But with a voice of most exceeding peace,
Out of the Shrine where unbeheld He broods,
God said, " What I have made, a living Soul,
Cannot be unmade, but endures for ever."
Then added, " Call the Man !"

      The Seraph heard,
And in a low voice named the lost one's name ;
The wild Wind that for ever beats the Gate
Caught up the word, and fled thro' the cold Void.
'Twas murmur'd on, as a lorn echo fading,
From peak to peak.   Swift as a wolf the Man
Was rushing o'er a waste, with shadow streaming
Backward 'gainst a frosty gleaming wind,
When like a fearful whisper in his ear
'Twas wafted ; then his blanch'd lips shook like leaves
In that chill wind, his hair was lifted up,

He paused, his shadow paused, like stone and shadow,
And shivering, glaring round him, the Man moan'd,
"Who calls?" and in a moment he was 'ware
Of the white light streaming from the far Gate,
And looming, blotted black against the light,
The Seraph with uplifted forefinger,
Naming his name !

           And ere the Man could fly,
The wild Wind in its circuit swept upon him,
And lifted him, and whirl'd him like a straw,
And cast him at the Gate,—a bloody thing—
Mad, moaning, horrible, obscene, unclean ;
A body swollen and stainëd like the wool
Of sheep that in the rainy season crawl
About the hills, and sleep on foul damp beds
Of bracken rusting red.   There, breathing hard,
Glaring with fiery eyes, panted the Man,
With scorch'd lips drooping, thirsting as he heard
The flowing of the Fountains far within.

Then said the Lord, "Is the Man there?" and "Yea,"
Answered the Seraph pale.   Then said the Lord,
"What doth the Man?"   The Seraph, frowning, said :
" O Master, in the belly of him is fire,
He thirsteth, fiercely thrusting out his hands,

And threateneth, seeking water!"   Then the Lord
Said, "Give him water—let him drink!"

                          The Seraph,
Stooping above him, with forefinger bright
Touched the gold kerbstone of the Gate, and lo!
Water gush'd forth and gleam'd ; and lying prone
The Man crawl'd thither, dipt his fever'd face,
Drank long and deeply ; then, his thirst appeased,
Thrust in his bloody hands unto the wrist,
And let the gleaming Fountain play upon them,
And looking up out of his dripping hair,
Grinn'd mockery at the Giver.

                        Then the Lord
Said low, "How doth the Man?"   The Seraph said :
"It is a Snake !   He mocketh all Thy gifts,
And, in a snake's voice, half articulate,
Blasphemeth !"   Then the Lord : " Doth the Man crave
To enter in ?"   " Not so," the Seraph said,
"He saith——"   "What saith he?"   "That his Soul
    is fill'd
With hate of Thee and of Thy ways ; he loathes
Pure pathways where the fruitage of the Stars
Hangeth resplendent, and he spitteth hate
On all Thy Children.   Send Thou forth Thy fire !

In no wise is he better than the beasts,
The gentle beasts, that come like morning dew
And vanish.   Let him die!"   Then said the Lord:
"What I have made endures; but 'tis not meet
This thing should cross my perfect work for ever.
Let him begone!"   Then cried the Seraph pale:
"O Master! at the frozen Clime he glares
In awe, shrieking at Thee!"   "What doth he crave?"
"Neither Thy Heaven nor Thy holy ways.
He murmureth out he is content to dwell
In the Cold Clime for ever, so Thou sendest
A face to look upon, a heart that beats,
A hand to touch—albeit like himself,
Black, venomous, unblest, exiled, and base:
Give him this thing, he will be very still,
Nor trouble Thee again."

The Lord mused.

Still,

Scarce audible, trembled the Waters of Life—
Over all Heaven the Snow of the same Thought
Which rose within the Spirit of the Lord
Fell hushedly; the innumerable Eyes
Swam in a lustrous dream.

      Then said the Lord:
" In all the waste of worlds there dwelleth not
Another like himself—behold he is
The basest Mortal born. Yet 'tis not meet
His cruel cry, for ever piteous,
Should trouble my eternal Sabbath-day.
Is there a Spirit here, a human thing,
Will pass this day from the Gate Beautiful
To share the exile of this Man accurst,—
That he may cease the shrill pain of his cry,
And I have peace ? "

      Hushedly, hushedly,
Snow'd down the Thought Divine—the living Waters
Murmur'd and darken'd. But like mournful mist
That hovers o'er an autumn pool, two Shapes,
Beautiful, human, glided to the Gate
And waited.
     "What art thou ? " in a stern voice
The Seraph said, with dreadful forefinger
Pointing to one. A gentle voice replied,
" I will go forth with him whom ye call curst !
He grew within my womb—my milk was white
Upon his lips. I will go forth with him ! "
" And *thou* ? " the Seraph said. The second Shape

Answer'd, " I also will go forth with him ;
I have kist his lips, I have lain upon his breast,
I bare him children, and I closed his eyes ;
I will go forth with him ! "

Then said the Lord,
" What Shapes are these which speak ? "   The Seraph
    answer'd :
" The woman who bore him and the wife he wed—
The one he slew in anger—the other he stript,
With ravenous claws, of raiment and of food."
Then said the Lord, " Doth the Man hear ? "   " He
    hears,"
Answer'd the Seraph ; " like a wolf he lies,
Venomous, bloody, dark, a thing accurst,
And hearkeneth with no sign ! "   Then said the Lord :
" Show them the Man," and the pale Seraph cried,
" Behold ! "
Hushedly, hushedly, hushedly,
In heaven fell the Snow of Thought Divine,
Gleaming upon the Waters of Life beneath,
And melting,—as with slow and lingering pace,
The Shapes stole forth into the windy cold,
And saw the thing that lay and throbb'd and lived,
And stoop'd above him.   Then one reach'd a hand

And touch'd him, and the fierce thing shrank and
    spat,
Hiding his face.

              " Have they beheld the Man ? "
The Lord said ; and the Seraph answer'd " Yea ; "
And the Lord said again, " What doth the Man ? "

" He lieth like a log in the wild blast,
And as he lieth, lo ! one sitting takes
His head into her lap, and moans his name,
And smooths his matted hair from off his brow,
And croons in a low voice a cradle song ;
And lo ! the other kneeleth at his side,
Half-shrinking in the old habit of her fear,
Yet hungering with her eyes, and passionately
Kissing his bloody hands."

              Then said the Lord,
" Will they go forth with him ? "   A voice replied,
" He grew within my womb—my milk was white
Upon his lips.   I will go forth with him ! "
And a voice cried, " I will go forth with him ;
I have kist his lips, I have lain upon his breast,
I bare him children, and I closed his eyes ;
I will go forth with him ! "

Still hushedly
Snow'd down the Thought Divine, the Waters of Life
Flow'd softly, sadly; for an alien sound,
A piteous human cry, a sob forlorn
Thrill'd to the heart of Heaven.

The Man wept.

And in a voice of most exceeding peace
The Lord said (while against the Breast Divine
The Waters of Life leapt, gleaming, gladdening):
" The Man is saved; let the Man enter in ! "

APPENDIX.

DAVID GRAY*

HIS BIRTHPLACE AND BOYHOOD.

Situated in a bye-road, about a mile from the small town of Kirkintilloch, and eight miles from the city of Glasgow, stands a cottage one storey high, roofed with slate, and surrounded by a little kitchen garden. A whitewashed lobby, leading from the front to the back door, divides this cottage into two sections ; to the right is a room fitted up as a hand-loom weaver's workshop ; to the left is a kitchen paved with stone, and opening into a tiny carpeted bedroom.

In this humble home, David Gray, a hand-loom weaver, resided for upwards of twenty years, and managed to rear a family of eight children—five boys and three girls. His eldest son, David, author of "The Luggie and other poems," is the hero of the present true history.

David was born on the 29th of January, 1838. He alone, of all the little household, was destined to receive a decent education. From early childhood, the dark-eyed little fellow was noted for his wit and cleverness ; and it was the dream of his father's life that he should become a scholar. At the parish school of Kirkintilloch he learned to read, write, and cast up accounts, and was, moreover, instructed in the Latin rudiments. Partly through the hard struggles of his parents, and partly through his own severe labours as a pupil-teacher and private tutor, he was afterwards enabled to attend the classes at the Glasgow University. In common with other rough country lads, who live up dark alleys, subsist chiefly on oatmeal and butter forwarded from home, and eventually distinguish themselves in

---

* This account of the poet David Gray is condensed from "The Life of David Gray," by Robert Buchanan. Without some knowledge of these facts, several of the preceding poems, –*e.g.*, "To David in Heaven," "The Snowdrop," etc. —can scarcely be understood.

the class-room, he had to fight his way onward amid poverty and pri-
vation ; but in his brave pursuit of knowledge nothing daunted him.
It had been settled at home that he should become a minister of
the Free Church of Scotland.   Unfortunately, however, he had no
love for the pulpit.   Early in life he had begun to hanker after the
delights of poetical composition.   He had devoured the poets from
Chaucer to Wordsworth.   The yearnings thus awakened in him had
begun to express themselves in many wild fragments—contributions,
for the most part, to the poet's corner of a local newspaper.

Up to this point there was nothing extraordinary in the career
or character of David Gray.   Taken at his best, he was an average
specimen of the persevering young Scottish student.   But his soul
contained wells of emotion which had not yet been stirred to their
depths.   When, at fourteen years of age, he began to study in Glasgow, it was his custom to go home every Saturday night in order
to pass the Sunday with his parents.   These Sundays at home were
chiefly occupied with rambles in the neighbourhood of Kirkintilloch ; wanderings on the sylvan banks of the Luggie, the beloved
little river which flowed close to his father's door.   On Luggieside
awakened one day the dream which developed all the hidden beauty
of his character, and eventually kindled all the faculties of his intel-
lect.   Had he been asked to explain the nature of this dream,
David would have answered vaguely enough, but he would have
said something to the following effect: " I'm thinking none of us
are quite contented ; there's a climbing impulse to heaven in us all
that won't let us rest for a moment.   Just now I would be happy if
I *knew* a little more.   I'd give ten years of life to see Rome, and
Florence, and Venice, and the grand places of old ; and to feel that
I wasn't a burden on the old folks.   I'll be a great man yet ! and
the old home, the Luggie and Gartshore wood shall be *famous* for
my sake."   He could only measure his ambition by the love he bore
his home.   " I was born, bred, and cared for here, and my folk are
buried here.   I know every nook and dell for miles around, and
they are all dear to me.   My own mother and father dwell here,
and in my own *wee* room " (the tiny carpeted room above alluded
to) " I first learned to read poetry.   I love my home ; and it is for
my home's sake that I love fame."

Nor were that home and its surroundings unworthy of such love. Tiny and unpretending as is Luggie stream, upon its banks lie many nooks of beauty, bowery glimpses of woodland, shady solitudes, places of nestling green for poets made. Not far off stretch the Campsie fells, with dusky nooks between, where the waterfall and the cascade make a silver pleasure in the heart of shadow ; and beyond, there are dreamy glimpses of the misty blue mountains themselves. Away to the south-west lies Glasgow, in its smoke, most hideous of cities, wherein the very clangour of church-bells is associated with abominations. Into the heart of that city David was to be slowly drawn, subject to a fascination only death could dispel— the desire to make deathless music, and the dream of moving therewith the mysterious heart of man.

HIS FIRST ACQUAINTANCE WITH ROBERT BUCHANAN.

Early in his teens David had made the acquaintance of a young man of Glasgow, with whom his fortunes were destined to be intimately woven. That young man was myself. We spent year after year in intimate communion, varying the monotony of our existence by reading books together, plotting great works, writing extravagant letters to men of eminence, and wandering about the country on vagrant freaks. Whole nights and days were often passed in seclusion, in reading the great thinkers, and pondering on their lives. Full of thoughts too deep for utterance, dreaming, David would walk at a swift pace through the crowded streets, with face bent down, and eyes fixed on the ground, taking no heed of the human beings passing to and fro. Then he would come to me crying, " I have had a dream," and would forthwith tell of visionary pictures which had haunted him in his solitary walk. This " dreaming," as he called it, consumed the greater portion of his hours of leisure.

GRAY AND BUCHANAN IN LONDON.

All at once there flashed upon David and myself the notion of going to London, and taking the literary fortress by storm. Again and again we talked the project over, and again we hesitated. In the spring of 1860, we both found ourselves without an anchorage; each found it necessary to do something for daily bread. For some little time the London scheme had been in abeyance; but on the 3rd of May, 1860, David came to me, his lips compressed, his eyes full of fire, saying, "Bob, I'm off to London." "Have you funds?" I asked. "Enough for one, not enough for two," was the reply. "If you can get the money anyhow, we'll go together." On parting, we arranged to meet on the evening of the 5th of May, in time to catch the five o'clock train. Unfortunately, however, we neglected to specify which of the two Glasgow stations was intended. At the hour appointed, David left Glasgow by one line of railway, in the belief that I had been unable to join him, but determined to try the venture alone. With the same belief and determination, I left at the same hour by the other line of railway, We arrived in different parts of London at about the same time. Had we left Glasgow in company, or had we met immediately after our arrival in London, the story of David's life might not have been so brief and sorrowful.

Though the month was May, the weather was dark, damp, cloudy. On arriving in the metropolis, David wandered about for hours, carpet-bag in hand. The magnitude of the place overwhelmed him; he was lost in that great ocean of life. He thought about Johnson and Savage, and how they wandered through London with pockets more empty than his own; but already he longed to be back in the little carpeted bedroom in the weaver's cottage. How lonely it seemed! Among all that mist of human faces there was not one to smile in welcome; and how was he to make his trembling voice heard above the roar and tumult of those streets? The very policemen seemed to look suspiciously at the stranger. To his sensitively Scottish ear the language spoken seemed quite strange and foreign; it had a painful, homeless sound about it that sank nervously on the heart-strings. As he wandered about the streets he glanced into coffee-shop after coffee-shop, seeing "beds" ticketed in each fly-blown window. His pocket contained a sovereign and a few shillings, but he would need every penny. Would not a bed be useless extravagance? he asked himself. Certainly. Where, then, should he pass the night ? In Hyde Park ! He had heard so much about this part of London that the name was quite familiar to him. Yes, he would pass the night in the park. Such a proceeding would save money, and be exceedingly romantic ; it would be just the right sort of beginning for a poet's struggle in London ! So he strolled into the great park, and wandered about its purlieus till morning. In remarking upon this foolish conduct, one must reflect that David was strong, heartsome, full of healthy youth. It was a frequent boast of his that he scarcely ever had a day's illness. Whether or not his fatal complaint was caught during this his first night in London is uncertain, but some few days afterwards David wrote thus to his father : " By-the-bye, I have had the worst cold I ever had in my life. I cannot get it away properly, but I feel a great deal better to-day." Alas ! violent cold had settled down upon his lungs, and insidious death was already slowly approaching him. So little conscious was he of his danger, however, that I find him writing to a friend : " What brought me here ? God knows, for I don't. *Alone* in such a place is a horrible thing. . . . People don't seem to understand me. . . . Westminster Abbey ; I was there all day yesterday. If I live I shall be buried there—so help me God ! A completely defined consciousness of great poetical genius is my only antidote against utter despair and despicable failure."

HIS FATAL ILLNESS.

It soon became evident that David's illness was of a most serious character. Pulmonary disease had set in ; medicine, blisterings, all remedies employed in the early stages of the complaint, seemed of little avail. Just then David read the " Life of John Keats," a book which impressed him with a nervous fear of impending dissolution. He began to be filled with conceits droller than any he had imagined in health. " If I were to meet Keats in heaven," he said one day, "I wonder if I should know his face from his pictures ? " Most frequently his talk was of labour uncompleted, hope deferred ; and he began to pant for free country air. " If I die," he said on a certain occasion, " I shall have one consolation,—Milnes * will

* Richard Monckton Milnes, now Lord Houghton.

write an introduction to the poems." At another time, with tears in his eyes, he repeated Burns's epitaph. Now and then, too, he had his fits of frolic and humour, and would laugh and joke over his unfortunate position. It cannot be said that Mr. Milnes and his friends were at all lukewarm about the case of their young friend; on the contrary, they gave him every practical assistance. Mr. Milnes himself, full of the most delicate sympathy, trudged to and fro between his own house and the invalid's lodging; his pockets laden with jelly and beef-tea, and his tongue tipped with kind comfort. His stay in these quarters was destined to be brief. Gradually, the invalid grew homesick. Nothing would content him but a speedy return to Scotland. He was carefully sent off by train, and arrived safely in his little cottage home far north. Here all was unchanged as ever. The beloved river was flowing through the same fields, and the same familiar faces were coming and going on its banks; but the whole meaning of the pastoral pageant had changed, and the colour of all was deepening towards the final sadness.

Great, meanwhile, had been the commotion in the hand-loom weaver's cottage, after the receipt of this bulletin: "I start off tonight at five o'clock by the Edinburgh and Glasgow Railway, right on to London in good health and spirits." A great cry arose in the household. He was fairly "daft;" he was throwing away all his chances in the world; the verse writing had turned his head. Father and mother mourned together. The former, though incompetent to judge literary merit of any kind, perceived that David was hot-headed, only half-educated, and was going to a place where thousands of people were starving daily. But the suspense was not to last long. The darling son, the secret hope and pride, came back to the old people, sick to death. All rebuke died away before the pale sad face and the feeble tottering body; and David was welcomed to the cottage hearth with silent prayers.

It was now placed beyond a doubt that the disease was one of mortal danger; yet David, surrounded again by his old *lares*, busied himself with many bright and delusive dreams of ultimate recovery. Pictures of a pleasant dreamy convalescence in a foreign clime floated before him morn and night.

HIS DEATH AND EPITAPH.

But ere long, David made up his mind that he must die ; and this feeling urged him to write something which would keep his memory green for ever. "I am working away at my old poem, Bob ; leavening it throughout with the pure beautiful theology of Kingsley." A little later : "By-the-bye, I have about 600 lines of my poem written, but the manual labour is so weakening that I do not go on." Nor was this all. In the very shadow of the grave, he began and finished a series of sonnets on the subject of his own disease and impending death. This increased literary energy was not, as many people imagined, a sign of increased physical strength ; it was merely the last flash upon the blackening brand. Gradually, but surely, life was ebbing away from the young poet.

At last, chiefly through the agency of the unwearying Dobell, the poem was placed in the hands of the printer. On the 2nd of December, 1861, a specimen-page was sent to the author. David, with the shadow of death even then dark upon him, gazed long and lingeringly at the printed page. All the mysterious past—the boyish yearnings, the flash of anticipated fame, the black surroundings of the great city—flitted across his vision like a dream. It was "good news," he said. The next day the complete silence passed over the weaver's household, for David Gray was no more. Thus, on the 3rd of December, 1861, in the 24th year of his age, he passed tranquilly away, almost his last words being, "God has love, and I have faith." The following epitaph, written out carefully, a few months before his decease, was found among his papers :

My Epitaph.

Below lies one whose name was traced in sand—
He died, not knowing what it was to live :
Died while the first sweet consciousness of manhood
And maiden thought electrified his soul :
Faint beatings in the calyx of the rose.
Bewildered reader, pass without a sigh
In a proud sorrow ! There is life with God,
In other kingdom of a sweeter air ;
In Eden every flower is blown. Amen.

Sept. 27, 1861. DAVID GRAY.

X

Draw a veil over the woe that day in the weaver's cottage, the wild broodings over the beloved face, white in the sweetness of rest after pain. A few days later, the beloved dust was shut for ever from the light, and carried a short journey, in ancient Scottish fashion, on handspokes, to the Auld Aisle Burial-Ground, a dull and lonely square upon an eminence, bounden by a stone wall, and deep with "the uncut hair of graves." Here, in happier seasons, had David often mused; for here slept dust of kindred, and hither in his sight the thin black line of rude mourners often wended with new burdens.

Standing on this eminence, one can gaze round upon the scenes which it is no exaggeration to say David has immortalised in song, —the Luggie flowing, the green woods of Gartshore, the smoke curling from the little hamlet of Merkland, and the faint blue misty distance of the Campsie Fells. The place though a lonely is a gentle and happy one, fit for a poet's rest; and there, while he was sleeping sound, a quiet company gathered ere long to uncover a monument inscribed with his name. The dying voice had been heard. Over the grave now stands a plain obelisk, publicly subscribed for, and inscribed with this epitaph, written by Lord Houghton :—

THIS MONUMENT OF

AFFECTION, ADMIRATION, AND REGRET,

IS ERECTED TO

DAVID GRAY,

THE POET OF MERKLAND,

BY FRIENDS FAR AND NEAR,

DESIROUS THAT HIS GRAVE SHOULD BE REMEMBERED

AMID THE SCENES OF HIS RARE GENIUS

AND EARLY DEATH,

AND BY THE LUGGIE NOW NUMBERED WITH THE

STREAMS ILLUSTRIOUS IN SCOTTISH SONG.

BORN, 29TH JANUARY, 1838; DIED, 3RD DECEMBER, 1861.

Butler & Tanner, The Selwood Printing Works, Frome, and London.

subtle, swift, and penetrating. . . . The subtle mingling of moral and physical contrasts is admirably worked out. . . . Almost perfect description. . . . The author of 'White Rose and Red' has written a fine dramatic poem ; his powers of humour, observation, construction, and character-painting ought to give him, if he pleased, a distinguished place as a writer of prose fiction."— *Pall Mall Gazette.*

"It shows so great an imaginative power, not merely for *painting* nature in her most beautiful and grandest forms, but for penetrating these poems with vivi-fying conceptions, that it will secure for itself a permanent name, and a long suc-cession of readers. . . . It is a poem to keep and read repeatedly, not a poem of which the enjoyment can be exhausted in one or two perusals."—*Spectator.*

"'St. Abe' was really a remarkable production, thoroughly original in every point of view. And 'White Rose and Red' is also no imitation. Its great characteristic is the author's passionate love for nature. He is no town poet ; he loves the backwoods. Here, for instance, is a Bird Chorus, such as has not been heard in literature since the days of Aristophanes. . . . His poetry is utterly unlike anything to which we have been accustomed. He is the first poet, too, who has really done Winter justice. The first canto of the Great Snow is one of the finest in the poem. . . . Thus the poet introduces us to one of the most vivid scenes—a storm in the backwoods—we have ever read. . . . What Thoreau has so worthily done for us in prose in ' Walden,' the author of 'White Rose and Red' has also equally well done in poetry. Each has opened up for us a new world for beauty."—*Westminster Review.*

"Grim tragi-comedy ! The metres are sparkling and facile, and the poet's humour plays like a lambent flame over all. There is a good deal of Chaucer, Burns, and Byron here ; yet the poem is thoroughly original—queer, sensuous, tender, serious, wonderful, like life !"—*Gentleman's Magazine.*

"One of the most remarkable poems issued for a long period. It has all the gorgeous colour of Titian, with the breadth of Rembrandt. . . . Never was anything more beautifully and accurately realized. . . . The poem is great—great in truthfulness, in conception, and in elaboration. The matter, however, in which we are most concerned is, that though its authorship has not been acknowledged, there are traces of workmanship about it which point to Mr. Buchanan as its author. . . . Besides Tennyson and Browning, there is no other person whose work we could consider it to be, and there are insuperable obstacles which would immediately forbid us to associate it with the Poet Laureate or the author of ' Pippa Passes.'"—*Contemporary Review.*

Fourth and enlarged Edition, 5s., with a Frontispiece by the late A. B. Houghton.

ST. ABE.
A Tale of Salt Lake City.
By the Author of "White Rose and Red."

" Amazingly clever."—*Nonconformist.*

"Would that in England we had humorists who could write as well ! But with Thackeray our last writer of humour left us."—*Temple Bar.*

"Fresh and salt as the sea. The work is masterly."—*Graphic.*

CHATTO AND WINDUS, PICCADILLY, W.

CHATTO & WINDUS'S
LIST OF BOOKS.

NEW FINE-ART WORK. Large 4to, bound in buckram, 21s.
Abdication, The; or, Time Tries All.
An Historical Drama. By W. D. SCOTT-MONCRIEFF. With Seven Etchings by JOHN PETTIE, R.A., W. Q. ORCHARDSON, R.A., J. MAC WHIRTER, A.R.A., COLIN HUNTER, R. MACBETH, and TOM GRAHAM.

Crown 8vo, Coloured Frontispiece and Illustrations, cloth gilt, 7s. 6d.
Advertising, A History of.
From the Earliest Times. Illustrated by Anecdotes, Curious Specimens, and Notices of Successful Advertisers. By HENRY SAMPSON.

Allen (Grant), Works by:
The Evolutionist at Large. Crown 8vo, cloth extra, 6s.
Vignettes from Nature. Crown 8vo, cloth extra, 6s.
"One of the best specimens of popular scientific exposition that we have ever had the good fortune to fall in with."—LEEDS MERCURY.

Crown 8vo, cloth extra, with 639 Illustrations, 7s. 6d.
Architectural Styles, A Handbook of.
From the German of A. ROSENGARTEN by W. COLLETT-SANDARS.

Crown 8vo, with Portrait and Facsimile, cloth extra, 7s. 6d.
Artemus Ward's Works:
The Works of CHARLES FARRER BROWNE, known as ARTEMUS WARD.

Crown 8vo, cloth extra, 7s. 6d.
Bankers, A Handbook of London;
With some Account of their Predecessors, the Early Goldsmiths; together with Lists of Bankers from 1677 to 1876. By F. G. HILTON PRICE.

Bardsley (Rev. C. W.), Works by:
English Surnames: Their Sources and Significations. Crown 8vo, cloth extra, 7s. 6d.
Curiosities of Puritan Nomenclature. Cr. 8vo, cl. extra, 7s. 6d.

Crown 8vo, cloth extra, Illustrated, 7s. 6d.

Bartholomew Fair, Memoirs of.

By HENRY MORLEY. New Edition, with One Hundred Illustrations.

Imperial 4to, cloth extra, gilt and gilt edges, 21s. per volume.

Beautiful Pictures by British Artists:

A Gathering of Favourites from our Picture Galleries. In Two Series.

The FIRST SERIES including Examples by WILKIE, CONSTABLE, TURNER, MULREADY, LANDSEER, MACLISE, E. M. WARD, FRITH, Sir JOHN GILBERT, LESLIE, ANSDELL, MARCUS STONE, Sir NOEL PATON, FAED, EYRE CROWE, GAVIN O'NEIL, and MADOX BROWN.

The SECOND SERIES containing Pictures by ARMITAGE, FAED, GOODALL, HEMSLEY, HORSLEY, MARKS, NICHOLLS, Sir NOEL PATON, PICKERSGILL, G. SMITH, MARCUS STONE, SOLOMON, STRAIGHT, E. M. WARD, and WARREN.

All engraved on Steel in the highest style of Art. Edited, with Notices of the Artists, by SYDNEY ARMYTAGE, M.A.

" This book is well got up, and good engravings by Jeens, Lumb Stocks, and others, bring back to us Royal Academy Exhibitions of past years."—TIMES.

Small 4to, green and gold, 6s. 6d. ; gilt edges, 7s. 6d.

Bechstein's As Pretty as Seven,

And other German Stories. Collected by LUDWIG BECHSTEIN. With Additional Tales by the Brothers GRIMM, and 100 Illustrations by RICHTER.

One Shilling Monthly, Illustrated.

Belgravia for 1882.

A New Serial Story, entitled "All Sorts and Conditions of Men," written by WALTER BESANT and JAMES RICE, Authors of " Ready-Money Mortiboy," "The Golden Butterfly," "The Chaplain of the Fleet," &c., and Illustrated by FRED. BARNARD, was begun in the JANUARY Number of BELGRAVIA ; which Number contained also the First Chapters of a New Novel, entitled "The Admiral's Ward," by Mrs. ALEXANDER, Author of "The Wooing o't," &c. ; the first portion of a Comedy in Two Parts, by OUIDA, entitled " Resurgo ;" and a Story by WILKIE COLLINS, entitled " How I Married Him : A Young Lady's Confession." In this Number was also given the First of a Series of Twelve Papers, by Mrs. MACQUOID, entitled "About Yorkshire," Illustrated by THOMAS R. MACQUOID.

*** *The FORTY-SIXTH Volume of BELGRAVIA, elegantly bound in crimson cloth, full gilt side and back, gilt edges, price 7s. 6d., is now ready.—Handsome Cases for binding volumes can be had at 2s. each.*

Folio, half-bound boards, India Proofs, 21s.

Blake (William):

Etchings from his Works. By W. B. SCOTT. With descriptive Text.

Crown 8vo, cloth extra, gilt, with Illustrations, 7s. 6d.

Boccaccio's Decameron ;

or, Ten Days' Entertainment. Translated into English, with an Introduction by THOMAS WRIGHT, Esq., M.A., F.S.A. With Portrait, and STOTHARD's beautiful Copperplates.

Demy 8vo, Illustrated, uniform in size for binding.

Blackburn's (Henry) Art Handbooks:

Academy Notes, 1875. With 40 Illustrations. 1*s.*
Academy Notes, 1876. With 107 Illustrations. 1*s.*
Academy Notes, 1877. With 143 Illustrations. 1*s.*
Academy Notes, 1878. With 150 Illustrations. 1*s.*
Academy Notes, 1879. With 146 Illustrations. 1*s.*
Academy Notes, 1880. With 126 Illustrations. 1*s.*
Academy Notes, 1881. With 128 Illustrations. 1*s.*
Grosvenor Notes, 1878. With 68 Illustrations. 1*s.*
Grosvenor Notes, 1879. With 60 Illustrations. 1*s.*
Grosvenor Notes, 1880. With 56 Illustrations. 1*s.*
Grosvenor Notes, 1881. With 74 Illustrations. 1*s.*
Pictures at the Paris Exhibition, 1878. 80 Illustrations. 1*s.*
Pictures at South Kensington. With 70 Illustrations. 1*s.*
The English Pictures at the National Gallery. 114 Illusts. 1*s.*
The Old Masters at the National Gallery. 128 Illusts. 1*s.* 6*d.*
Academy Notes, 1875–79. Complete in One Volume, with nearly 600 Illustrations in Facsimile. Demy 8vo, cloth limp, 6*s.*
A Complete Illustrated Catalogue to the National Gallery. With Notes by H. BLACKBURN, and 242 Illusts. Demy 8vo, cloth limp, 3*s.*

UNIFORM WITH "ACADEMY NOTES."

Royal Scottish Academy Notes, 1878. 117 Illustrations. 1*s.*
Royal Scottish Academy Notes, 1879. 125 Illustrations. 1*s.*
Royal Scottish Academy Notes, 1880. 114 Illustrations. 1*s.*
Royal Scottish Academy Notes, 1881. 104 Illustrations. 1*s.*
Glasgow Institute of Fine Arts Notes, 1878. 95 Illusts. 1*s.*
Glasgow Institute of Fine Arts Notes, 1879. 100 Illusts. 1*s.*
Glasgow Institute of Fine Arts Notes, 1880. 120 Illusts. 1*s.*
Glasgow Institute of Fine Arts Notes, 1881. 108 Illusts. 1*s.*
Walker Art Gallery Notes, Liverpool, 1878. 112 Illusts. 1*s.*
Walker Art Gallery Notes, Liverpool, 1879. 100 Illusts. 1*s.*
Walker Art Gallery Notes, Liverpool, 1880. 100 Illusts. 1*s.*
Royal Manchester Institution Notes, 1878. 88 Illustrations. 1*s.*
Society of Artists Notes, Birmingham, 1878. 95 Illusts. 1*s.*
Children of the Great City. By F. W. LAWSON. 1*s.*

Bowers' (G.) Hunting Sketches:

Canters in Crampshire. By G. BOWERS. I. Gallops from Gorseborough. II. Scrambles with Scratch Packs. III. Studies with Stag Hounds. Oblong 4to, half-bound boards, 21*s.*
Leaves from a Hunting Journal. By G. BOWERS. Coloured in facsimile of the originals. Oblong 4to, half-bound, 21*s.*

Crown 8vo, cloth extra, gilt, 7*s.* 6*d.*

Brand's Observations on Popular Antiquities,

chiefly Illustrating the Origin of our Vulgar Customs, Ceremonies, and Superstitions. With the Additions of Sir HENRY ELLIS. An entirely New and Revised Edition, with fine full-page Illustrations.

Bret Harte, Works by:

Bret Harte's Collected Works.   Arranged and Revised by the Author.   Complete in Five Vols., crown 8vo, cloth extra, 6s. each.
> Vol.   I. COMPLETE POETICAL AND DRAMATIC WORKS. With Steel Plate Portrait, and an Introduction by the Author.
> Vol.   II. EARLIER PAPERS—LUCK OF ROARING CAMP, and other Sketches —BOHEMIAN PAPERS—SPANISH and AMERICAN LEGENDS.
> Vol. III. TALES OF THE ARGONAUTS—EASTERN SKETCHES.
> Vol. IV. GABRIEL CONROY.
> Vol. V. STORIES—CONDENSED NOVELS, &c.

The Select Works of Bret Harte, in Prose and Poetry. With Introductory Essay by J. M. BELLEW, Portrait of the Author, and 50 Illustrations.   Crown 8vo, cloth extra, 7s. 6d.

An Heiress of Red Dog, and other Stories. By BRET HARTE. Post 8vo, illustrated boards, 2s. ; cloth limp, 2s. 6d.

The Twins of Table Mountain.   By BRET HARTE.   Fcap. 8vo, picture cover, 1s. ; crown 8vo, cloth extra, 3s. 6d.

The Luck of Roaring Camp, and other Sketches.   By BRET HARTE.   Post 8vo, illustrated boards, 2s.

Jeff Briggs's Love Story. By BRET HARTE. Fcap. 8vo, picture cover, 1s. ; cloth extra, 2s. 6d.

Small crown 8vo, cloth extra, gilt, with full-page Portraits, 4s. 6d.

Brewster's (Sir David) Martyrs of Science.

Small crown 8vo, cloth extra, gilt, with Astronomical Plates, 4s. 6d.

Brewster's (Sir D.) More Worlds than One,
the Creed of the Philosopher and the Hope of the Christian.

A HANDSOME GIFT-BOOK.—Small 4to, cloth extra, 6s.

Brushwood.
By T. BUCHANAN READ.   Illustrated from Designs by FREDERICK DIELMAN.

Crown 8vo, cloth extra, 6s.

Buchanan.—Ballads of Life, Love & Humour.
By ROBERT BUCHANAN, Author of "God and the Man," &c.

THE STOTHARD BUNYAN.—Crown 8vo, cloth extra, gilt, 7s. 6d.

Bunyan's Pilgrim's Progress.
Edited by Rev. T. SCOTT.   With 17 beautiful Steel Plates by STOTHARD, engraved by GOODALL ; and numerous Woodcuts.

Demy 8vo, cloth extra, 7s. 6d.

Burton's Anatomy of Melancholy:
A New Edition, complete, corrected and enriched by Translations of the Classical Extracts.

Crown 8vo, cloth extra, gilt, with Illustrations, 7s. 6d.

Byron's Letters and Journals.
With Notices of his Life. By THOMAS MOORE. A Reprint of the Original Edition, newly revised, with Twelve full-page Plates.

Demy 8vo, cloth extra, 14*s.*
Campbell's (Sir G.) White and Black:
Travels in the United States. By Sir GEORGE CAMPBELL, M.P.

Demy 8vo, cloth extra, with Illustrations, 7*s.* 6*d.*
Caravan Route (The) between Egypt and
Syria. By His Imperial and Royal Highness the ARCHDUKE LUDWIG SALVATOR of AUSTRIA. With 23 full-page Illustrations by the Author.

Post 8vo, cloth extra, 1*s.* 6*d.*
Carlyle (Thomas) On the Choice of Books.
With a Life of the Author by R. H. SHEPHERD. Entirely New and Revised Edition.

Two Vols., demy 8vo, cloth extra, 21*s.*
Cavalry Life;
Or, Sketches and Stories in Barracks and Out. By J. S. WINTER.

Crown 8vo, cloth extra, 7*s.* 6*d.*
Century (A) of Dishonour:
A Sketch of the United States Government's Dealings with some of the Indian Tribes.

Crown 8vo, cloth extra, with Illustrations, 7*s.* 6*d.*
Chap-Books.—A History of the Chap-Books
of the Eighteenth Century. By JOHN ASHTON. With nearly 400 Illustrations, engraved in facsimile of the originals.   [*In the press.*
₄ A few Large-Paper copies will be carefully printed on hand-made paper, for which early application should be made.

Large 4to, half-bound, profusely Illustrated, 28*s.*
Chatto and Jackson.—A Treatise on Wood
Engraving; Historical and Practical. By WILLIAM ANDREW CHATTO and JOHN JACKSON. With an Additional Chapter by HENRY G. BOHN; and 450 fine Illustrations. A reprint of the last Revised Edition.

Small 4to, cloth gilt, with Coloured Illustrations, 10*s.* 6*d.*
Chaucer for Children:
A Golden Key. By Mrs. H. R. HAWEIS. With Eight Coloured Pictures and numerous Woodcuts by the Author.

Demy 8vo, cloth limp, 2*s.* 6*d.*
Chaucer for Schools.
By Mrs. HAWEIS, Author of "Chaucer for Children."

Crown 8vo, cloth extra, gilt, 7*s.* 6*d.*
Colman's Humorous Works:
"Broad Grins," "My Nightgown and Slippers," and other Humorous Works, Prose and Poetical, of GEORGE COLMAN. With Life by G. B. BUCKSTONE, and Frontispiece by HOGARTH.

Post 8vo, cloth limp, 2s. 6d.

Convalescent Cookery:

A Family Handbook. By CATHERINE RYAN.

"Full of sound sense and useful hints."—SATURDAY REVIEW.

Conway (Moncure D.), Works by:

Demonology and Devil-Lore. By MONCURE D. CONWAY, M.A. Two Vols., royal 8vo, with 65 Illustrations, 28s.

A Necklace of Stories. By MONCURE D. CONWAY, M.A. Illustrated by W. J. HENNESSY. Square 8vo, cloth extra, 6s.

The Wandering Jew. By MONCURE D. CONWAY, M.A. Crown 8vo, cloth extra, 6s.

Thomas Carlyle: Letters and Recollections. By MONCURE D. CONWAY, M.A. With Illustrations. Crown 8vo, cloth extra, 6s.

Two Vols., crown 8vo, cloth extra, 21s.

Cook (Dutton).—Hours with the Players.

By DUTTON COOK.

" Mr. Dutton Cook has more dramatic lore than any living English writer, and his style is always easy and pleasant. . . . To all with any feeling for the stage the book will prove delightful reading."—WORLD.

Post 8vo, cloth limp, 2s. 6d.

Copyright.—A Handbook of English and

Foreign Copyright in Literary and Dramatic Works. By SIDNEY JERROLD, of the Middle Temple, Esq., Barrister-at-Law.

" Till the time arrives when copyright shall be so simple and so uniform that it can be generally understood and enjoyed, such a handbook as this will prove of great value. It is correct as well as concise, and gives just the kind and quantity of information desired by persons who are ignorant of the subject, and turn to it for information and guidance."—ATHENÆUM.

Crown 8vo, cloth extra, 7s. 6d.

Cornwall.—Popular Romances of the West

of England ; or, The Drolls, Traditions, and Superstitions of Old Cornwall. Collected and Edited by ROBERT HUNT, F.R.S. New and Revised Edition, with Additions, and Two Steel-plate Illustrations by GEORGE CRUIKSHANK.

Crown 8vo, cloth extra, gilt, with 13 Portraits, 7s. 6d.

Creasy's Memoirs of Eminent Etonians ;

with Notices of the Early History of Eton College. By Sir EDWARD CREASY, Author of " The Fifteen Decisive Battles of the World."

Crown 8vo, cloth extra, with Etched Frontispiece, 7s. 6d.

Credulities, Past and Present.

By WILLIAM JONES, F.S.A., Author of " Finger-Ring Lore," &c.

Crown 8vo, cloth extra, 6s.

Crimes and Punishments.

Including a New Translation of Beccaria's " Dei Delitti e delle Pene." By JAMES ANSON FARRER.

Crown 8vo, cloth gilt, Two very thick Volumes, 7s. 6d. each.

Cruikshank's Comic Almanack.

Complete in TWO SERIES: The FIRST from 1835 to 1843; the SECOND from 1844 to 1853. A Gathering of the BEST HUMOUR of THACKERAY, HOOD, MAYHEW, ALBERT SMITH, A'BECKETT, ROBERT BROUGH, &c. With 2,000 Woodcuts and Steel Engravings by CRUIKSHANK, HINE, LANDELLS, &c.

Two Vols., crown 8vo, cloth extra, with Illustrations, 24s.

Cruikshank (The Life of George).

In Two Epochs. By BLANCHARD JERROLD, Author of "The Life of Napoleon III.," &c. With numerous Illustrations, and a List of his Works.   *[In the press.*

Crown 8vo, cloth extra, 7s. 6d.

Cussans.—Handbook of Heraldry;

with Instructions for Tracing Pedigrees and Deciphering Ancient MSS. &c. By JOHN E. CUSSANS. Entirely New and Revised Edition. Illustrated with over 400 Plates and Woodcuts.   *[In the press.*

Two Vols., demy 4to, handsomely bound in half-morocco, gilt, profusely Illustrated with Coloured and Plain Plates and Woodcuts, price £7 7s.

Cyclopædia of Costume;

or, A Dictionary of Dress—Regal, Ecclesiastical, Civil, and Military—from the Earliest Period in England to the reign of George the Third. Including Notices of Contemporaneous Fashions on the Continent, and a General History of the Costumes of the Principal Countries of Europe. By J. R. PLANCHÉ, Somerset Herald.

The Volumes may also be had *separately* (each Complete in itself) at £3 13s. 6d. each :

    Vol. I. THE DICTIONARY.
    Vol. II. A GENERAL HISTORY OF COSTUME IN EUROPE.
       Also in 25 Parts, at 5s. each. Cases for binding, 5s. each.

"*A comprehensive and highly valuable book of reference. . . . We have rarely failed to find in this book an account of an article of dress, while in most of the entries curious and instructive details are given. . . . Mr. Planché's enormous labour of love, the production of a text which, whether in its dictionary form or in that of the 'General History,' is within its intended scope immeasurably the best and richest work on Costume in English. . . . This book is not only one of the most readable works of the kind, but intrinsically attractive and amusing.*"—ATHENÆUM.

"*A most readable and interesting work—and it can scarcely be consulted in vain, whether the reader is in search for information as to military, court, ecclesiastical, legal, or professional costume. . . . All the chromo-lithographs, and most of the woodcut illustrations—the latter amounting to several thousands —are very elaborately executed; and the work forms a livre de luxe which renders it equally suited to the library and the ladies' drawing-room.*"—TIMES.

Entirely New Edition, crown 8vo, cloth extra, Illustrated, 7s. 6d.

Doran's Memories of our Great Towns.

With Anecdotic Gleanings concerning their Worthies and their Oddities. By Dr. JOHN DORAN, F.S.A. With nearly 50 Illustra-tions.   *[In the press*

Two Vols., crown 8vo, cloth extra, 21s.

Drury Lane, Old:

Fifty Years' Recollections of Author, Actor, and Manager. By EDWARD STIRLING.

Demy 8vo, cloth, 16s.

Dutt's India, Past and Present;

with Minor Essays on Cognate Subjects. By SHOSHEE CHUNDER DUTT, Rái Báhádoor.

Crown 8vo, cloth boards, 6s. per Volume.

Early English Poets.

Edited, with Introductions and Annotations, by Rev. A. B. GROSART.

1. **Fletcher's (Giles, B.D.) Complete Poems:** Christ's Victorie in Heaven, Christ's Victorie on Earth, Christ's Triumph over Death, and Minor Poems. With Memorial-Introduction and Notes. One Vol.

2. **Davies' (Sir John) Complete** Poetical Works, including Psalms I. to L. in Verse, and other hitherto Unpublished MSS., for the first time Collected and Edited. Memorial-Introduction and Notes. Two Vols.

3. **Herrick's (Robert) Hesperi**des, Noble Numbers, and Complete Collected Poems. With Memorial-Introduction and Notes, Steel Portrait, Index of First Lines, and Glossarial Index, &c. Three Vols.

4. **Sidney's (Sir Philip) Com**plete Poetical Works, including all those in "Arcadia." With Portrait, Memorial-Introduction, Essay on the Poetry of Sidney, and Notes. Three Vols.

Crown 8vo, cloth extra, gilt, with Illustrations, 6s.

Emanuel On Diamonds and Precious

Stones ; their History, Value, and Properties ; with Simple Tests for ascertaining their Reality. By HARRY EMANUEL, F.R.G.S. With numerous Illustrations, Tinted and Plain.

Crown 8vo, cloth extra, with Illustrations, 7s. 6d.

Englishman's House, The:

A Practical Guide to all interested in Selecting or Building a House, with full Estimates of Cost, Quantities, &c. By C. J. RICHARDSON. Third Edition. With nearly 600 Illustrations.

Crown 8vo, cloth extra, with nearly 300 Illustrations, 7s. 6d.

Evolution, Chapters on;

A Popular History of the Darwinian and Allied Theories of Development. By ANDREW WILSON, Ph.D., F.R.S. Edin. &c. [*In preparation.*

Crown 8vo, cloth extra, with Illustrations, 6s.

Fairholt's Tobacco :

Its History and Associations ; with an Account of the Plant and its Manufacture, and its Modes of Use in all Ages and Countries. By F. W. FAIRHOLT, F.S.A. With Coloured Frontispiece and upwards of 100 Illustrations by the Author.

Crown 8vo, cloth extra, 7s. 6d.

Familiar Allusions:

A Handbook of Miscellaneous Information ; including the Names of Celebrated Statues, Paintings, Palaces, Country Seats, Ruins, Churches, Ships, Streets, Clubs, Natural Curiosities, and the like. By WILLIAM A. WHEELER, Author of "Noted Names of Fiction;" and CHARLES G. WHEELER. [*In the press.*

Crown 8vo, cloth extra, with Illustrations, 4s. 6d.

Faraday's Chemical History of a Candle.

Lectures delivered to a Juvenile Audience. A New Edition. Edited by W. CROOKES, F.C.S. With numerous Illustrations.

Crown 8vo, cloth extra, with Illustrations, 4s. 6d.

Faraday's Various Forces of Nature.

New Edition. Edited by W. CROOKES, F.C.S. Numerous Illustrations.

Crown 8vo, cloth extra, with Illustrations, 7s. 6d.

Finger-Ring Lore:

Historical, Legendary, and Anecdotal. By WM. JONES, F.S.A. With Hundreds of Illustrations of Curious Rings of all Ages and Countries.

"One of those gossiping books which are as full of amusement as of instruc-tion."—ATHENÆUM.

Two Vols., crown 8vo, cloth extra, 21s.

Fitzgerald.—Recreations of a Literary Man;

or, Does Writing Pay? With Recollections of some Literary Men, and a View of a Literary Man's Working Life. By PERCY FITZ-GERALD. [*In preparation.*

Gardening Books:

A Year's Work in Garden and Greenhouse : Practical Advice to Amateur Gardeners as to the Management of the Flower, Fruit, and Frame Garden. By GEORGE GLENNY. Post 8vo, cloth limp, 2s. 6d.

Our Kitchen Garden : The Plants we Grow, and How we Cook Them. By TOM JERROLD, Author of "The Garden that Paid the Rent," &c. Post 8vo, cloth limp, 2s. 6d.

Household Horticulture : A Gossip about Flowers. By TOM and JANE JERROLD. Illustrated. Post 8vo, cloth limp, 2s. 6d.

My Garden Wild, and What I Grew there. By FRANCIS GEORGE HEATH. Crown 8vo, cloth extra, 5s.

One Shilling Monthly.

Gentleman's Magazine (The) for 1882.

The JANUARY Number of this Periodical contained the First Chapters of a New Serial Story, entitled "Dust," by JULIAN HAWTHORNE, Author of "Garth," &c. "Science Notes," by W. MATTIEU WILLIAMS, F.R.A.S., will also be continued monthly.

** *Now ready, the Volume for* JULY *to* DECEMBER, *1881, cloth extra, price 8s. 6d.; and Cases for binding, price 2s. each.*

THE RUSKIN GRIMM.—Square 8vo, cl. ex., 6s. 6d. ; gilt edges, 7s. 6d.

German Popular Stories.

Collected by the Brothers GRIMM, and Translated by EDGAR TAYLOR. Edited with an Introduction by JOHN RUSKIN. With 22 Illustrations after the inimitable designs of GEORGE CRUIKSHANK. Both Series Complete.

" The illustrations of this volume . . . are of quite sterling and admirable art, of a class precisely parallel in elevation to the character of the tales which they illustrate; and the original etchings, as I have before said in the Appendix to my ' Elements of Drawing,' were unrivalled in masterfulness of touch since Rembrandt (in some qualities of delineation, unrivalled even by him). . . . To make somewhat enlarged copies of them, looking at them through a magnifying glass, and never putting two lines where Cruikshank has put only one, would be an exercise in decision and severe drawing which would leave afterwards little to be learnt in schools."—Extract from Introduction by JOHN RUSKIN.

Square 16mo (Tauchnitz size), cloth extra, 2s. per volume.

Golden Library, The:

Ballad History of England. By W. C. BENNETT.

Bayard Taylor's Diversions of the Echo Club.

Byron's Don Juan.

Emerson's Letters and Social Aims.

Godwin's (William) Lives of the Necromancers.

Holmes's Autocrat of the Breakfast Table. With an Introduction by G. A. SALA.

Holmes's Professor at the Breakfast Table.

Hood's Whims and Oddities. Complete. With all the original Illustrations.

Irving's (Washington) Tales of a Traveller.

Irving's (Washington) Tales of the Alhambra.

Jesse's (Edward) Scenes and Occupations of Country Life.

Lamb's Essays of Elia. Both Series Complete in One Vol.

Leigh Hunt's Essays : A Tale for a Chimney Corner, and other Pieces. With Portrait, and Introduction by EDMUND OLLIER.

Mallory's (Sir Thomas) Mort d'Arthur : The Stories of King Arthur and of the Knights of the Round Table. Edited by B. MONTGOMERIE RANKING.

Pascal's Provincial Letters. A New Translation, with Historical Introduction and Notes, by T. M'CRIE, D.D.

Pope's Poetical Works. Complete.

Rochefoucauld's Maxims and Moral Reflections. With Notes, and an Introductory Essay by SAINTE-BEUVE.

St. Pierre's Paul and Virginia, and The Indian Cottage. Edited. with Life, by the Rev. E. CLARKE.

Shelley's Early Poems, and Queen Mab, with Essay by LEIGH HUNT.

Shelley's Later Poems : Laon and Cythna, &c.

Shelley's Posthumous Poems, the Shelley Papers, &c.

Shelley's Prose Works, including A Refutation of Deism, Zastrozzi, St. Irvyne, &c.

White's Natural History of Selborne. Edited, with Additions, by THOMAS BROWN, F.L.S.

Crown 8vo, cloth gilt and gilt edges, 7s. 6d.

Golden Treasury of Thought, The:

An ENCYCLOPÆDIA OF QUOTATIONS from Writers of all Times and Countries. Selected and Edited by THEODORE TAYLOR.

Post 8vo, cloth limp, 2s. 6d.

Glenny's A Year's Work in Garden and

Greenhouse : Practical Advice to Amateur Gardeners as to the Management of the Flower, Fruit, and Frame Garden. By GEORGE GLENNY.

"A great deal of valuable information, conveyed in very simple language. The amateur need not wish for a better guide."—LEEDS MERCURY.

New and Cheaper Edition, demy 8vo, cloth extra, with Illustrations, 7s. 6d.

Greeks and Romans, The Life of the,

Described from Antique Monuments. By ERNST GUHL and W. KONER. Translated from the Third German Edition, and Edited by Dr. F. HUEFFER. With 545 Illustrations.

"Must find a place, not only upon the scholar's shelves, but in every well-chosen library of art."—DAILY NEWS.

Crown 8vo, cloth extra, gilt, with Illustrations, 4s. 6d.

Guyot's Earth and Man;

or, Physical Geography in its Relation to the History of Mankino. With Additions by Professors AGASSIZ, PIERCE, and GRAY ; 12 Maps and Engravings on Steel, some Coloured, and copious Index.

Crown 8vo, 1s.

Hair (The): Its Treatment in Health, Weak-

ness, and Disease. Translated from the German of Dr. J. PINCUS, of Berlin.　　*[In the press.*

Hake (Dr. Thomas Gordon), Poems by:

Maiden Ecstasy. Small 4to, cloth extra, 8s.
New Symbols. Crown 8vo, cloth extra, 6s.
Legends of the Morrow. Crown 8vo, cloth extra, 6s.

Two Vols., crown 8vo, cloth extra, 12s.

Half-Hours with Foreign Novelists.

With Notices of their Lives and Writings. By HELEN and ALICE ZIMMERN. A New Edition.

Medium 8vo, cloth extra, gilt, with Illustrations, 7s. 6d.

Hall's (Mrs. S. C.) Sketches of Irish Character.

With numerous Illustrations on Steel and Wood by MACLISE, GILBERT, HARVEY, and G. CRUIKSHANK.

"The Irish Sketches of this lady resemble Miss Mitford's beautiful English sketches in 'Our Village,' but they are far more vigorous and picturesque and bright."—BLACKWOOD'S MAGAZINE.

Crown 8vo, cloth extra, 5s.

Heath (F. G.)—My Garden Wild,

And What I Grew there. By FRANCIS GEORGE HEATH, Author of "The Fern World," &c.

Haweis (Mrs.), Works by:

The Art of Dress. By Mrs. H. R. HAWEIS. Illustrated by the Author. Small 8vo, illustrated cover, 1s.; cloth limp, 1s. 6d.

"*A well-considered attempt to apply canons of good taste to the costumes of ladies of our time. . . . . Mrs. Haweis writes frankly and to the point, she does not mince matters, but boldly remonstrates with her own sex on the follies they indulge in. . . . . We may recommend the book to the ladies whom it concerns.*"—ATHENÆUM.

The Art of Beauty. By Mrs. H. R. HAWEIS. Square 8vo, cloth extra, gilt, gilt edges, with Coloured Frontispiece and nearly 100 Illustrations, 10s. 6d.

The Art of Decoration. By Mrs. H. R. HAWEIS. Square 8vo, handsomely bound and profusely Illustrated, 10s. 6d.

*** *See also* CHAUCER, *p. 5 of this Catalogue.*

SPECIMENS OF MODERN POETS.—Crown 8vo, cloth extra, 6s.

Heptalogia (The); or, The Seven against Sense.

A Cap with Seven Bells.

"*The merits of the book cannot be fairly estimated by means of a few extracts; it should be read at length to be appreciated properly, and, in our opinion, its merits entitle it to be very widely read indeed.*"—ST. JAMES'S GAZETTE.

Cr. 8vo, bound in parchment, 8s.; Large-Paper copies (only 50 printed), 15s.

Herbert.—The Poems of Lord Herbert of Cherbury. Edited, with an Introduction, by J. CHURTON COLLINS.

Complete in Four Vols., demy 8vo, cloth extra, 12s. each.

History of Our Own Times, from the Accession of Queen Victoria to the General Election of 1880. By JUSTIN McCARTHY, M.P.

"*Criticism is disarmed before a composition which provokes little but approval. This is a really good book on a really interesting subject, and words piled on words could say no more for it.*"—SATURDAY REVIEW.

New Work by the Author of "A HISTORY of OUR OWN TIMES."

Four Vols. demy 8vo, cloth extra, 12s. each.

History of the Four Georges.

By JUSTIN McCARTHY, M.P.   [*In preparation.*

Crown 8vo, cloth limp, with Illustrations, 2s. 6d.

Holmes's The Science of Voice Production

and Voice Preservation : A Popular Manual for the Use of Speakers and Singers. By GORDON HOLMES, L.R.C.P.E.

Crown 8vo, cloth extra, gilt, 7s. 6d.

Hood's (Thomas) Choice Works,

In Prose and Verse. Including the CREAM OF THE COMIC ANNUALS. With Life of the Author, Portrait, and Two Hundred Illustrations.

Square crown 8vo, cloth extra, gilt edges, 6s.

Hood's (Tom) From Nowhere to the North

Pole: A Noah's Arkæological Narrative. With 25 Illustrations by W. BRUNTON and E. C. BARNES.

"The amusing letterpress is profusely interspersed with the jingling rhymes which children love and learn so easily. Messrs. Brunton and Barnes do full justice to the writer's meaning, and a pleasanter result of the harmonious co-operation of author and artist could not be desired."—TIMES.

Crown 8vo, cloth extra, gilt, 7s. 6d.

Hook's (Theodore) Choice Humorous Works,

including his Ludicrous Adventures, Bons-mots, Puns, and Hoaxes: With a new Life of the Author, Portraits, Facsimiles, and Illustrations.

Crown 8vo, cloth extra, 7s.

Horne's Orion:

An Epic Poem in Three Books. By RICHARD HENGIST HORNE. With a brief Commentary by the Author. With Photographic Portrait from a Medallion by SUMMERS. Tenth Edition.

Crown 8vo, cloth extra, 7s. 6d.

Howell's Conflicts of Capital and Labour

Historically and Economically considered. Being a History and Review of the Trade Unions of Great Britain, showing their Origin, Progress, Constitution, and Objects, in their Political, Social, Economical, and Industrial Aspects. By GEORGE HOWELL.

"This book is an attempt, and on the whole a successful attempt, to place the work of trade unions in the past, and their objects in the future, fairly before the public from the working man's point of view."—PALL MALL GAZETTE.

Demy 8vo, cloth extra, 12s. 6d.

Hueffer's The Troubadours:

A History of Provencal Life and Literature in the Middle Ages. By FRANCIS HUEFFER.

Crown 8vo, cloth extra, 6s.

Janvier.—Practical Keramics for Students.

By CATHERINE A. JANVIER.

"Will be found a useful handbook by those who wish to try the manufacture or decoration of pottery, and may be studied by all who desire to know something of the art."—MORNING POST.

A NEW EDITION, Revised and partly Re-written, with several New Chapters and Illustrations, crown 8vo, cloth extra, 7s. 6d.

Jennings' The Rosicrucians:

Their Rites and Mysteries. With Chapters on the Ancient Fire and Serpent Worshippers. By HARGRAVE JENNINGS. With Five full-page Plates and upwards of 300 Illustrations.

Two Vols. 8vo, with 52 Illustrations and Maps, cloth extra, gilt, 14s.

Josephus, The Complete Works of.

Translated by WHISTON. Containing both "The Antiquities of the Jews" and "The Wars of the Jews."

Jerrold (Tom), Works by:

Household Horticulture: A Gossip about Flowers. By TOM and JANE JERROLD. Illustrated. Post 8vo, cloth limp, 2s.6d.

Our Kitchen Garden: The Plants we Grow, and How we Cook Them. By TOM JERROLD, Author of "The Garden that Paid the Rent," &c. Post 8vo, cloth limp, 2s. 6d.

"The combination of hints on cookery with gardening has been very cleverly carried out, and the result is an interesting and highly instructive little work. Mr. Jerrold is correct in saying that English people do not make half the use of vegetables they might ; and by showing how easily they can be grown, and so obtained fresh, he is doing a great deal to make them more popular."—DAILY CHRONICLE.

Small 8vo, cloth, full gilt, gilt edges, with Illustrations, 6s.

Kavanaghs' Pearl Fountain,

And other Fairy Stories. By BRIDGET and JULIA KAVANAGH. With Thirty Illustrations by J. MOYR SMITH.

"Genuine new fairy stories of the old type, some of them as delightful as the best of Grimm's ' German Popular Stories.' . . . . For the most part the stories are downright, thorough-going fairy stories of the most admirable kind. . . . Mr. Moyr Smith's illustrations, too, are admirable."—SPECTATOR.

Square 8vo, cloth extra, with Illustrations, 6s.

Knight (The) and the Dwarf.

By CHARLES MILLS. With numerous Illustrations by THOMAS LINDSAY.

Crown 8vo, illustrated boards, with numerous Plates, 2s. 6d.

Lace (Old Point), and How to Copy and

Imitate it. By DAISY WATERHOUSE HAWKINS. With 17 Illustrations by the Author.

Crown 8vo, cloth extra, gilt, with Portraits, 7s. 6d.

Lamb's Complete Works,

In Prose and Verse, reprinted from the Original Editions, with many Pieces hitherto unpublished. Edited, with Notes and Introduction, by R. H. SHEPHERD. With Two Portraits and Facsimile of a Page of the "Essay on Roast Pig."

"A complete edition of Lamb's writings, in prose and verse, has long been wanted, and is now supplied. The editor appears to have taken great pains to bring together Lamb's scattered contributions, and his collection contains a number of pieces which are now reproduced for the first time since their original appearance in various old periodicals."—SATURDAY REVIEW.

Crown 8vo, cloth extra, with numerous Illustrations, 10s. 6d.

Lamb (Mary and Charles):

Their Poems, Letters, and Remains. With Reminiscences and Notes by W. CAREW HAZLITT. With HANCOCK'S Portrait of the Essayist, Facsimiles of the Title-pages of the rare First Editions of Lamb's and Coleridge's Works, and numerous Illustrations.

" Very many passages will delight those fond of literary trifles ; hardly any portion will fail in interest for lovers of Charles Lamb and his sister."—STANDARD.

Small 8vo, cloth extra, 5*s.*
Lamb's Poetry for Children, and Prince

Dorus. Carefully Reprinted from unique copies.

"The quaint and delightful little book, over the recovery of which all the heart of his lovers are yet warm with rejoicing."—A. C. SWINBURNE.

Crown 8vo, cloth extra, 6*s.*
Lares and Penates;

Or, The Background of Life. By FLORENCE CADDY.

" The whole book is well worth reading, for it is full of practical suggestions. . . . . We hope nobody will be deterred from taking up a book which teaches a good deal about sweetening poor lives as well as giving grace to wealthy ones."—GRAPHIC.

Crown 8vo, cloth, full gilt, 6*s.*
Leigh's A Town Garland.

By HENRY S. LEIGH, Author of "Carols of Cockayne."

"If Mr. Leigh's verse survive to a future generation—and there is no reason why that honour should not be accorded productions so delicate, so finished, and so full of humour—their author will probably be remembered as the Poet of the Strand."—ATHENÆUM.

SECOND EDITION.—Crown 8vo, cloth extra, with Illustrations, 6*s.*
Leisure-Time Studies, chiefly Biological.

By ANDREW WILSON, F.R.S.E., Lecturer on Zoology and Comparative Anatomy in the Edinburgh Medical School.

"It is well when we can take up the work of a really qualified investigator, who in the intervals of his more serious professional labours sets himself to impart knowledge in such a simple and elementary form as may attract and instruct, with no danger of misleading the tyro in natural science. Such a work is this little volume, made up of essays and addresses written and delivered by Dr. Andrew Wilson, lecturer and examiner in science at Edinburgh and Glasgow, at leisure intervals in a busy professional life. . . . Dr. Wilson's pages teem wit h matter stimulating to a healthy love of science and a reverence for the truths of nature."—SATURDAY REVIEW.

Crown 8vo, cloth extra, with Illustrations, 7*s.* 6*d.*
Life in London;

or, The History of Jerry Hawthorn and Corinthian Tom. With the whole of CRUIKSHANK'S Illustrations, in Colours, after the Originals

Crown 8vo, cloth extra, 6*s.*
Lights on the Way:

Some Tales within a Tale. By the late J. H. ALEXANDER, B.A. Edited, with an Explanatory Note, by H. A. PAGE, Author of "Thoreau: A Study."

Crown 8vo, cloth extra, with Illustrations, 7*s.* 6*d.*
Longfellow's Complete Prose Works.

Including "Outre Mer," "Hyperion," "Kavanagh," "The Poets and Poetry of Europe," and "Driftwood." With Portrait and Illustrations by VALENTINE BROMLEY.

Crown 8vo, cloth extra, gilt, with Illustrations, 7s. 6d.

Longfellow's Poetical Works.

Carefully Reprinted from the Original Editions. With numerous fine Illustrations on Steel and Wood.

Crown 8vo, cloth extra, 5s.

Lunatic Asylum, My Experiences in a.

By a SANE PATIENT.

" The story is clever and interesting, sad beyond measure though the subject be. There is no personal bitterness, and no violence or anger. Whatever may have been the evidence for our author's madness when he was consigned to an asylum, nothing can be clearer than his sanity when he wrote this book; it is bright, calm, and to the point."—SPECTATOR.

Demy 8vo, with Fourteen full-page Plates, cloth boards, 18s.

Lusiad (The) of Camoens.

Translated into English Spenserian verse by ROBERT FFRENCH DUFF, Knight Commander of the Portuguese Royal Order of Christ.

Crown 8vo, cloth extra, 7s. 6d.

Maclise Gallery (The) of Illustrious Literary

Characters: 84 fine Portraits, with Descriptive Text, Anecdotal and Biographical. By WILLIAM BATES, B.A.   *[In preparation.*

Handsomely printed in facsimile, price 5s.

Magna Charta.

An exact Facsimile of the Original Document in the British Museum, printed on fine plate paper, nearly 3 feet long by 2 feet wide, with the Arms and Seals emblazoned in Gold and Colours.

Mallock's (W. H.) Works:

Is Life Worth Living? By WILLIAM HURRELL MALLOCK. New Edition, crown 8vo, cloth extra, 6s.

" This deeply interesting volume. . . . . It is the most powerful vindication of religion, both natural and revealed, that has appeared since Bishop Butler wrote, and is much more useful than either the Analogy or the Sermons of that great divine, as a refutation of the peculiar form assumed by the infidelity of the present day. . . . . Deeply philosophical as the book is, there is not a heavy page in it. The writer is 'possessed,' so to speak, with his great subject, has sounded its depths, surveyed it in all its extent, and brought to bear on it all the resources of a vivid, rich, and impassioned style, as well as an adequate acquaintance with the science, the philosophy, and the literature of the day."—IRISH DAILY NEWS.

The New Republic; or, Culture, Faith, and Philosophy in an English Country House. By W. H. MALLOCK. Post 8vo, cloth limp, 2s. 6d.

The New Paul and Virginia; or, Positivism on an Island. By W. H. MALLOCK. Post 8vo, cloth limp, 2s. 6d.

Poems. By W. H. MALLOCK. Small 4to, bound in parchment, 8s.

A Romance of the Nineteenth Century. By W. H. MALLOCK. Second Edition, with a Preface. Two Vols., crown 8vo, 21s.

Macquoid (Mrs.), Works by:

In the Ardennes. By KATHARINE S. MACQUOID. With 50 fine Illustrations by THOMAS R. MACQUOID. Uniform with "Pictures and Legends." Square 8vo, cloth extra, 10s. 6d.

"This is another of Mrs. Macquoid's pleasant books of travel, full of useful information, of picturesque descriptions of scenery, and of quaint traditions respecting the various monuments and ruins which she encounters in her tour. . . . To such of our readers as are already thinking about the year's holiday, we strongly recommend the perusal of Mrs. Macquoid's experiences. The book is well illustrated by Mr. Thomas R. Macquoid."—GRAPHIC.

Pictures and Legends from Normandy and Brittany. By KATHARINE S. MACQUOID. With numerous Illustrations by THOMAS R. MACQUOID. Square 8vo, cloth gilt, 10s. 6d.

Through Normandy. By KATHARINE S. MACQUOID. With 90 Illustrations by T. R. MACQUOID. Square 8vo, cloth extra, 7s. 6d.

"One of the few books which can be read as a piece of literature, whilst at the same time handy in the knapsack."—BRITISH QUARTERLY REVIEW.

Through Brittany. By KATHARINE S. MACQUOID. With numerous Illustrations by T. R. MACQUOID. Sq. 8vo, cloth extra, 7s. 6d.

"The pleasant companionship which Mrs. Macquoid offers, while wandering from one point of interest to another, seems to throw a renewed charm around each oft-depicted scene."—MORNING POST.

Mark Twain's Works:

The Choice Works of Mark Twain. Revised and Corrected throughout by the Author. With Life, Portrait, and numerous Illustrations. Crown 8vo, cloth extra, 7s. 6d.

The Adventures of Tom Sawyer. By MARK TWAIN. With 100 Illustrations. Small 8vo, cloth extra, 7s. 6d. CHEAP EDITION, illustrated boards, 2s.

A Pleasure Trip on the Continent of Europe : The Innocents Abroad, and The New Pilgrim's Progress. By MARK TWAIN. Post 8vo, illustrated boards, 2s.

An Idle Excursion, and other Sketches. By MARK TWAIN. Post 8vo, illustrated boards, 2s.

The Prince and the Pauper. By MARK TWAIN. With nearly 200 Illustrations. Crown 8vo, cloth extra, 7s. 6d. Uniform with "A Tramp Abroad."

The Innocents Abroad; or, The New Pilgrim's Progress : Being some Account of the Steamship "Quaker City's" Pleasure Excursion to Europe and the Holy Land, with descriptions of Countries, Nations, Incidents, and Adventures, as they appeared to the Author. With 234 Illustrations. By MARK TWAIN. Crown 8vo, cloth extra, 7s. 6d. Uniform with "A Tramp Abroad."

A Tramp Abroad. By MARK TWAIN. With 314 Illustrations. Crown 8vo, cloth extra, 7s. 6d.

"The fun and tenderness of the conception, of which no living man but Mark Twain is capable, its grace and fantasy and slyness, the wonderful feeling for animals that is manifest in every line, make of all this episode of Jim Baker and his jays a piece of work that is not only delightful as mere reading, but also of a high degree of merit as literature. . . . The book is full of good things, and contains passages and episodes that are equal to the funniest of those that have gone before."—ATHENÆUM.

Post 8vo, cloth limp, 2s. 6d. per volume.

Mayfair Library, The:

The New Republic. By W. H. MALLOCK.

The New Paul and Virginia. By W. H. MALLOCK.

The True History of Joshua Davidson. By E. LYNN LINTON.

Old Stories Re-told. By WALTER THORNBURY.

Thoreau: His Life and Aims. By H. A. PAGE.

By Stream and Sea. By WILLIAM SENIOR.

Jeux d'Esprit. Edited by HENRY S. LEIGH.

Puniana. By the Hon. HUGH ROWLEY.

More Puniana. By the Hon. HUGH ROWLEY.

Puck on Pegasus. By H. CHOLMONDELEY-PENNELL.

The Speeches of Charles Dickens.

Muses of Mayfair. Edited by H. CHOLMONDELEY-PENNELL.

Gastronomy as a Fine Art. By BRILLAT-SAVARIN.

The Philosophy of Hand-writing. By DON FELIX DE SALA-MANCA.

Curiosities of Criticism. By HENRY J. JENNINGS.

Literary Frivolities, Fancies, Follies, Frolics. By W. T. DOBSON.

Poetical Ingenuities and Eccentricities. Selected and Edited by W. T. DOBSON.

Pencil and Palette. By ROBERT KEMPT.

Latter-Day Lyrics. Edited by W. DAVENPORT ADAMS.

Original Plays by W. S. GILBERT. FIRST SERIES. Containing: The Wicked World—Pygmalion and Galatea — Charity — The Princess—The Palace of Truth—Trial by Jury.

Original Plays by W. S. GILBERT. SECOND SERIES. Containing: Broken Hearts — Engaged — Sweethearts — Dan'l Druce — Gretchen—Tom Cobb—The Sorcerer—H.M.S. Pinafore—The Pirates of Penzance.

Carols of Cockayne. By HENRY S. LEIGH.

The Book of Clerical Anecdotes. By JACOB LARWOOD.

The Agony Column of "The Times," from 1800 to 1870. Edited, with an Introduction, by ALICE CLAY.

The Cupboard Papers. By FIN-BEC.

Pastimes and Players. By ROBERT MACGREGOR.

Balzac's "Comédie Humaine" and its Author. With Translations by H. H. WALKER.

Melancholy Anatomised: A Popular Abridgment of "Burton's Anatomy of Melancholy."

Quips and Quiddities. Selected by W. DAVENPORT ADAMS.

Leaves from a Naturalist's Note-Book. By ANDREW WILSON, F.R.S.E.

The Autocrat of the Breakfast-Table. By OLIVER WENDELL HOLMES. Illustrated by J. GORDON THOMSON.

Forensic Anecdotes; or, Humour and Curiosities of the Law and the Men of Law. By JACOB LARWOOD.

⁎⁎⁎ Other Volumes are in preparation.

Small 8vo, cloth limp, with Illustrations, 2s. 6d.

Miller's Physiology for the Young;

Or, The House of Life: Human Physiology, with its Applications to the Preservation of Health. For use in Classes and Popular Reading. With numerous Illustrations. By Mrs. F. FENWICK MILLER.

"An admirable introduction to a subject which all who value health and enjoy life should have at their fingers' ends."—ECHO.

Milton (J. L.), Works by:

The Hygiene of the Skin. A Concise Set of Rules for the Management of the Skin; with Directions for Diet, Wines, Soaps, Baths, &c. By J. L. MILTON, Senior Surgeon to St. John's Hospital. Small 8vo, 1*s.*; cloth extra, 1*s.* 6*d.*

The Bath in Diseases of the Skin. Small 8vo, 1*s.*; cloth extra, 1*s.* 6*d.*

Square 8vo, cloth extra, with numerous Illustrations, 7*s.* 6*d.*

North Italian Folk.

By Mrs. COMYNS CARR. Illustrated by RANDOLPH CALDECOTT.

" A delightful book, of a kind which is far too rare. If anyone wants to really know the North Italian folk, we can honestly advise him to omit the journey, and read Mrs. Carr's pages instead. . . Description with Mrs. Carr is a real gift. . It is rarely that a book is so happily illustrated."—CONTEMPORARY REVIEW.

New Novels:

IN MAREMMA.
By OUIDA. 3 vols., crown 8vo. *[Shortly.*

GOD AND THE MAN.
By ROBERT BUCHANAN, Author of "The Shadow of the Sword," &c. 3 vols., crown 8vo. With 11 Illustrations by FRED. BARNARD.

THE COMET OF A SEASON.
By JUSTIN McCARTHY, M.P., Author of "Miss Misanthrope." 3 vols., crown 8vo.

JOSEPH'S COAT.
By DAVID CHRISTIE MURRAY, Author of "A Life's Atonement," &c. With 12 Illustrations by FRED. BARNARD.

A HEART'S PROBLEM.
By CHARLES GIBBON, Author of "Robin Gray," &c. 2 vols. crown 8vo.

THE BRIDE'S PASS.
By SARAH TYTLER, 2 vols., crown 8vo.

PRINCE SARONI'S WIFE, and other Stories.
By JULIAN HAWTHORNE. 3 vols., crown 8vo. *[Shortly.*

SOMETHING IN THE CITY.
By GEORGE AUGUSTUS SALA. 3 vols. crown 8vo. *[In preparation.*

THE MARTYRDOM OF MADELINE.
By ROBERT BUCHANAN. 3 vols., crown 8vo. *[Shortly.*

Crown 8vo, cloth extra, with Vignette Portraits, price 6*s.* per Vol.

Old Dramatists, The:

Ben Jonson's Works.
With Notes, Critical and Explanatory, and a Biographical Memoir by WILLIAM GIFFORD. Edited by Colonel CUNNINGHAM. Three Vols.

Chapman's Works.
Now First Collected. Complete in Three Vols. Vol. I. contains the Plays complete, including the doubtful ones; Vol. II. the Poems and Minor Translations, with an Introductory Essay by ALGERNON CHARLES SWINBURNE. Vol. III. the Translations of the Iliad and Odyssey.

Marlowe's Works.
Including his Translations. Edited, with Notes and Introduction, by Col. CUNNINGHAM. One Vol.

Massinger's Plays.
From the Text of WILLIAM GIFFORD. With the addition of the Tragedy of "Believe as you List." Edited by Col. CUNNINGHAM. One Vol.

O'Shaughnessy (Arthur) Works by:

Songs of a Worker. By ARTHUR O'SHAUGHNESSY. Fcap. 8vo, cloth extra, 7s. 6d.

Music and Moonlight. By ARTHUR O'SHAUGHNESSY. Fcap. 8vo, cloth extra, 7s. 6d.

Lays of France. By ARTHUR O'SHAUGHNESSY. Crown 8vo, cloth extra, 10s. 6d.

Crown 8vo, red cloth extra, 5s. each.

Ouida's Novels.—Library Edition.

Held in Bondage.	By OUIDA.	Pascarel.	By OUIDA.
Strathmore.	By OUIDA.	Two Wooden Shoes.	By OUIDA.
Chandos.	By OUIDA.	Signa.	By OUIDA.
Under Two Flags.	By OUIDA.	In a Winter City.	By OUIDA.
Idalia.	By OUIDA.	Ariadne.	By OUIDA.
Cecil Castlemaine.	By OUIDA.	Friendship.	By OUIDA.
Tricotrin.	By OUIDA.	Moths.	By OUIDA.
Puck.	By OUIDA.	Pipistrello.	By OUIDA.
Folle Farine.	By OUIDA.	A Village Commune.	By OUIDA.
Dog of Flanders.	By OUIDA.		

. Also a Cheap Edition of all but the last, post 8vo, illustrated boards, 2s. each.

Post 8vo, cloth limp, 1s. 6d.

Parliamentary Procedure, A Popular Handbook of. By HENRY W. LUCY.

Large 4to, cloth extra, gilt, beautifully Illustrated, 31s. 6d.

Pastoral Days;

Or, Memories of a New England Year. By W. HAMILTON GIBSON. With 76 Illustrations in the highest style of Wood Engraving.

"*The volume contains a prose poem, with illustrations in the shape of wood engravings more beautiful than it can well enter into the hearts of most men to conceive.*"—SCOTSMAN.

Crown 8vo, cloth extra, 6s.

Payn.—Some Private Views.

Being Essays contributed to *The Nineteenth Century* and to *The Times.* By JAMES PAYN. Author of "High Spirits," "By Proxy," "Lost Sir Massingberd," &c.

Two Vols. 8vo, cloth extra, with Portraits, 10s. 6d.

Plutarch's Lives of Illustrious Men.

Translated from the Greek, with Notes, Critical and Historical, and a Life of Plutarch, by JOHN and WILLIAM LANGHORNE.

Crown 8vo, cloth extra, with Portrait and Illustrations, 7s. 6d.

Poe's Choice Prose and Poetical Works.

With BAUDELAIRE'S "Essay."

LIBRARY EDITIONS, many Illustrated, crown 8vo, cloth extra, 3s. 6d. each.

Piccadilly Novels, The.

𝔓opular 𝔖tories by the 𝔅est 𝔄uthors.

Maid, Wife, or Widow? By Mrs. ALEXANDER.

Ready-Money Mortiboy. By W. BESANT and JAMES RICE.

My Little Girl. By W. BESANT and JAMES RICE.

The Case of Mr. Lucraft. By W. BESANT and JAMES RICE.

This Son of Vulcan. By W. BESANT and JAMES RICE.

With Harp and Crown. By W. BESANT and JAMES RICE.

The Golden Butterfly. By W. BESANT and JAMES RICE.

By Celia's Arbour. By W. BESANT and JAMES RICE.

The Monks of Thelema. By W. BESANT and JAMES RICE.

'Twas in Trafalgar's Bay. By W. BESANT and JAMES RICE.

The Seamy Side. By WALTER BESANT and JAMES RICE.

The Chaplain of the Fleet. By WALTER BESANT and JAMES RICE.

The Ten Years' Tenant. By WALTER BESANT and JAMES RICE.

A Child of Nature. By ROBERT BUCHANAN.

Antonina. By WILKIE COLLINS.

Basil. By WILKIE COLLINS.

Hide and Seek. By WILKIE COLLINS.

The Dead Secret. W. COLLINS.

Queen of Hearts. W. COLLINS.

My Miscellanies. W. COLLINS.

The Woman in White. By WILKIE COLLINS.

The Moonstone. W. COLLINS.

Man and Wife. W. COLLINS.

Poor Miss Finch. W. COLLINS.

Miss or Mrs. ? By W. COLLINS.

The New Magdalen. By WILKIE COLLINS.

The Frozen Deep. W. COLLINS.

The Law and the Lady. By WILKIE COLLINS.

The Two Destinies. By WILKIE COLLINS.

The Haunted Hotel. By WILKIE COLLINS.

The Fallen Leaves. By WILKIE COLLINS.

Jezebel's Daughter. W. COLLINS.

The Black Robe. By WILKIE COLLINS.

Deceivers Ever. By Mrs. H. LOVETT CAMERON.

Juliet's Guardian. By Mrs. H. LOVETT CAMERON.

Felicia. M. BETHAM-EDWARDS.

Archie Lovell. By Mrs. ANNIE EDWARDES.

Olympia. By R. E. FRANCILLON.

Queen Cophetua. By R. E. FRANCILLON.

The Capel Girls. By EDWARD GARRETT.

Robin Gray. CHARLES GIBBON.

For Lack of Gold. By CHARLES GIBBON.

In Love and War. By CHARLES GIBBON.

What will the World Say ? By CHARLES GIBBON.

For the King. CHARLES GIBBON.

In Honour Bound. By CHARLES GIBBON.

Queen of the Meadow. By CHARLES GIBBON.

In Pastures Green. By CHARLES GIBBON.

Under the Greenwood Tree. By THOMAS HARDY.

Garth. By JULIAN HAWTHORNE.

Ellice Quentin. By JULIAN HAWTHORNE.

Sebastian Strome. By JULIAN HAWTHORNE.

Thornicroft's Model. By Mrs. ALFRED HUNT.

The Leaden Casket. By Mrs. ALFRED HUNT.

Fated to be Free. By JEAN INGELOW.

Confidence. HENRY JAMES, Jun.

PICCADILLY NOVELS—*continued.*

The Queen of Connaught. By HARRIETT JAY.

The Dark Colleen. By H. JAY.

Number Seventeen. By HENRY KINGSLEY.

Oakshott Castle. H. KINGSLEY.

Patricia Kemball. By E. LYNN LINTON.

The Atonement of Leam Dundas. By E. LYNN LINTON.

The World Well Lost. By E. LYNN LINTON.

Under which Lord? By E. LYNN LINTON.

With a Silken Thread. By E. LYNN LINTON.

The Rebel of the Family. By E. LYNN LINTON.

"My Love!" By E. LYNN LINTON.

The Waterdale Neighbours. By JUSTIN MCCARTHY.

My Enemy's Daughter. By JUSTIN MCCARTHY.

Linley Rochford. By JUSTIN MCCARTHY.

A Fair Saxon. J. MCCARTHY.

Dear Lady Disdain. By JUSTIN MCCARTHY.

Miss Misanthrope. By JUSTIN MCCARTHY.

Donna Quixote. J. MCCARTHY.

Quaker Cousins. By AGNES MACDONELL.

Lost Rose. By KATHARINE S. MACQUOID.

The Evil Eye. By KATHARINE S. MACQUOID.

Open! Sesame! By FLORENCE MARRYAT.

Written in Fire. F. MARRYAT.

Touch and Go. By JEAN MIDDLEMASS.

A Life's Atonement. By D. CHRISTIE MURRAY.

Whiteladies. Mrs. OLIPHANT.

Lost Sir Massingberd. By JAMES PAYN.

The Best of Husbands. By JAMES PAYN.

Fallen Fortunes. JAMES PAYN.

Halves. By JAMES PAYN.

Walter's Word. JAMES PAYN.

What He Cost Her. By JAMES PAYN.

Less Black than we're Painted. By JAMES PAYN.

By Proxy. By JAMES PAYN.

Under One Roof. JAMES PAYN.

High Spirits. By JAMES PAYN.

From Exile. By JAMES PAYN.

Carlyon's Year. By JAMES PAYN.

A Confidential Agent. By JAMES PAYN.

Put Yourself in his Place. By CHARLES READE.

Her Mother's Darling. By Mrs. J. H. RIDDELL.

Bound to the Wheel. By JOHN SAUNDERS.

Guy Waterman. J. SAUNDERS.

One Against the World. By JOHN SAUNDERS.

The Lion in the Path. By JOHN SAUNDERS.

The Two Dreamers. By JOHN SAUNDERS.

Proud Maisie. By BERTHA THOMAS.

Cressida. By BERTHA THOMAS.

The Violin-Player. By BERTHA THOMAS.

The Way We Live Now. By ANTHONY TROLLOPE.

The American Senator. By ANTHONY TROLLOPE.

Diamond Cut Diamond. By T. A. TROLLOPE.

What She Came through. By SARAH TYTLER.

Crown 8vo, cloth extra, 6*s.*

Planché.—Songs and Poems, from 1819 to 1879.

By J. R. PLANCHE. Edited, with an Introduction, by his Daughter, Mrs. MACKARNESS.

Post 8vo, illustrated boards, 2s. each.

Popular Novels, Cheap Editions of.

[WILKIE COLLINS' NOVELS and BESANT and RICE'S NOVELS may also be had in cloth limp at 2s. 6d. *See, too, the* PICCADILLY NOVELS, *for Library Editions.*]

Confidences. HAMILTON AÏDÉ.
Carr of Carrlyon. H. AÏDÉ.
Maid, Wife, or Widow? By Mrs. ALEXANDER.
Ready-Money Mortiboy. By WALTER BESANT and JAMES RICE.
With Harp and Crown. By WALTER BESANT and JAMES RICE.
This Son of Vulcan. By W. BESANT and JAMES RICE.
My Little Girl. By the same.
The Case of Mr. Lucraft. By WALTER BESANT and JAMES RICE.
The Golden Butterfly. By W. BESANT and JAMES RICE.
By Celia's Arbour. By WALTER BESANT and JAMES RICE.
The Monks of Thelema. By WALTER BESANT and JAMES RICE.
'Twas in Trafalgar's Bay. By WALTER BESANT and JAMES RICE.
Seamy Side. BESANT and RICE.
Grantley Grange. By SHELSLEY BEAUCHAMP.
An Heiress of Red Dog. By BRET HARTE.
The Luck of Roaring Camp. By BRET HARTE.
Gabriel Conroy. BRET HARTE.
Surly Tim. By F. E. BURNETT.
Deceivers Ever. By Mrs. L. CAMERON.
Juliet's Guardian. By Mrs. LOVETT CAMERON.
The Cure of Souls. By MAC-LAREN COBBAN.
The Bar Sinister. By C. ALLSTON COLLINS.
Antonina. By WILKIE COLLINS.
Basil. By WILKIE COLLINS.
Hide and Seek. W. COLLINS.
The Dead Secret. W. COLLINS.
Queen of Hearts. W. COLLINS.
My Miscellanies. W. COLLINS.
Woman in White. W. COLLINS.
The Moonstone. W. COLLINS.

Man and Wife. W. COLLINS.
Poor Miss Finch. W. COLLINS.
Miss or Mrs. ? W. COLLINS.
New Magdalen. W. COLLINS.
The Frozen Deep. W. COLLINS.
Law and the Lady. W. COLLINS.
Two Destinies. W. COLLINS.
Haunted Hotel. W. COLLINS.
Fallen Leaves. By W. COLLINS.
Leo. By DUTTON COOK.
A Point of Honour. By Mrs. ANNIE EDWARDES.
Archie Lovell. Mrs A. EDWARDES
Felicia. M. BETHAM-EDWARDS.
Roxy. By EDWARD EGGLESTON.
Polly. By PERCY FITZGERALD.
Bella Donna. P. FITZGERALD.
Never Forgotten. FITZGERALD.
The Second Mrs. Tillotson. By PERCY FITZGERALD.
Seventy-Five Brooke Street. By PERCY FITZGERALD.
Filthy Lucre. By ALBANY DE FONBLANQUE.
Olympia. By R. E. FRANCILLON.
The Capel Girls. By EDWARD GARRETT.
Robin Gray. By CHAS. GIBBON.
For Lack of Gold. C. GIBBON.
What will the World Say? By CHARLES GIBBON.
In Honour Bound. C. GIBBON.
The Dead Heart. By C. GIBBON.
In Love and War. C. GIBBON.
For the King. By C. GIBBON.
Queen of the Meadow. By CHARLES GIBBON.
Dick Temple. By JAMES GREENWOOD.
Every-day Papers. By ANDREW HALLIDAY.
Paul Wynter's Sacrifice. By Lady DUFFUS HARDY.
Under the Greenwood Tree. By THOMAS HARDY.

POPULAR NOVELS—*continued.*

Garth. By JULIAN HAWTHORNE.

Golden Heart. By TOM HOOD.

The Hunchback of Notre Dame. By VICTOR HUGO.

Thornicroft's Model. By Mrs. ALFRED HUNT.

Fated to be Free. By JEAN INGELOW.

Confidence. By HENRY JAMES, Jun.

The Queen of Connaught. By HARRIETT JAY.

The Dark Colleen. By H. JAY.

Number Seventeen. By HENRY KINGSLEY.

Oakshott Castle. H. KINGSLEY.

Patricia Kemball. By E. LYNN LINTON.

Leam Dundas. E. LYNN LINTON.

The World Well Lost. By E. LYNN LINTON.

Under which Lord? By E. LYNN LINTON.

The Waterdale Neighbours. By JUSTIN MCCARTHY.

Dear Lady Disdain. By the same.

My Enemy's Daughter. By JUSTIN MCCARTHY.

A Fair Saxon. J. MCCARTHY.

Linley Rochford. MCCARTHY.

Miss Misanthrope. MCCARTHY.

Donna Quixote. J. MCCARTHY.

The Evil Eye. By KATHARINE S. MACQUOID.

Lost Rose. K. S. MACQUOID.

Open! Sesame! By FLORENCE MARRYAT.

Harvest of Wild Oats. By FLORENCE MARRYAT.

A Little Stepson. F. MARRYAT.

Fighting the Air. F. MARRYAT.

Touch and Go. By JEAN MIDDLEMASS.

Mr. Dorillion. J. MIDDLEMASS.

Whiteladies. By Mrs. OLIPHANT.

Held in Bondage. By OUIDA.

Strathmore. By OUIDA.

Chandos. By OUIDA.

Under Two Flags. By OUIDA.

Idalia. By OUIDA.

Cecil Castlemaine. By OUIDA.

Tricotrin. By OUIDA.

Puck. By OUIDA.

Folle Farine. By OUIDA.

A Dog of Flanders. By OUIDA.

Pascarel. By OUIDA.

Two Little Wooden Shoes. By Signa. By OUIDA. [OUIDA.

In a Winter City. By OUIDA.

Ariadne. By OUIDA.

Friendship. By OUIDA.

Moths. By OUIDA.

Lost Sir Massingberd. J. PAYN.

A Perfect Treasure. J. PAYN.

Bentinck's Tutor. By J. PAYN.

Murphy's Master. By J. PAYN.

A County Family. By J. PAYN.

At Her Mercy. By J. PAYN.

A Woman's Vengeance. J. PAYN.

Cecil's Tryst. By JAMES PAYN.

The Clyffards of Clyffe. J. PAYN.

Family Scapegrace. J. PAYN.

The Foster Brothers. J. PAYN.

Found Dead. By JAMES PAYN.

Gwendoline's Harvest. J. PAYN.

Humorous Stories. J. PAYN.

Like Father, Like Son. J. PAYN.

A Marine Residence. J. PAYN.

Married Beneath Him. J. PAYN.

Mirk Abbey. By JAMES PAYN.

Not Wooed, but Won. J. PAYN.

Two Hundred Pounds Reward. By JAMES PAYN.

Best of Husbands. By J. PAYN.

Walter's Word. By J. PAYN.

Halves. By JAMES PAYN.

Fallen Fortunes. By J. PAYN.

What He Cost Her. J. PAYN.

Less Black than We're Painted. By JAMES PAYN.

By Proxy. By JAMES PAYN.

Under One Roof. By J. PAYN.

High Spirits. By JAS. PAYN.

Paul Ferroll.

Why P. Ferroll Killed his Wife.

The Mystery of Marie Roget. By EDGAR A. POE.

POPULAR NOVELS—*continued.*

Put Yourself in his Place By CHARLES READE.

Her Mother's Darling. By Mrs. J. H. RIDDELL.

Gaslight and Daylight. By GEORGE AUGUSTUS SALA.

Bound to the Wheel. By JOHN SAUNDERS.

Guy Waterman. J. SAUNDERS.

One Against the World. By JOHN SAUNDERS.

The Lion in the Path. By JOHN and KATHERINE SAUNDERS.

A Match in the Dark. By A. SKETCHLEY.

Tales for the Marines. By WALTER THORNBURY.

The Way we Live Now. By ANTHONY TROLLOPE.

The American Senator. Ditto.

Diamond Cut Diamond. Ditto.

A Pleasure Trip in Europe. By MARK TWAIN.

Tom Sawyer. By MARK TWAIN.

An Idle Excursion. M. TWAIN.

Sabina. By Lady WOOD.

Castaway. By EDMUND YATES.

Forlorn Hope. EDMUND YATES.

Land at Last. EDMUND YATES.

NEW TWO-SHILLING NOVELS IN THE PRESS.

Pipistrello. By OUIDA.

The Ten Years' Tenant. By BESANT and RICE.

Jezebel's Daughter. By WILKIE COLLINS.

Queen Cophetua. By R. E. FRANCILLON.

In Pastures Green. By CHAS. GIBBON.

A Confidential Agent. By JAS. PAYN.

Ellice Quentin. By JULIAN HAWTHORNE.

With a Silken Thread. By E. LYNN LINTON.

Quaker Cousins. By AGNES MACDONELL.

Written in Fire. By FLORENCE MARRYAT.

A Life's Atonement. By D. CHRISTIE MURRAY.

Carlyon's Year. By J. PAYN.

Fcap. 8vo, picture covers, 1*s.* each.

Jeff Briggs's Love Story. By BRET HARTE.

The Twins of Table Mountain. By BRET HARTE.

Mrs. Gainsborough's Diamonds. By JULIAN HAWTHORNE.

Kathleen Mavourneen. By the Author of "That Lass o' Lowrie's."

Lindsay's Luck. By the Author of "That Lass o' Lowrie's."

Pretty Polly Pemberton. By Author of "That Lass o' Lowrie's."

Trooping with Crows. By Mrs. PIRKIS.

The Professor's Wife. By LEONARD GRAHAM.

A Double Bond. By LINDA VILLARI.

Crown 8vo, cloth extra, 7*s.* 6*d.*

Primitive Manners and Customs.

By JAMES A. FARRER.

Small 8vo, cloth extra, with 130 Illustrations, 3*s.* 6*d.*

Prince of Argolis, The:

A Story of the Old Greek Fairy Time. By J. MOYR SMITH.

Crown 8vo, cloth extra, gilt, 7*s.* 6*d.*

Pursuivant of Arms, The;

or, Heraldry founded upon Facts. By J. R. PLANCHE, Somerset Herald. With Coloured Frontispiece and 200 Illustrations.

Proctor's (R. A.) Works:

Easy Star Lessons. With Star Maps for Every Night in the Year, Drawings of the Constellations, &c. Crown 8vo, cloth extra, 6s.

Familiar Science Studies. Crown 8vo, cloth extra, 7s. 6d.

Saturn and its System. By RICHARD A. PROCTOR. New and Revised Edition, demy 8vo, cloth extra, 10s. 6d. *[In preparation.*

Myths and Marvels of Astronomy. By RICH. A. PROCTOR, Author of "Other Worlds than Ours," &c. Crown 8vo, cloth extra, 6s.

Pleasant Ways in Science. Crown 8vo, cloth extra, 6s.

Rough Ways made Smooth: A Series of Familiar Essays on Scientific Subjects. By R. A. PROCTOR. Crown 8vo, cloth extra, 6s.

Our Place among Infinities: A Series of Essays contrasting our Little Abode in Space and Time with the Infinities Around us. By RICHARD A. PROCTOR. Crown 8vo, cloth extra, 6s.

The Expanse of Heaven: A Series of Essays on the Wonders of the Firmament. By RICHARD A. PROCTOR. Crown 8vo, cloth, 6s.

Wages and Wants of Science Workers. Crown 8vo, 1s. 6d.

Crown 8vo, cloth extra, with Illustrations, 7s. 6d.

Rabelais' Works.

Faithfully Translated from the French, with variorum Notes, and numerous characteristic Illustrations by GUSTAVE DORE.

Crown 8vo, cloth gilt, with numerous Illustrations, and a beautifully executed Chart of the various Spectra, 7s. 6d.

Rambosson's Popular Astronomy.

By J. RAMBOSSON, Laureate of the Institute of France. Translated by C. B. PITMAN. Profusely Illustrated.

Entirely New Edition, Revised, crown 8vo, 1,400 pages, cloth extra, 7s. 6d.

Reader's Handbook (The) of Allusions, Re-

ferences, Plots, and Stories. By the Rev. Dr. BREWER. Third Edition, revised throughout, with a new Appendix containing a Complete English Bibliography. *[In the press.*

Crown 8vo, cloth extra, 6s.

Richardson's (Dr.) A Ministry of Health,

and other Papers. By BENJAMIN WARD RICHARDSON, M.D., &c.

Rimmer (Alfred), Works by:

Our Old Country Towns. With over 50 Illustrations. By ALFRED RIMMER. Square 8vo, cloth extra, gilt, 10s. 6d.

Rambles Round Eton and Harrow. By ALFRED RIMMER. With 50 Illustrations by the Author. Square 8vo, cloth gilt, 10s. 6d. Also an EDITION DE LUXE, in 4to (only a limited number printed), with the Illusts. beautifully printed on China paper, cloth bds., edges uncut, 42s. *[Shortly.*

About England with Dickens. With Illustrations by ALFRED RIMMER and C. A. VANDERHOOF, Sq. 8vo, cloth gilt, 10s. 6d. *[In the press.*

Crown 8vo, cloth extra, 6s. per volume.

Robinson.—Natural History of the Poets.

By PHIL. ROBINSON, Author of "Under the Punkah," &c. In Four Volumes. Vol. I. The Birds. Vol. II. The Beasts. Vol. III. The Fauna of Fancy. Vol. IV. The Flora of Poetry. *[In the press.*

Handsomely printed, price 5s.

Roll of Battle Abbey, The;

or, A List of the Principal Warriors who came over from Normandy with William the Conqueror, and Settled in this Country, A.D. 1066-7. With the principal Arms emblazoned in Gold and Colours.

Two Vols., large 4to, profusely Illustrated, half-morocco, £2 16s.

Rowlandson, the Caricaturist.

A Selection from his Works, with Anecdotal Descriptions of his Famous Caricatures, and a Sketch of his Life, Times, and Contemporaries. With nearly 400 Illustrations, mostly in Facsimile of the Originals. By JOSEPH GREGO, Author of "James Gillray, the Caricaturist; his Life, Works, and Times."

Crown 8vo, cloth extra, profusely Illustrated, 4s. 6d. each.

"Secret Out" Series, The.

The Pyrotechnist's Treasury;
or, Complete Art of Making Fireworks. By THOMAS KENTISH. With numerous Illustrations.

The Art of Amusing:
A Collection of Graceful Arts, Games, Tricks, Puzzles, and Charades. By FRANK BELLEW. 300 Illustrations.

Hanky-Panky:
Very Easy Tricks, Very Difficult Tricks, White Magic, Sleight of Hand. Edited by W. H. CREMER. 200 Illusts.

The Merry Circle:
A Book of New Intellectual Games and Amusements. By CLARA BELLEW. Many Illustrations.

Magician's Own Book:
Performances with Cups and Balls, Eggs, Hats, Handkerchiefs, &c. All from Actual Experience. Edited by W. H. CREMER. 200 Illustrations.

Magic No Mystery:
Tricks with Cards, Dice, Balls, &c., with fully descriptive Directions; the Art of Secret Writing; Training of Performing Animals, &c. Coloured Frontispiece and many Illustrations.

The Secret Out:
One Thousand Tricks with Cards, and other Recreations; with Entertaining Experiments in Drawing-room or "White Magic." By W. H. CREMER. 300 Engravings.

Shakespeare:

Shakespeare, The First Folio. Mr. WILLIAM SHAKESPEARE'S Comedies, Histories, and Tragedies. Published according to the true Originall Copies. London, Printed by ISAAC IAGGARD and ED. BLOUNT, 1623.—A Reproduction of the extremely rare original, in reduced facsimile by a photographic process—ensuring the strictest accuracy in every detail. Small 8vo, half-Roxburghe, 7s. 6d.

Shakespeare, The Lansdowne. Beautifully printed in red and black, in small but very clear type. With engraved facsimile of DROESHOUT'S Portrait. Post 8vo, cloth extra, 7s. 6d.

Shakespeare for Children: Tales from Shakespeare. By CHARLES and MARY LAMB. With numerous Illustrations, coloured and plain, by J. MOYR SMITH. Crown 4to, cloth gilt, 10s. 6d.

Shakespeare Music, The Handbook of. Being an Account of 350 Pieces of Music, set to Words taken from the Plays and Poems of Shakespeare, the compositions ranging from the Elizabethan Age to the Present Time. By ALFRED ROFFE. 4to, half-Roxburghe, 7s.

Shakespeare, A Study of. By ALGERNON CHARLES SWINBURNE. Crown 8vo, cloth extra 8s.

Crown 8vo, cloth extra, 6s.

Senior's Travel and Trout in the Antipodes.

An Angler's Sketches in Tasmania and New Zealand. By WILLIAM SENIOR ("Red Spinner"), Author of "By Stream and Sea."

Crown 8vo, cloth extra, gilt, with 10 full-page Tinted Illustrations, 7s. 6d.

Sheridan's Complete Works,

with Life and Anecdotes. Including his Dramatic Writings, printed from the Original Editions, his Works in Prose and Poetry, Translations, Speeches, Jokes, Puns, &c. ; with a Collection of Sheridaniana.

Crown 8vo, cloth extra, with 100 Illustrations, 7s. 6d.

Signboards:

Their History. With Anecdotes of Famous Taverns and Remarkable Characters. By JACOB LARWOOD and JOHN CAMDEN HOTTEN

Crown 8vo, cloth extra, gilt, 6s. 6d.

Slang Dictionary, The:

Etymological, Historical, and Anecdotal.. An ENTIRELY NEW EDITION, revised throughout, and considerably Enlarged.

Exquisitely printed in miniature, cloth extra, gilt edges, 2s. 6d.

Smoker's Text-Book, The. By J. HAMER, F.R.S.L.

Crown 8vo, cloth extra, 5s.

Spalding's Elizabethan Demonology:

An Essay in Illustration of the Belief in the Existence of Devils, and the Powers possessed by them. By T. ALFRED SPALDING, LL.B.

Crown 4to, with Coloured Illustrations, cloth gilt, 10s. 6d.

Spenser for Children.

By M. H. TOWRY. Illustrations in Colours by WALTER J. MORGAN.

A New Edition, small crown 8vo, cloth extra, 5s.

Staunton.—Laws and Practice of Chess;

Together with an Analysis of the Openings, and a Treatise on End Games. By HOWARD STAUNTON. Edited by ROBERT B. WORMALD.

Crown 8vo, cloth extra, 9s.

Stedman.—Victorian Poets:

Critical Essays. By EDMUND CLARENCE STEDMAN.

Crown 8vo, cloth extra, 6s.

Stevenson.—Familiar Studies in Men and

Books. By R. LOUIS STEVENSON, Author of "With a Donkey in the Cevennes," &c.   [*Nearly ready.*

Post 8vo, cloth extra, 5s.

Stories about Number Nip,

The Spirit of the Giant Mountains. Retold for Children, by WALTER GRAHAME. With Illustrations by J. MOYR SMITH.

Two Vols., crown 8vo, cloth extra, 21s.

Stories from the State Papers.

By ALEX. CHARLES EWALD, F.S.A., Author of "The Life of Prince Charles Stuart," &c. With an Autotype Facsimile.

Two Vols., crown 8vo, with numerous Portraits and Illustrations, 24s.

Strahan.—Twenty Years of a Publisher's

Life. By ALEXANDER STRAHAN. *[In the press.*

Crown 8vo, cloth extra, with Illustrations, 7s. 6d.

Strutt's Sports and Pastimes of the People

of England; including the Rural and Domestic Recreations, May Games, Mummeries, Shows, Processions, Pageants, and Pompous Spectacles, from the Earliest Period to the Present Time. With 140 Illustrations. Edited by WILLIAM HONE.

Crown 8vo, with a Map of Suburban London, cloth extra, 7s. 6d.

Suburban Homes (The) of London:

A Residential Guide to Favourite London Localities, their Society, Celebrities, and Associations. With Notes on their Rental, Rates, and House Accommodation.

Crown 8vo, cloth extra, with Illustrations, 7s. 6d.

Swift's Choice Works,

In Prose and Verse. With Memoir, Portrait, and Facsimiles of the Maps in the Original Edition of "Gulliver's Travels."

Swinburne's Works:

The Queen Mother and Rosamond. Fcap. 8vo, 5s.

Atalanta in Calydon.
A New Edition. Crown 8vo, 6s.

Chastelard.
A Tragedy. Crown 8vo, 7s.

Poems and Ballads.
FIRST SERIES. Fcap. 8vo, 9s. Also in crown 8vo, at same price.

Poems and Ballads.
SECOND SERIES. Fcap. 8vo, 9s. Also in crown 8vo, at same price.

Notes on "Poems and Ballads." 8vo, 1s.

William Blake:
A Critical Essay. With Facsimile Paintings. Demy 8vo, 16s.

Songs before Sunrise.
Crown 8vo, 10s. 6d.

Bothwell:
A Tragedy. Crown 8vo, 12s. 6d.

George Chapman:
An Essay. Crown 8vo, 7s.

Songs of Two Nations.
Crown 8vo, 6s.

Essays and Studies.
Crown 8vo, 12s.

Erechtheus:
A Tragedy. Crown 8vo, 6s.

Note of an English Republican
on the Muscovite Crusade. 8vo, 1s.

A Note on Charlotte Brontë.
Crown 8vo, 6s.

A Study of Shakespeare.
Crown 8vo, 8s.

Songs of the Springtides.
Crown 8vo, 6s.

Studies in Song.
Crown 8vo, 7s.

Mary Stuart:
A Tragedy. Crown 8vo, 8s.

Small 4to, cloth extra, Illustrated, 25s.

Sword, The Book of the:

Being a History of the Sword, and its Use, in all Countries from the Earliest Times. By Captain RICHARD BURTON. With over 400 Illustrations. *[In preparation.*

Medium 8vo, cloth extra, with Illustrations, 7s. 6d.

Syntax's (Dr.) Three Tours,

In Search of the Picturesque, in Search of Consolation, and in Search of a Wife. With the whole of ROWLANDSON's droll page Illustrations, in Colours, and Life of the Author by J. C. HOTTEN.

Four Vols. small 8vo, cloth boards, 30s.

Taine's History of English Literature.

Translated by HENRY VAN LAUN.

. Also a POPULAR EDITION, in Two Vols. crown 8vo, cloth extra, 15s.

Crown 8vo, cloth gilt, profusely Illustrated, 6s.

Tales of Old Thule.

Collected and Illustrated by J. MOYR SMITH.

One Vol. crown 8vo, cloth extra, 7s. 6d.

Taylor's (Tom) Historical Dramas:

" Clancarty," " Jeanne Darc," " 'Twixt Axe and Crown," " The Fool's Revenge," " Arkwright's Wife," " Anne Boleyn," " Plot and Passion."

*** The Plays may also be had separately, at 1s. each.

Crown 8vo, cloth extra, with Coloured Frontispiece and numerous Illustrations, 7s. 6d.

Thackerayana:

Notes and Anecdotes. Illustrated by a profusion of Sketches by WILLIAM MAKEPEACE THACKERAY, depicting Humorous Incidents in his School-life, and Favourite Characters in the books of his every-day reading. With Hundreds of Wood Engravings, facsimiled from Mr. Thackeray's Original Drawings.

Crown 8vo, cloth extra, gilt edges, with Illustrations, 7s. 6d.

Thomson's Seasons and Castle of Indolence.

With a Biographical and Critical Introduction by ALLAN CUNNING-HAM, and over 50 fine Illustrations on Steel and Wood.

Crown 8vo, cloth extra, with numerous Illustrations, 7s. 6d.

Thornbury's (Walter) Haunted London.

A New Edition, Edited by EDWARD WALFORD, M.A., with numerous Illustrations by F. W. FAIRHOLT, F.S.A.

Crown 8vo, cloth extra, with Illustrations, 7s. 6d.

Timbs' Clubs and Club Life in London.

With Anecdotes of its famous Coffee-houses, Hostelries, and Taverns. By JOHN TIMBS, F.S.A. With numerous Illustrations.

Crown 8vo, cloth extra, with Illustrations, 7s. 6d.

Timbs' English Eccentrics and Eccentrici-

ties: Stories of Wealth and Fashion, Delusions, Impostures, and Fanatic Missions, Strange Sights and Sporting Scenes, Eccentric Artists, Theatrical Folks, Men of Letters, &c. By JOHN TIMBS, F.S.A. With nearly 50 Illustrations.

Demy 8vo, cloth extra, 14s.

Torrens' The Marquess Wellesley,

Architect of Empire. An Historic Portrait. *Forming Vol. I. of* PRO-CONSUL and TRIBUNE: WELLESLEY and O'CONNELL: Historic Portraits. By W. M. TORRENS, M.P. In Two Vols.

Demy 8vo, cloth extra, with Illustrations, 9s.
Tunis : the Land and the People.
By ERNST VON HESSE-WARTEGG. With 22 fine Illustrations.

Crown 8vo, cloth extra, with Coloured Illustrations, 7s. 6d.
Turner's (J. M. W.) Life and Correspondence:
Founded upon Letters and Papers furnished by his Friends and fellow-Academicians. By WALTER THORNBURY. A New Edition, considerably Enlarged. With numerous Illustrations in Colours, facsimiled from Turner's original Drawings.

Two Vols., crown 8vo, cloth extra, with Map and Ground-Plans, 14s.
Walcott's Church Work and Life in English
Minsters ; and the English Student's Monasticon. By the Rev. MACKENZIE E. C. WALCOTT, B.D.

Large crown 8vo, cloth antique, with Illustrations, 7s. 6d.
Walton and Cotton's Complete Angler;
or, The Contemplative Man's Recreation : being a Discourse of Rivers, Fishponds, Fish and Fishing, written by IZAAK WALTON ; and Instructions how to Angle for a Trout or Grayling in a clear Stream, by CHARLES COTTON. With Original Memoirs and Notes by Sir HARRIS NICOLAS, and 61 Copperplate Illustrations.

The Twenty-second Annual Edition, for 1882, cloth, full gilt, 50s.
Walford's County Families of the United
Kingdom. By EDWARD WALFORD, M. A. Containing Notices of the Descent, Birth, Marriage, Education, &c., of more than 12,000 distinguished Heads of Families, their Heirs Apparent or Presumptive, the Offices they hold or have held, their Town and Country Addresses, Clubs, &c. *[Just ready.*

Crown 8vo, cloth extra, 3s. 6d. per volume.
Wanderer's Library, The :

Merrie England in the Olden Time. By GEORGE DANIEL. With Illustrations by ROBT. CRUIKSHANK.

The Old Showmen and the Old London Fairs. By THOMAS FROST.

The Wilds of London. By JAMES GREENWOOD.

Tavern Anecdotes and Sayings; Including the Origin of Signs, and Reminiscences connected with Taverns, Coffee Houses, Clubs, &c. By CHARLES HINDLEY. With Illusts.

Circus Life and Circus Celebrities. By THOMAS FROST.

The Lives of the Conjurers. By THOMAS FROST.

The Life and Adventures of a Cheap Jack. By One of the Fraternity. Edited by CHARLES HINDLEY.

The Story of the London Parks. By JACOB LARWOOD. With Illusts.

Low-Life Deeps. An Account of the Strange Fish to be found there. By JAMES GREENWOOD.

Seven Generations of Executioners: Memoirs of the Sanson Family (1688 to 1847). Edited by HENRY SANSON.

The World Behind the Scenes. By PERCY FITZGERALD.

London Characters. By HENRY MAYHEW. Illustrated.

The Genial Showman : Life and Adventures of Artemus Ward. By E. P. HINGSTON. Frontispiece.

Wanderings in Patagonia ; or, Life among the Ostrich Hunters. By JULIUS BEERBOHM. Illustrated.

Summer Cruising in the South Seas. By CHARLES WARREN STODDARD. Illustrated by WALLIS MACKAY.

Carefully printed on paper to imitate the Original. 22 in. by 14 in., 2s.

Warrant to Execute Charles I.

An exact Facsimile of this important Document, with the Fifty-nine Signatures of the Regicides, and corresponding Seals.

Beautifully printed on paper to imitate the Original MS., price 2s.

Warrant to Execute Mary Queen of Scots.

An exact Facsimile, including the Signature of Queen Elizabeth, and a Facsimile of the Great Seal.

Crown 8vo, cloth limp, with numerous Illustrations, 4s. 6d.

Westropp's Handbook of Pottery and Porcelain ; or, History of those Arts from the Earliest Period. By HODDER

M. WESTROPP. With numerous Illustrations, and a List of Marks.

Post 8vo, cloth limp, 2s. 6d.

What shall my Son be ?

Hints for Parents on the Choice of a Profession or Trade for their Sons. By FRANCIS DAVENANT, M.A.

SEVENTH EDITION. Square 8vo, 1s.

Whistler v. Ruskin: Art and Art Critics.

By J. A. MACNEILL WHISTLER.

A VERY HANDSOME VOLUME.— Large 4to, cloth extra, 31s. 6d.

White Mountains (The Heart of the):

Their Legend and Scenery. By SAMUEL ADAMS DRAKE. With nearly 100 Illustrations by W. HAMILTON GIBSON, Author of "Pastoral Days."

Crown 8vo, cloth limp, with Illustrations, 2s. 6d.

Williams' A Simple Treatise on Heat.

By W. MATTIEU WILLIAMS, F.R.A.S., F.C.S.

Small 8vo, cloth extra, Illustrated, 6s.

Wooing (The) of the Water-Witch:

A Northern Oddity. By EVAN DALDORNE. Illust. by J. MOYR SMITH.

Crown 8vo, half-bound, 12s. 6d.

Words, Facts, and Phrases:

A Dictionary of Curious, Quaint, and Out-of-the-Way Matters. By ELIEZER EDWARDS.

Crown 8vo, cloth extra, with Illustrations, 7s. 6d.

Wright's Caricature History of the Georges.

(The House of Hanover.) With 400 Pictures, Caricatures, Squibs, Broadsides, Window Pictures, &c. By THOMAS WRIGHT, M.A., F.S.A.

Large post 8vo, cloth extra, gilt, with Illustrations, 7s. 6d.

Wright's History of Caricature and of the

Grotesque in Art, Literature, Sculpture, and Painting. By THOMAS WRIGHT, F.S.A. Profusely Illustrated by F. W. FAIRHOLT, F.S.A.

J. OGDEN AND CO., PRINTERS, 172, ST. JOHN STREET, E.C.